PLANET CAT

SHIFTERS WORLD

REBECCA ROYCE

Planet Cat (Shifters World)

Copyright @ 2021 by Rebecca Royce

Cover art by Virginia Nelson

Content Editing: Claire Young

Copy Editing: Jennifer Jones at Bookends Editing

Final Proof Editing: Meghan Leigh Daigle of Bookish Dreams Editing

Formatting: Ripley Proserpina

Published by Rebecca Royce

www.rebeccaroyce.com

 Created with Vellum

1

I was either going to conquer this wave or end up dead on the rocks. There was no in between for me. *The Cyclops.* One of the few waves left on Planet Earth that was still worth surfing, still worth the risk of death. After traveling planet to planet for so long, there was so little left for me to do at home that was of any interest. But this was one of them. I was going to conquer the Cyclops today.

The second I'd gotten off Earth, I'd discovered how much prettier the planets we'd terraformed over the years had turned out to be. Mostly because we'd terraformed them and then left the settlers on them alone. Not by choice, mind you. No, we'd left them alone because we'd been screwing up our own world, and during those years, we hadn't been able to screw up theirs. All I knew was the people on them had been devoid of our government fucking them up. They were what Earth should have been. We'd meant to use them for our own benefit, but our wars had kept us from doing that.

I shook my head. Surfing always brought out the philosopher in me. It was the only time I could think my own thoughts and not concentrate on what others needed from me. Surfing brought back the days that my father had been alive and we'd done this together. Well...not this. My father had never been good enough to attempt the Cyclops. He might have dreamed about it, but it never happened. And that was why I was here today.

"Tiffany." The boat captain who had brought me out here—because even the advanced jet skis couldn't make this trek—called my name. I was on the water, and it was a good thing I hadn't moved too far away to hear him yet. Some things were automated, but on Earth, there were some traditions that remained as they had always been. Captains still took people out here. A spray of ocean water hit me in the face, and I squinted in his general direction because the glare made it hard to see him. Where were my sunglasses? Oh yes, on my head. Not very secure for surfing. I should probably have left them home. That was a distracted error on my part. I never knew where the hell my sunglasses were. Maybe I should just have the operation that would make my eyes automatically adjust to the sun.

But that kind of thing skeeved me out. I never wanted anything attached permanently to my eyes.

"Yes?" I called back to him, quickly cataloging all the things he could want from me. I'd paid and tipped him directly into his account so that I didn't have to deal with it later. All things I'd done when I got up this morning. It couldn't be that. I was leaving with everything I'd brought with me. And if he thought he was going to hold me hostage in some sort of extortion for gold credits, he had another think coming. The knife I'd taped to my body under my wetsuit was right where I needed it to be. Sheathed so it couldn't hurt me by accident, but there just the same. I was always armed with some kind of weapon. Hell, I was a lethal one all on my own.

"Someone is calling you on the communicator. Says it's an emergency."

Who the hell even knew I was here? Most of my friends —the ones I still had left after years of being off-grid—had moved on to start families and careers that didn't include time to see me when I breezed in and out of their lives. That was okay. I got paid a lot of money by the Union to keep their interests working on other planets. Since the Union was basically the only government ruling Earth right now, it meant most Earthlings could thank me for their current prosperity. Whether they knew it or not.

I pushed my hair off my face from where the wind had blown it into my eyes. I paddled closer to the boat until it was easier to hear before I answered. "Who is it?"

"Someone named Ferguson. Do you want me to tell him to go away? We don't get many calls on the boat."

"No, I'd imagine you don't. And, no, I'll take his call."

I had no choice. That fucker was my boss. I paddled my board back to the boat and, with some help, pulled both it and myself back onto the vessel. I grabbed the mid-level communicator that looked an awful lot like my tablet and was probably ten years out of date. Still, it worked and was obviously good enough for how the captain used it. This model would adjust to tune out the background noise, so I didn't need to struggle to hear over the loud waves or the noises off the boat. "Bad moment, Ferguson."

He was whom I answered to, but both he and I knew I didn't like it. How could I? When I'd been knee deep in diplomatic negotiations over sugar capsules on Nester 5, he'd snaked the job he now had right out from under me.

But he couldn't manage it without me, and he knew it. Mutual fucking hate.

"You're not answering your messages."

I shook my head. "V.A.C.A.T.I.O.N." I spelled the letters for him. "I don't have to."

"This is an emergency. Section five of the code of obligation lets me call you back in."

I closed my eyes and bit back what I wanted to say. Asking him if he needed me to help him wipe his ass was probably not going to be conducive right now. We had lines with each other. I could push him with rudeness to a point but not further. If he reported me to his superiors, all these years of sacrifice would be for naught. I'd given everything to the Union, and they'd give me what I wanted back—lots and lots of gold credits to live my days comfortably and easily on a resort planet. I was only twenty-eight years old, but I'd been at this for a decade. Ten more years, and I could retire early and figure out what I wanted for the first time in my life.

Something neither my mother, father, grandfather, or any relatives I'd ever heard of had gotten to enjoy. I'd done what so few could do. I'd gotten out of the Dead Zone to make something of myself.

"Okay. Hold on one minute." I put my hand over the speaker to address the boat captain. "Take me back. I'll pay you for the return trip, obviously." Everything had a price, and his transporting me back hadn't been part of the deal. "I'm not doing the Cyclops today."

He nodded once. "Right."

Leaning back on the side of the boat, I stared at my unused surfboard. All those years on Jackson-3 that had the same gravity and a similar enough ecosystem that I'd trained for this. And it wouldn't be today that I succeeded. Oh fucking well.

I had to get back to my call. "What's the problem?" I asked Ferguson finally. "How can I help?"

"The Cats."

I closed my eyes. Well, that sucked. So far, I'd avoided the shifter planets like the plague that they were. The Union stayed in their lane and made no trouble for them. They left us alone. There had been that very weird thing that no one spoke about where some of the Bears had left their planet—something that was practically unheard of—attacked an asylum, and then moved off their home world to a planet on the other side of the galaxy. No one had heard from them since. Internal intelligence had advised the Union not to pursue them. Just to pretend it hadn't happened and hope it was a one-time thing that no one would have to deal with anymore.

It hadn't cost us anything but lives, and as I'd learned early on, the Union considered certain lives of more value than others. The ones that had been taken in that event didn't add up to enough of a deficit to make the powers that be interested in pursuing it. If they had, someone like me would have been sent out to deal with them.

I considered myself lucky they hadn't wanted follow-up. Those people—if they could be called that—shifted from humans to animals. How did that even work? There was little that freaked me out in this universe, but that was one of those things. There was no logical explanation for it. Our scientists understood nothing about how it worked. And just the idea that they could become an animal... No. I didn't want to think about it a second more than I had to.

"What happened?"

"There was some kind of incident. Missiles are being

launched from their planet, but the governing body, if you can call it that, is denying that happened at all. Two of our transports were hit, and one supply ship is missing."

Well...that was a problem. We carried some valuable goods through that sector. If something were missing, we'd have to find it.

"You want me to go recover the goods?"

"I want you to go down there, prove to them that they have a missile problem, find out who is doing that, and put a stop to it in any way you want."

So I could kill someone if I needed to. "Right. I'll be on the next transport. I'm in Australia, so I'll need to..."

"I've had your things shipped onto the vessel coming for you. Everything you need."

I bit my cheek purposely. "Ferguson, we have talked about how I don't like my privacy invaded like that."

"I don't care."

No, he didn't. And I knew it too. If Ferguson wanted to send people into my apartment to pack my underwear, he could do just that. I was worth a great deal of money to the Union. They didn't want to lose me. But not enough to warrant staying out of my shit. Someday though, my value would rank C class and they'd stay away because I wanted them to.

Ferguson and all his ilk would know better than to get in my way.

That day was coming.

If dealing with the Cats got me one step closer, then so be it. "On my way."

The Cyclops would wait for another day.

~

I RUBBED the back of my neck as we approached Planet Cat. The view screen in my cabin showed me everything I needed to see. The planet was predictably blue and green with pretty clouds covering the atmosphere. From this view, it looked like Earth. Although intelligence insisted the Shifter Planets—Bear, Cat, and Wolf—all genuinely believed that they'd been here before humans were on Earth, that seemed like local bullshit to me, giving themselves some kind of import they certainly didn't have. Like everyone else, they lived on planets we had terraformed hundreds of years ago and then couldn't afford to keep up. Settlers were left there, and they somehow evolved. If the people who lived there during that time developed some kind of shifting ability based on local conditions and mutations of their sun or some such crap, that really wasn't so strange. On Terra-9, they spoke in each other's heads. Weird things happened on these planets. I didn't believe for one second that the shifters had terraformed us millions of years ago and somehow, we'd lost our shifting abilities. That was just nonsense.

Wasn't it?

Earth was downright boring these days. With the plagues, poverty for those not affiliated with the Union, and war against anyone who challenged the Union. Predictable human behavior. Eventually, we'd kill each other. But I'd be somewhere else and that would be someone else's problem.

The gravity was heavier down there on what we called Planet Cat. Heavy wasn't the technical term, but I'd worry about being correct and accurate when I arrived. For now, the fake gravity we had on our ships was starting to prepare me for the transition. Hence, the back pain. I rubbed again. Better to get the aches over with now. I knew how to distract myself from noticing.

Every planet had its challenges, and I was lucky we'd figured out how to mitigate them over the years. This would be easier than the time I had to stay awake for thirty hours at a time to fit in with the population. This planet at least had a twenty-six-hour day. I wouldn't notice the difference, even if others would have a huge problem with it. I'd long ago learned how to not get caught up in the problems that came with circadian rhythms.

It was all pretty interesting, actually. The government on the Cat Planet changed rather regularly. About every five years, give or take a few months. I couldn't make sense of how they decided when that would happen. There weren't any elections that we saw. We had so few spies down there. Sometimes, we'd be allowed to come for a small reason, like when the Cats wanted to help with a crisis on another planet, they'd sometimes let us pick something up to help. But our spies never lasted long, so we really only had bits and pieces of information here and there.

But as far as we could tell, one group of males would leave their home to aggressively take over other family groups. Before they could do that, however, they had to take over and run the whole planet. Sort of like they were a central authority that dealt with world issues as opposed to regional ones. While this was highly sought after on Earth, on the Cat planet, they seemed to prefer to be the regional authority, like it was higher up. But they had to earn that by being the bureaucrats who looked after planetary issues first. For the most part, they seemed like basically family tribes that were ever shifting. The goal wasn't to rule the planet, it was to have ownership over their tribes. Whoever was running the planet now was just biding their time until they could take over leadership in a smaller, regional area.

It wasn't clear if they killed the people they'd eventually

replace. Or what happened to the men who didn't end up leading at all. What did they do with them?

So much of the Shifter worlds remained totally secret. It was my misfortune to have to go try to make sense of this so I didn't step in any pitfalls while I found out who was shooting missiles at us. Did they have factions?

Just then, the ship bayed left. I grabbed on to my desk. "Captain?" I called into the communicator in my room. "What is happening?"

I traveled almost constantly. That kind of abrupt movement wasn't normal.

"Someone shot at us, ma'am. We were prepared. Buckle in. We're going to land now because I can't be sure they won't keep doing it."

I was supposed to have another day in orbit. Bracing myself, I buckled in. This was bound to be bouncy. And being shot at by a missile actually made my case better for me. Hard for them to argue that there were no missiles when I'd been shot at. "Captain, after you drop me off, go find that missile. I want it analyzed and a forensic report sent to me and the Union rep when you're done."

"I'm going to get you down safely now and worry about that later." He clearly spoke through gritted teeth. In the background, I could hear the other three crewmembers talking back and forth in loud voices, like they had to shout to be heard. All of them were very well trained. We might be a civilian company, but sometimes, we acted like military. When it came down to it, the Union was both.

I sat back in my chair. The way I'd spoken to the captain wasn't well done of me. I should not be barking orders while he was saving my life. Fuck. Sometimes, I wondered if I was human myself. Where was my common sense? I had to remember what really mattered—not dying. When I was working, I wanted to be efficient. I wanted things to be orderly. That was how I got things done. But it didn't always work in every situation.

This was real life, and real life was messy. That was why I loved surfing when I was off work. Then, I could embrace chaos. Here, I had to find the balance between inserting order and not pissing everyone I worked with off.

A lesson I kept having to learn over and over. I rubbed my eyes and then gripped my chair as it got even bouncier. Landings sucked, always, but this one was going to be particularly bad.

With no time to get used to the gravity ahead of time, it was going to be a bitch to deal with once I stepped off the ship. Not to mention the timing was wrong. The people who should be meeting me might not be there yet.

Three females who had some kind of familial relationships with the current government were supposed to be my guides. What was going to happen now? I hated not knowing. With nothing to do, I closed my eyes and waited for this whole thing to be over. At least if the missile had taken us out, it would have been fast. The dark thought crossed my mind and fled just as fast. Sometimes I was like that. Always had been. I would think really awful things that should get some kind of emotional response from me but wouldn't at all. It was like my mind could travel to dark places and bring back a sense of nothingness from there that should have made me horrified. Only it didn't. Just a sense of futility that I would have to push away before I could get on with my day. I got it from my mother. She was always like that too. Only with her, it wasn't fleeting.

And not that I could blame her. Life in the Dead Zone had been hell.

Minutes later, we were on the ground. The fact that we

were in one piece was impressive. Being shot at usually ended up with the person dead. I straightened and closed my tablets to put away the information I had on the Cats. At this point, whatever I knew, I knew. I wasn't going to be able to learn anything else until I was settled somewhere. The question was, where to go and what to do.

I was a day early, and I hadn't gotten to adjust to the gravity.

When we were officially on the ground, I rose from where I'd strapped in. This captain and I had traveled together before. He chauffeured people at my level around. That meant his ship was pretty comfortable but not luxurious. I'd seen C level transportation once when I'd had to take a meeting with someone at that level. Wow. I hadn't known it was possible to be that indulged while working. A spa? But I was also better than the people who had to fly in what essentially amounted to steerage. Those ships wouldn't have had a chance in hell of missing the missile. They were bigger, bulkier ships, harder to maneuver in emergencies.

And that was why I was here.

"Ms. Keyes." The captain took his hat off his head to speak to me. He was endlessly polite, which was why when he'd spoken to me earlier in clear frustration, it had really hit home to me that he had. I knew nothing about his life because I never asked, and he showed me the same courtesy. Others might not like that, but I had no room in my head for polite details that wouldn't matter one way or another when it came down to it.

"Captain, thanks for getting us down safely."

He nodded. "I'm concerned that I don't have a place to leave you."

Yes, I'd had that thought myself. But it wouldn't do in

this situation to share that with him. He might tell my superiors I had faltered, and then I'd be demoted. In front of others, I had it all together. Always and forever.

I shook my head. "I assure you it won't be a problem."

It was going to be one, though. A huge problem. A big fucking problem. First, I didn't know who had shot at us. And second, unlike most places, I had no ability to find the Cats I was to meet with. They were supposed to find me tomorrow. I'd never worked with so many loose ends, but these were different circumstances. Still, I'd pretend things were fine just as I was supposed to.

He smiled at me. "Great. Then I'll have the crew take your bag out."

I followed him outside, digging deep inside of myself in the ways I'd learned since I was a child to push down my anxiety until I couldn't feel it anymore. There was a deep, dark hole in the center of my soul, and it held every bad thing I wasn't able to deal with. I had to believe it would never get too full, because otherwise I couldn't function.

It would catch me at some point. I knew that intellectually. It always did for everyone. But I had been trained to take care of myself. I might look like a person who had to be taken care of, but the truth was I could manage on my own in almost every situation. There had only been once I'd fallen apart, and that was a long time ago. This wouldn't break me. I wasn't the first human to come to this planet. Visits were few and far between, but the general consensus was that the Cats were scary, secretive, and anxious to be rid of newcomers. They didn't want us around, but that didn't mean they were going to harm me.

More likely, they'd eject me from the place on the first transport they could find—or try to—after the people I was meeting tomorrow cleared the whole thing up in one conversation.

The only trouble with this was when I stepped outside, there was no one there at all. The space shuttle landing pad we found ourselves on was completely devoid of anyone. This was a new one for me. Space ports were always bustling with excitement, day and night. Shops. People trying to get here, there, and everywhere.

But not here.

There was such silence that the small hum of the ship seemed like an invasion of the night air around us. I turned around. It was dark, nighttime. Had I known that? I really hadn't focused on where we were landing and what time it was currently because I'd expected to land the next day when I was due to arrive at high noon.

I straightened my back. What did I know about this area? Well, it was supposed to be on the outskirts of a city. I didn't see any lights, but the landing area should have been due west of it. I pulled out my tablet and oriented myself. Okay. At least I should know which way to walk.

"I have to leave you now if you want me to get that missile." He made a face. "I can leave one of the crew here with you."

There were three other crew members, and one of them was dragging my bag over to me right now. He nodded, and I did the same as a form of greeting without having to speak. Sometimes, less said the better.

The last thing I needed was to have to cart around a crew member who was not licensed or certified to be here with me in the same way that he had just dragged my Union assigned bag. It had wheels and it converted to a backpack if I required it. But he'd had no way of knowing that since the bag was above his pay grade, and despite the fact that it was going to irk me from now until forever that there were scuff marks on my bag, I was going to pretend everything was fine.

"I'm good to go on my own. Thank you, Captain. I assume that they'll send you to pick me up when I'm done, so I'll look forward to that and hearing your report on the missile when you send it to me."

He looked left and right once before nodding. I could read his body language, the way his shoulders slumped, the way he ran a hand over his forehead. He wasn't comfortable leaving me here. That was kind. We were rarely that way to each other in the Union. It would never have occurred to me to do the same for him.

"I'll be okay."

He stepped away from me. "Call for pickup whenever you're ready. Be careful. These shifters...they're dangerous. That's why we stay away from them."

"We stay away from them because they've never been interested in joining the Union. They don't trade with us, maybe they trade with other shifters, I don't know, and our advances to reach out to them have been met with hostility. They are, it seems, basically isolationists, except when they pop their heads up to help with a crisis that we don't know how they hear about to begin with." I took a long breath. "Perhaps we are all losing out because of the lack of contact. In this case, they are initiating hostilities as per what just happened to us."

The captain sighed. "If you say so. You took that very calmly. Have you been shot at before?"

That wasn't a question he got to know the answer to. Some secrets were just my own. "Good luck finding that missile, Captain."

He took that as I'd meant it and reentered his ship. I bent

over to play with my bag. Fuck this fucking mess. Okay. I'd thought that. Now I'd find my calm again and play the good little company employee that I was. No one ever knew just how messed up I was inside. No one would believe my internal dialogue. To make sure of that, I spent a lot of time not even letting myself think much of anything at all.

I'd swung the bag up and on my back when I felt the eyes on me. It was a strange sensation and one I was sure could be traced back anthropologically in many ways. Still, it would always be impossible to describe it other than I just *knew* someone—or many people—was looking at me.

I felt for my weapon taped to my body. I could get off eight shots of the laser before it would have to be recharged. Eight, and then I could run. If I had to use it at all. The ship that brought me took off as I considered stopping it. The Union couldn't object to me bailing out if I were in danger. It would cost them credits to rescue me. Better to spare them that.

But it was too late now. By the time they landed again, I'd be facing whatever this was anyway.

And maybe these people didn't have hostile intent. Only the hair on the back of my neck stood at attention, and it really, really felt like this wasn't someone looking to welcome me with handshakes and hugs.

Not that I wanted to be hugged. Ever.

"Hello," I called out to the night, to whoever was listening. "My name is Tiffany Keyes. I come as representative of the Union. I'm expected tomorrow. But, as my ship was shot at, we landed early." The gravity of the planet lay solidly on my joints. They hurt like someone was crushing them. They were going to hurt until they didn't anymore. In the meantime, I had to pretend that I was fine.

Fuck.

"Could you kindly direct me to someone to speak to that could be made aware of my arrival? And, if anything...upsetting were to happen to me, my people know where I am. There are repercussions for hurting a Union representative while they are on official duty."

There was silence to my announcement and question. Moments passed. It was in those long seconds that I saw the eyes. Three sets of them. They seemed to glow in the darkness. Red and staring at me. I caught my breath.

I'd assumed I was talking to people who would be in their human form. But maybe I wasn't. Maybe out there in the darkness were shifters watching me in their big Cat form. Lions. That was what they were here. They sometimes were Lions, although they rarely let anyone other than their kind see them like that.

I caught my breath, and the red eyes vanished, replaced by three men who walked toward me almost in unison before they broke apart, so they ultimately came toward me from three different directions, which would block my way to reach the city if I had to make a run for it.

"Technically," the one who was south of me said first. "You're not on official duty until tomorrow. Technically, tonight, you are trespassing on our planet before you were invited. And as you said, we are, how did you put it, isolationists."

I tilted my head. At least they were human-looking. They walked toward me on two feet. Not four. Thanks to the device in my ear, I could understand anything said to me in most known languages. Presumably, since they could understand me, they could do the same.

It was hard to make them out in the dark. Maybe I really should have my eyes worked on. Seeing-in-the-dark implants. They'd be very helpful right now.

"It wasn't meant to be rude. Just a statement of fact." My anxiety rose again, I could feel it in the way my hands wanted to clench on their own. I shoved down the sensation. That dark pit. It could hold anything.

"And a true one," the one who was west of me answered. "Don't mind him, Tiffany Keyes. He just likes to be difficult. We are, as you said, isolationists. And I'm very happy to see that you didn't blow up."

This day was not going at all the way I thought it was going to. I really hoped I could continue my usual ability to pretend all was well, because otherwise this really might all blow up in my face.

2

My mind raced, full of thoughts that rapidly came and went. One jumped in and another fled. I wasn't easily scared. I guessed I had known from the moment I was born that death was a factor in life and mine might be sooner rather than later. And I didn't think that was an exaggeration. With a mother who had never been really okay and a father who came and went, I'd almost assumed there was a fifty-fifty chance that I would perish. We all did eventually. In fact, the countdown on when our hearts would stop beating started the second we were born.

It was the impermanence of things that made us the same. The rich would die. The poor would die. We all just did. But it was how we enjoyed ourselves in the meantime that mattered. I intended to get to my goal of luxury and not die standing here with three Lion shifters blocking my way and being somewhat aggressive in what they were saying. I'd dealt with lots of other cultures on other planets, and I'd learned to trust myself. If people seemed like they were being rude to me, then they probably were.

These guys were making a scene. The first and most pressing question was who was I talking to. Yes, I needed to be wary because they could kill, but ultimately, did they have the power to get me where I needed to go if I could get past this initial aggression? I had to stay logical. Giving in to terror would solve nothing right now. Not that it ever really did. Were these men worth me spending my time trying to negotiate with, or were they three nothings who had no reason to be here except to harass me and needed to be dealt with accordingly? There was no criminal system on this planet as far as I could tell. Truth was, I had no idea what dealing with them would mean or if there would be ramifications for doing so. Maybe they could just be made to go away.

I changed my stance, just slightly. I couldn't see them other than their outlines, but they looked strong. Muscular. Three to one, they'd beat me in a physical fight, and with what little I knew about shifters, I wouldn't be able to outrun them.

If it came down to it, I would have to outthink them. I'd been doing that with almost every person I'd met my whole life.

"Are you three the welcoming committee? Do you greet all the visitors like this, or am I special tonight?"

The one north of me finally spoke. "You've landed on our planet. A day before you're welcome. And as far as I can tell, you have no way to remedy that. Your ride left you. They must not like you very much."

"Maybe not. I'm not very likeable. But I am useful. Let's cut to the chase. Are you here to hurt me, or can we stop the grandstanding and you let me do what I was sent here to do?"

Frank. Direct. I wasn't sure what they would have said

because a gust of wind hit me in the face right then, blowing my hair out of its wildly disordered bun. I went to grab it when the wind shifted again, this time blowing the now loose blonde strands right back into my eyes. I pushed it away, righting it myself. Was that normal here? The back and forth of the wind gusts? For a person as orderly as I tended to be, my hair was forever the bane of my existence.

There was a storm coming in. I couldn't look up at the sky right then, but I could feel it on my skin, like electricity had built up in the air. It matched a battle that raged inside of me to keep my cool. Something might explode.

It was a quick moment, but maybe they hated the wind because all three of them sucked in air like they'd been deprived for hours, and almost simultaneously, their eyes turned red. Oh, that couldn't be good. I looked quickly, practically spinning in a circle, to see that it had happened to all three of them and then listened to the loud voice in my head that had managed to keep me alive all these years telling me to run. My whole body jolted. When my instincts said go, I went.

Backing up fast, I turned east and grabbed my laser. From the depths of human instinct, I knew I was prey surrounded by predators. There was no choice but to try to survive. I ran as fast as I could, knowing it wouldn't be good enough. My weapon wouldn't put them down if they were in their Lion bodies, but it might...

Two strong hands wrenched me to a stop, their hold firm but not painful as I suddenly came face-to-face with a man who was not winded at all. One who held me so close, our noses practically touched. He smelled like cinnamon. I had a lot more pressing on me than what the scent on this man happened to be. Still, it was soothing. I blinked and shook my head clear of it. This was not the time for me to suddenly go gooey over the way some man—a practically alien man—smelled.

"Easy, now. We're not going to hurt you."

Flanked on both sides by the appearance of the other two, I didn't feel like it was the time to go easy. "Oh no? Could have fooled me."

My hand was still on my laser. It would just take one flick. With it, I could take out the one in front of me and maybe the second one to my left before the third took me down. But maybe I'd have more luck than that.

"Things have changed." The one who might live through this spoke low. "In an unexpected, interesting manner. Sure, we thought to play with you for a little bit. But that has changed now. What is your name, female?"

Such a condescending way to speak to me. I took a deep breath. "I gave you my name when I first arrived. I'm Tiffany Keyes. If you have a problem with your short-term memory, I'd suggest finding some kind of healer. Now let go of my arm," that was to the one holding me, "or I'm going to lose my patience any second now."

The one right in front of me twitched his lips. He dropped his arm from where he held me. "If you run again, we will catch you, easily. Every time. You are not fast, although I appreciated the attempt. You have a brave soul, Tiffany. And that laser in your hand will only make us annoyed. We all wear shielding to protect us from your human toys, sorry, weapons. You can put it away. I hate the sulfur smell after those things are fired."

"William, brother, for the love of all things holy, stop yammering on and let the woman breathe." The one to the left groaned. "You are going to scare her, and then I am going to have to fix all of that. It would just be so much easier to begin as we intend to go, and since things are... different now...whatever brought you here, we'll just say thank you."

I had no idea what any of that meant. I really didn't. But I also didn't trust the idea that my laser wouldn't work on them. Sure, maybe—and it was a big maybe—they had some sort of material that made them resistant to lasers, but I doubted they could survive mine. I had things that weren't on the market for other people.

And I was done with this and whatever was going on.

I pointed my weapon right into the chest of the one who had been holding me. What had they called him? William. That was right. An old-fashioned Earth name that I didn't hear very much but wasn't totally gone. Interesting. That was either his name or just how the translator made me hear it. I'd probably never know which.

But in the meantime, I had other things to think about. "Listen to me, the easiest way to convince a person not to shoot me would be for me to tell them that their weapons don't work. I'd be a fool to fall for that. I am many things, but none of them are foolish. In fact, some people have suggested it is what is missing in my life. But let me be clear. I will shoot you and risk it not working because maybe it will. Now, I have a meeting tomorrow I intend to make. I'm not going to let three" —I kept my gaze where it was, even as I addressed all of them. I didn't dare lose eye contact with the one that I had— "annoyances get in my way of doing my job. So let me go, or I'm going to blast you."

The one with the gun pointed right in his chest grinned at me slowly. "Oh, we won't be letting you go. I can assure you of that. But go ahead and shoot me. I'd like to know if you would."

He wanted to know if I would? He'd picked the wrong woman to fuck with today. The fact that I had done so many times before was why I was still alive and such a high up Union rep. I didn't even hesitate before I pulled the trigger, yanking my arm back when I did and leveling it at the other two, back and forth, fast.

Only the one I had shot was laughing instead of lying on the ground near death and wishing the seconds until he was officially gone were over.

"So you do have it in you, little human. Interesting." He rubbed his chest. "But I never lie. You can't hurt me with that. Now hand it to Casper before you hurt yourself with it. I do like to see you have claws, even if you aren't technically a Cat." He dropped my arm.

"Enough of that." The one he'd called Casper pulled the gun from my hand. I let him. Maybe it was shocking that William was fine or just the futility of the whole thing dawning on me, but I opened my hand and let him take it without any struggle. "You can feel free to believe us when we speak to you. Lying is a Canine problem."

It was so weird to hear them talk to me like that. Cats. Canines. They looked like men. Sure, their eyes glowed red and apparently their clothes resisted weaponry, but no one in front of me seemed like the housecat I'd encountered the last time I'd gone to a company party at the head of human resources' home.

The anxiety I'd swallowed wanted to force its way back up. I pushed it down. No. I couldn't lose it now. I was trained to deal with cultures on foreign planets. This wasn't going to be any different. I just had to, somehow, keep it together.

Somehow being the key word in that thought.

"What do you plan on doing with me?" It was better to get that out there now, so I knew what to expect and I could gear up inside for how much I'd have to fight back. So far, they'd been honest. And they said they didn't lie, which for now, I had to believe. What was I going to have to do to survive? Kidnapped for money or something much more nefarious.

The one to my right stroked my back. I was so worked up, I could barely feel it. "Do with you? Well, right now, I think we are going to bring you some place so you can be warm for the night. There is a storm coming in. Then tomorrow, we're all going to figure out who shot missiles at your spaceship. Such a thing is completely forbidden, and if our people are breaking the law, then they are to be dealt with. Harshly. You're going to be comfortable and well looked after. For now, that is what we are going to do. Things have taken a sharp left turn with you for us and all of us—we need to take a breath."

I didn't have the slightest idea what he meant by that, but he continued to speak, and I didn't have a chance to ask him as I tried to process all the new information being thrown at me.

"Let's start again. We scared you." He pointed at his eyes. "It was the red glow, right? Humans don't do that. We do. The why and how we can explain another time. Generally, we don't to humans, but you're different."

I was? How so and...

"Let me introduce myself. That's how civilized people start. My name is Oscar. The man you just tried to shoot—and bravo at that—is my brother William. And over there holding the weapon is my other brother Casper. We are very pleased to meet you, Tiffany Keyes."

The way he said my name, it sounded like he rolled it around in his mouth. It was musical in a way I'd never heard before. I shook my head.

"You three...you can find out about the missiles because they're your people?"

I wanted to be clear on those points. The rest of it I could untangle later. There were facts to deal with.

Casper nodded. "Yes. The storm, remember, we need to go. Now."

The three younger males who ran things until they took over an older man's family. Was it possible I had just stumbled upon them? Or were they hanging out by the airfield on purpose? Had they shot missiles at me?

This was interesting. "I'm supposed to meet with three women tomorrow."

Oscar shook his head. "That's canceled. We didn't believe there were missiles being fired. Thought to pawn you off on others to deal with. But now that has changed."

I raised an eyebrow. "You didn't believe there were missiles, but now you do just because I said that it happened?"

Perhaps I was looking a gift horse—sorry, cat—in the mouth, but I was skeptical by nature and this seemed a little bit too convenient for my taste.

William took a long, deep, audible breath. Did he want me to hear him do that? So I'd know I was frustrating him? Or was I reading into something that wasn't there? "Lies taste bitter. That's why we don't do it. Every person you encounter on this planet can smell if you're lying. It's better not to do it. You aren't lying, beautiful. Something else that smells very awful to our senses is rainstorms."

He took my arm and, in a firm but not painful embrace, hustled me with him down the road in the direction I'd wanted to walk anyway. This wasn't okay, but I had nothing I could do about it at the moment. He wasn't hurting me. For now, I'd leave it alone until I could think of a better solution.

And then there was the fact that my anxiety had actually cooled a little. I didn't want to clench my fists. Why was that happening? I cleared my throat. "How was it that you three happened to be here right now?"

"We detected a ship landing. Unauthorized. We came to look." William had me, but Casper was very close. In fact, Oscar was too. All three of them were pretty invasive of my personal space, as far as my comfort level for it went. That could vary based on planetary custom.

Thunder cracked in the sky, and William's body stiffened. These guys really didn't like rain. That might be an important thing to remember later. Truthfully, I couldn't remember the last time I'd been this flabbergasted. For the most part, I never got rattled. But these three were really throwing me off my game in a way I couldn't remember being for a very long time.

Why that was would have to be examined later. I'd long ago learned to compartmentalize my emotions.

I wouldn't lose it here.

With no choice but to trust them—if they'd wanted to kill, maim, or do something awful to me, they could have more easily accomplished that alone on the airfield. We were walking in the direction of the city. It made sense to at least go this far because I could escape more easily there if I needed to.

I chewed on my lip and then stopped. That was a tell that I couldn't afford to have right now. I had to keep my face blank, my emotions low. If they could smell lies, what else could they scent that I couldn't?

After a moment, William pulled my bag off my back. I whirled to grab it back, and he held up his hands, smiling again. "Don't get your fur ruffled, kitten. I'm just carrying it for you because it looks heavy."

The endearments had to stop now. "I am not a kitten. Or beautiful. Or anything like that. My name, as you know, is Tiffany Keyes, and I am a Union representative here to—"

"Investigate missiles, yes, we know." William smiled as he interrupted me, which didn't make the fact that he did it any less rude. What was more was that even though I'd never be able to describe how I knew it, I was fully sure that he was completely aware of just how rude he had been.

Finally, he sighed. "Please go on."

But I didn't want to just then. Instead, I swung around to look at the city we'd just walked into. There had been nothing around us, just a lot of trees everywhere as we'd walked, but then we'd come to the top of a path and right in front of us was a city. When I was done with this mission, I was going to go see a doctor. I'd never been so off in my life, so completely distracted that I was missing my surroundings, which was a big no-no.

The city, or so it had been described, wouldn't have qualified on Earth under the designation. We'd have called it a big town. It really was amazing. We'd walked for a few minutes and arrived here, but I hadn't been able to see this place from the road leading up to it because the lights on the small buildings all had a glow that kept them from shining upward, only down to illuminate the streets around us once we'd arrived. As though they meant to keep the skies bright. On Earth, we couldn't see the stars anymore except in deserted places. Being able to see those glowing orbs usually meant you weren't somewhere safe.

I'd seen the night sky from all over the universe, but I'd never gotten over that sensation. Resisting the urge to rub my arms, I continued to make note of what I saw. Mid-sized buildings. Wide open spaces everywhere else.

"Hey." Oscar nudged my arm. "What just made you scared?"

I stared at him. "Emotions have scents?"

He nodded. "They do."

That was going to be a problem. Lies had scents. Emotions had scents. How did people here do anything at all? Did they silently feel nothing and never have to tell anyone something that wasn't true? This was going to be hard. I did lie on these kinds of jobs. Often and very well.

I swallowed. "My emotions are my own and not your business. We're here to get something done together. If you can't do that, give me to the people who I was supposed to see, and I'm sure it will be fine."

William grinned next to him, his face illuminated by the dash of light coming off the closest building. "Don't mind my brother. We're raised to leave emotions alone. To ignore the scents and mind our business. It's just that you are so... surprising. Not someone we ever expected to meet."

The sky lit up with lightning, and they once again hustled me along. Once I was settled, wherever we were going, I might consider checking in with my superiors. I never did. It was one of the reasons that they liked me. I just got things done.

But they might want to send someone else.

Something was wrong with me. I shouldn't be so thrown off just because things were new. I never had been before.

I shook my head as they ushered me inside of a building before closing the door behind them. I caught my breath as I took in the warmth of the home in front of me. If these men wanted to kidnap me, they'd taken me to a palace-like place to do so.

"This is your home?" I took a hesitant step and stopped. There were rules to these things. Only I didn't know them here. I'd not expected to be staying in anyone's house. Protocols I hadn't studied...

Casper touched the small of my back. "Come, Tiffany. Let me show you to your room."

The colors in the rooms we passed were warm. Someone had painted the walls, as they weren't just white. My home back on Earth was starkly untouched. I'd taken no time to do anything with them. But here, there was ivory, beige, and even rustic reds on the walls. That was all I had time to note before we kept going to where I would sleep.

"You live here all the time? This is where you run things?"

William spoke from behind me. "We are right now. Wherever we go, we have a home. But these are held for the current rulers at all times. When we choose a pack and take it, we will have a permanent place. We haven't yet decided where that will be."

Oscar brushed my side. "You'll have a say in that."

I would? "Why would I get any say in where you choose to permanently place yourselves?"

Casper opened a door. "Because you are our mate."

His words threw me for such a loop, I tripped over my own feet, nearly falling on my face, which I would have done if William hadn't grabbed me by the arm and hauled me back up. "Careful, you're breakable. Which is going to make this complicated."

I shook my head, wrenching my arm back. "I am not. Absolutely not. Without the slightest doubt, your mate."

His smile was slow. "You are. And it's highly unusual. We all hope for a true mating, but in reality, they almost never happen anymore. Our Lions recognized your scent, and it is real. You are the first true mate in generations, actually. Thank you for existing."

I swallowed to give myself a second since I had absolutely no idea what the fuck to say. "I don't have it in me to unpack what you just said to me. I can't do that. But you are mistaken. I'm not anyone's mate, and frankly, the fact that you call it that—Hold on...wait a second. There are three of you. I can't belong to all three of you."

Oscar sighed. "You can. That is how we do things here. It has to do with our Pride. There is some account of one female mating with twenty men of the same pride. That was quite a thing, I imagine, but it may be just a story. Most matings are three to five men with a woman."

Twenty? Oh, no. Absolutely not. I didn't like sex, and I was certainly not going to do it with twenty men. Over my dead body. I would...destroy this place...somehow...before I let that happen.

They looked at each other. Yes, they could smell emotion. Casper opened and closed his mouth. Okay, they weren't going to comment on it. Then I would.

"Whatever you're smelling, that's how I feel right now. I expect you to stay away from me. There won't be any mating. Not now. Not ever. And if you try, I will have the might of the Union reign down on your heads." I wasn't sure I could actually do that. It would really depend on how the valuation came back on me. Likelihood was that I wasn't worth the effort they'd have to put in to do that. But they didn't need to know that.

William's face fell. "No one would ever touch you without your permission here. That isn't how this works. And it breaks my heart just a little that you live in such a place where that might happen to you."

I sucked in a breath. "There is one universal truth everywhere I go. There are always people who are willing to take what they want despite not having permission. That much I know. We aren't mates. You're confused."

I shut the door on them then. What had happened here? I leaned my head against the wall. In a million years, I couldn't have imagined this. Mate? Three men? No. That wouldn't be happening. Not now. Not ever.

3

I considered blockading the door, but as I forced myself to breathe, hearing no sounds from outside, I decided against it. I was here to do a job. I could handle all sorts of things. The trouble was that I'd gone all over the universe with my laser, and it had offered me the kind of security that came with knowing I was more lethal than anyone would think.

Truth was, I was tiny. Had been by Earth standards at five feet tall. Here on this planet, if all the men were as big as the three out there in the hall, I would be considered even smaller by comparison. I hadn't investigated the sheer size of the population here before arrival. Those three were brothers. Maybe they were just really tall—six foot seven inches tall at least, each. But if everyone was like that here, I was going to be extra short for sure.

And I didn't have a working weapon. Out of everything that had happened, that was the most bizarre. First of all, I'd pulled the trigger. I didn't know what had possessed me to do so, except that in that moment, he had really seemed like a threat. Or maybe I'd wanted to prove something. That was more concerning. There were darker sides of my personality, sides I kept to myself, sides I'd long since conquered. Was my darkness rising from where I kept it far away from the universe?

I did like to win. More than I should.

Like I was going to conquer that wave.

The way my father never had.

I put my hand on the wall and pounded it once. Then twice. I had no business discharging that weapon. It was a completely unprofessional thing to do.

I took two deep breaths. Doing things like that would have me removed. I couldn't fuck this up now. I was too close to making all my dreams come true. I could have the life I wanted if I just didn't blow this and whatever came next. I had an end date when this would stop if I could just get there.

Okay. These people were strange. Their natural mutations made their eyes turn red. They talked about themselves as being Cats. I hadn't seen anyone turn into a Lion. What did it mean to be a shifter? They were confused about me, thinking I was their mate.

So far, no one was trying to have sex with me. I didn't even know what being a mate entailed. Maybe it meant nothing I needed to worry about. They wanted me to help them pick their home. Well, they'd have to move on from that.

I took another deep breath. Prepare and be ready. That was the mantra of someone like me. That was how I got out of my meager beginnings when so few ever did before me. Okay. I stepped back from the door. I needed my stuff. One of them still had it. William.

I cracked open the door to find all three of them lined up, staring at me. Were they just going to stand there?

Casper raised an eyebrow. "Are you hungry? Is there anything I can do to make you more comfortable?"

I reached out for my bag. "I'll take that back now, William. Thank you."

He handed it to me. "What else can we do?"

"You should...go about your night. We can talk tomorrow morning about the missiles. Thanks."

They didn't take their eyes off of me, and yet I couldn't help feeling that it was as though they'd shared a look among themselves I couldn't understand. I stepped back, ready to close the door again. Surely they couldn't spend the whole night lined up outside of my room. I'd told them I was fine, they'd been polite, they had to get on with their night. I'd been clear about my boundaries and said no.

But just to be safe, I did move the desk on the side of the room in front of the door.

I turned around and examined the room. My head was clearer. I could think. It was gorgeous. I blinked to make sure I hadn't imagined the space. I'd actually never seen anything like it. The bed was low, the bedframe a dark wood and practically on the floor. It was more than big enough for two people. A group could sleep comfortably on it.

The bed itself was covered in a white sheet with four pillows that were also draped in the same soft-looking white sheet. On the end of the bed was a brown blanket folded on the edge like I might like to use it if I was cold or leave it alone if I wasn't. Two white chairs, matching the bed, were on the other side of the room, one where the brown desk would have been before I pushed it in front of the door. The walls were painted ivory, and the shades of the drapes matched the bed, covering huge windows.

Compelled like I couldn't explain, I strode to the window and looked out. The sky I'd been staring at outside was illuminated right there in front of me in the floor to ceiling windows. It was like being outside without being outside. I stared up at the stars.

A thousand worlds with stories and miserable people living miserable lives. It was the same everywhere I went. I found the washroom through a door and quickly washed up, taking the makeup off my face. It had been the same look for years. Professional, unless I was going to swim, I took it off to sleep and reapplied it the next morning. The same small amount that said I meant business. It was what some people called severe, making me look older than I was.

My hands shook as I rinsed my face, and I ignored the sensation. Nervous? No, I was fine. If I said it enough, maybe I would believe it. Fine. Fine. Fine.

I opened my bag and pulled out my night clothes. Some women had hot and sexy. But that wasn't what I did. Since I could never be sure what might happen at night, I was always practical with it. Long pants that were close to leggings without quite being that tight and a long white T-shirt that went past my rear end. Bulky and easy if I had to run.

That had happened just once when I was first starting out. I shook my head. I dressed for what might happen. And why was I even thinking about this?

I actually had to lower myself to get into the low bed. Usually, I had to climb up onto things, but not this bed. That was when I realized the lights were on. I chewed on my lip. Almost universally, this was a problem. I could figure out showers, baths, and food everywhere, but the lighting was never the same on any two planets. How did the lights go off in this room?

I rose, strangely since the position was so new to me, and examined the walls until I found a button. Pushing it, I waited to see what would happen, and three seconds later, the room was drenched in darkness.

That was on the easier side. I'd been unable to turn off the lights in UA-542 once. I never did figure it out, since the people there viewed asking questions as weakness. On that planet, my data devices hadn't synced to space-operations. I'd been really out of luck there. I just dealt with the light. But now I was bathed in darkness, except that the window drapes were open. The starlight bled into the room like its own light source, and I was grateful for the intrusion. Catching sight of the stars without any light at all stole my breath from my body and brought tears to my eyes.

What was the matter with me? I wiped at my eyes, sucking back those tears. A noise in the hall caught my attention, but it immediately passed. I shook my head. They couldn't possibly be able to smell my emotions through a closed door. Had to be a coincidence.

I decided right then and there to leave the drapes open. I wanted that light in the room. If I rolled over and looked, I wanted to see those stars in the room with me, twinkling lights of places I could pretend were beautiful.

Getting back in my low bed, I turned my back on the decision I'd just made and stared at the wall instead. Sometimes, I didn't even understand myself.

I closed my eyes. There were missiles to find tomorrow. Missiles that had fired at me and almost ended my life.

Somehow, I had to pull it together. I'd just keep reminding myself that Tiffany Keyes didn't fall apart. I was a survivor. Nothing was going to change that, ever.

～

"DADDY, couldn't you take me with you?" The ocean covered my legs up to my knees where I straddled the slightly too big for me surfboard, moving gently over a rare patch of easy waves for the Pacific Ocean. The sun beat down on my head, and I wished I had a hat I could wear on the waves that wouldn't fall off. But it cost a fortune to buy hats. We got allotments for clothes, and a hat wasn't included. I couldn't afford to lose one in the ocean. So I'd probably come home from this adventure with my dad with my arms tanned and my head red, shining through my blonde hair for the world to see.

It wasn't healthy to get sunburned. The rich could get their skin fixed. Lasers, creams. Maybe even some rich person voodoo. I didn't know what people did, only that they could do it. My education was lacking. I knew they weren't teaching us very well. They didn't spend much on teaching those they thought were going to be dead before they were twenty.

Not me. I had plans.

"Dad? Did you hear me?"

My father looked up from his surfboard and smiled at me. He was always so relaxed on the water, happy. So completely different than the few times I saw him on land. But this was our thing. Our only thing. He came and picked me up twice during the summer, and we went surfing.

He'd probably buy me an ice cream. Although last time, he hadn't.

"I heard you, Tiff."

He was the only one who called me Tiff. Everyone else used my full name. I loved when my father called me Tiff. It filled me up inside. I didn't have much of a father, but when he was there, he was spectacular. The other dads looked worn down by life, but not mine. He was strong, healthy. He drove trucks over the mountains between here and some of the colony towns. A person had to be tough to do his job. There were so many people who died doing it. They were robbed or they drove off the road. Or they were kidnapped from their trucks and forced to work in the space fleet hauling supplies for the Union until they died.

But not my father. He made it every year and came back here every summer to feel the sun, surf, and see his Tiff. These were my moments with him.

"Dad?"

He flipped his hair out of his eyes, the spray of salt showing in his blond locks as he regarded me. I got my coloring from him. Blonde hair, blue eyes. Mom had brown hair and chestnut-colored eyes. I was tiny like her. Dad was tall. I hadn't gotten those genes.

"You can't. You know it's not possible, and you know why."

I nodded. "I can study in the truck. I won't even bother you. Much." I smiled. I might have to bother him some-times. It wouldn't be realistic to say that I never could. Everyone was a bother sometimes, even though I tried so hard never to be.

He shook his head. "Not possible. Can't take a kid on the road."

His tone suggested there would be no moving him on this subject, and I knew when to leave things alone. Most of the time. "She's bad, Dad. I'm not sure... I'm not sure she's going to make it another year. And then what? Where do I go if she's dead?"

My father sighed loudly. "Let's hope that doesn't happen."

Hope? I wasn't sure what that was exactly. I'd never had any. He didn't have answers for me, and so he was changing the subject. He didn't care that my mother wanted to be dead so much that I wasn't sure she wasn't going to do things to make that happen. Staying alive for me would only sustain her for so long. My mother had no hope. No future to look forward to. Not even any faith that I had a good one coming.

She never went out on the ocean with us. Dad didn't invite her, and they barely spoke the few times he picked me up. But even if he had, she'd have turned him down. There was no joy for her.

"Come on, let's paddle. There are waves to catch, and my Tiff can ride them better than any other little girl her age."

I'd gotten my period. I wasn't such a little girl anymore. And he either couldn't see it, or he didn't care.

I WOKE up with my heart racing in my chest and quickly pushed my head against my knees to stop the sensation. I had to breathe. Why was I freaked out? I'd had a dream, well a memory. Of my father. It hadn't even been a bad one. Not that I had any of those of my dad. I'd never seen him enough to make any. Just surfing. Until he'd missed a summer. Then he'd shown up the next one and never again.

I'd heard years later when I'd hired an investigator to find him that he'd been found dead on the road. His throat had been cut. Maybe he'd been right—the road was no place for a kid. Then there had been the other matter of his real family. Wife. Three sons. I'd never met them. They didn't know about me, and I'd never have known they existed if not for that investigation I'd been able to do because of my Union job.

His real family didn't know I existed.

My mom had been a woman he'd been fucking for a while. How he'd ended up with me when birth control was one of the few things people from my place in the world could get easily, I didn't know. The Union didn't want too many of us around. A small amount so that we could do their menial labor. Not so many they had to lose money on feeding us.

I sucked in my breath. The sun was coming up in the room. It was great to leave the drapes open for the stars, not that I'd looked, but the morning sun was another thing. I rose, which wasn't hard since I was so low to begin with and finally used to it, and walked to the window. Vast open nothingness was everywhere. Pinks and golds greeted the day.

With a shake to snap out of whatever was coming over me, I shut those drapes and the sun away from my life. Flipping on the fake lights, I padded to the bathroom. I didn't know if the Lion brothers were earlier risers, but I was getting up regardless of their schedule. If they were who they said they were, it was time to find missiles.

If they weren't, I was getting out of their beautiful home to meet the women who expected me.

I showered and dressed quickly. My hair was still wet, so I braided it. If I left it like this, it would be slightly curly when I pulled it out later. I'd have to deal with straightening it then, but I'd worry about that then.

One thing at a time. I always had to do the next right thing.

Missiles. Then on to the next mission. Then the next one. I'd put Lion-shifters-thought-I-was-their-mate into the category of weird assignments and laugh at it someday.

Mate...it was so animalistic. Wasn't that what wolves did? We still had those on Earth. In zoos. I'd never seen a lion except in pictures. I thought there were some somewhere in a preserve. But I wasn't sure. I'd never given it the least bit of thought.

And for some reason, guilt came with that realization. I shoved away that sensation. There were plenty of things to feel guilty about, but that wasn't going to be one of them. I didn't have much to do with animals. When I'd been growing up, they'd just been another mouth to feed.

So we'd never had any around and certainly had no resources to go look at ones that others paid to observe from the safety of their concrete paths. Observed as they gazed at the false surroundings someone had taken the time to carve out for the beasts. No one was fooled into thinking it was real, particularly not the animals themselves.

At least that had been my disgruntled impression the one time I'd gone. Looking at the animals whose names they'd forced us to learn but never allowed us to really see—when the rich kids from other zones had had the opportunity—had pissed me off as a grown up. I didn't like to remember the disparity of my past.

Anything that brought up those thoughts and memories needed to be avoided. That included zoos.

After I pushed the desk back where it belonged—thank goodness it was light enough for me to do that—I opened the door to find William on the floor. He looked up when I stepped into the hallway, slowly moving his gaze from my sensible flat black shoes up to my black pants suit with the Union insignia on my arm, to my braided blonde hair and severely dark makeup. He lifted an eyebrow, but I wasn't sure he approved of my look.

Not that I wanted any of that from him.

I cleared my throat. "Good morning."

He rose, slowly, in a way I wasn't sure I'd ever seen anyone do before. William didn't so much stand up as he slid, the wall at his back, in a way that had to be from pure core strength. "Good morning, Tiffany."

In the light of day, in his house, I could make things out about William that I hadn't focused on in the rush and suddenness of the day before. He was dark-haired, they all were, but his face was slightly longer than his brothers, if I was recalling them exactly correctly. Also, he was at least one inch taller than they were too.

Dark whiskers had grown in overnight, coating his cheeks. The effect was striking. Along with his dark brown eyes that contained a gold rim on the outside, he would be the type of man that I stared too long at in the few times I had to do such things. I didn't like sex, but I did like admiring the beauty of the male form.

"Did you spend the whole night out here?"

He tilted his head slightly. "Of course."

I opened and closed my mouth. "Where I come from, that isn't something we do. We don't sit outside of guest's rooms all night. Is that customary here?"

There. I'd regained my equilibrium. That was exactly how I should have handled that. My diplomatic abilities were back in place. Since I knew so little about things here, maybe it was absolutely normal for him to have done this.

"You aren't a guest." He motioned his hand to the hall. "Are you hungry?"

My stomach growled, answering for me before I could tell him that I was. I smiled. "Sure. I could eat." Since he wasn't going to walk in front of me, I had no choice but to go first. The kitchen wasn't far, and when I stepped inside, I sucked in a breath. It was huge, and there were devices I'd never seen anywhere before. Multiple things that could be stoves and then some other electronics I'd never be able to describe.

I swung around. "This is a beautiful room."

William nodded again. "I am enormously glad to hear approval in your voice. Although, I can't say that I had anything to do with it. As I told you last night, this place is kept for us. It isn't of our design or even our style. But I'll remember that you like this."

I took a deep breath. "William, I ignored the not-a-guest remark. But I now have to say something. What I like doesn't matter. I'm not your mate. I'm just a human woman who happens to be here looking for answers. After I get those, I'll leave. You'll forget me, and that will be that. Perhaps my scent, one you're not used to, is confusing all of you."

His laugh surprised me. What was funny about what I'd just said? "I'm never confused. Not when it comes to scents. I'm remarkably clearheaded, and as I've been around many, many humans from Earth, I think that it is probably safe to say that I'm not misconstruing what I smell from you."

Putting aside the mate part of that, I stared at him. "How? I was under the impression your planet was very..."

"Isolationist. Yes, I remember from last night. We don't get humans here, but some of us leave for a while to explore our universe. I lived on Earth for a year."

Lived on Earth? We didn't have shifters there. It would have to be reported. "How is that possible? Earth requires shifters to check in."

His smile was slow as he opened up what I quickly discovered was their equivalent of a fridge. It just blended into the cabinets in such a way I'd never have been able to tell. "How would you know? Or not you specifically, but how would anyone know if I was there?"

I pointed at my eyes to indicate. "Yours turn red."

"Yes, but I can control that. They only do that if I let

them. A male Lion shifter learns to control his shifting instincts when he is twenty years old. I came to Earth at thirty. My eyes stayed brown the whole time. And I never felt the need to shift into my Lion form, although I missed it. So I'll ask again. How would you know?"

I supposed I wouldn't. If I passed him on the streets, he'd seem human to me. A gorgeous human. I shoved away that thought. Not helpful. "Where on Earth did you go?"

"All the big sites. The former cities. The Pacific rim. The polar conservatory. The hub of government." He held up an egg—they looked the same everywhere—and when I nodded, he cracked it into a pan.

Those were the big sites, that was for sure. "I was just in the Pacific rim before I came here."

"Is that where you're from?" The egg sizzled in the pan. Did this place have coffee? Some places did, some didn't. Or some kind of equivalent. Anything caffeine would do.

"No, I'm not from there. I grew up in a place called the Dead Zone." He was going to burn my egg. I walked over and took the pan from him, which he smirked at but let me do. This wasn't a restaurant, he didn't have to cook for me. I turned down the heat on the pan. His oven worked just like my own at home.

"I don't know that place, never heard of it. Why is it called the Dead Zone?"

"Well, they say you're born dead there. Don't worry. It would never be on a list of places you'd have seen." The egg was done. "So you spent a year undiscovered on Earth. That's interesting. Why there?"

He leaned over and breathed me in, loudly. I froze at the action. There was something sensual about it, even as he invaded my personal space. I caught my breath.

"You smell plenty alive to me, Tiffany."

I forced my attention back to the egg and not what his strange, non-human behavior did to me. My nipples hardened, which was a very new experience. Maybe sometimes that happened when I was cold, but not otherwise.

"It's an expression that those of us who are from there use to describe it. It means that we are born basically for the purpose of dying. Nothing else in life." I wished I'd never said anything, and I wasn't sure why I had at this point to begin with. It had just slipped out. Why had I told him when I didn't give out personal information to people I met on missions?

I took the pan with the egg off the fire, turned the stove off, and looked around for a plate that William was suddenly holding right out in front of me. "Thank you. Are you going to eat?"

"I ate earlier."

The day had just begun. They must eat before the sun rose. That was a good note to make going forward. Pointing at the counter, I asked one more question. "Okay to sit there to eat?"

"That is what it is there for."

His words made sense, but he might be surprised how many things were different on other planets. Like maybe this was a place they only ate lunch, and it would be deeply offensive if I sat there now.

"Why did you go to Earth?"

He hadn't done anything but answer me since the smelling me moment, not engaging me in conversation. Maybe I'd already upset him. This wasn't going to do. Not if we were going to get through this together. I needed him, or I had to find someone else to help me. My discomfort had nothing to do with his dark smoldering eyes and the way they seemed to watch every breath I took like it was interesting to him.

My host—well, the one currently with me—sat down next to me. "Some of it was wanderlust. We're very happy here on this planet, compared to how I hear it is other places. But I wanted to see if what they told us about how nice it is here was true. I don't tend to take truth as truth without looking into things on my own. If something feels off, I want to know why. The other part was the issue of mating that you keep avoiding—and good job on the way you ignore or shift on that—was that it has always bothered me that we didn't have true mating anymore. Why had it stopped? I wondered if it was because we had so little to do with other planets. That didn't used to be the case."

"You thought if you found yours, then you could make a case for letting others back here?"

His grin surprised me. "And she pivots again. Yes, I did. But make no mistake. I didn't think I'd have to make a case. What I planned to do was take control, as I have done, and announce to everyone we were opening our borders. But I found no one because, of course, what I needed to do was sit here and wait for you to simply arrive."

I needed to push harder on understanding how their government worked for my report when I was out of here, but it was clear I was going to have to address this head-on because it wasn't going away.

"William." I took a bite of my egg. It was perfect. Eggs really did taste the same everywhere. Although I didn't know if it was a chicken who had made this or if I was eating something else. Sometimes, it was better not to know. "I'm not from here. I don't have mates. If I were to meet someone, it would be a choice I would make. Like, oh I like him or I like her. I'd get to know them, and if we liked each other enough that we wanted to spend permanent time together, we'd make that decision and get to it. There is no such thing as true mates for me. So I can't be that for you. Something is wrong. Besides, I can't possibly be mated to three of you. That isn't how it works for us either."

He walked to the fridge-like machine, took out a drink that was dark brown, poured it into a glass, and then handed it to me. I took a sip. It was sweet, like an iced coffee. Apparently, he wasn't going to answer what I'd said. "Is this caffeinated?"

"Yes." He nodded his head. "I thought you might like some of that. Coffee was a big deal on Earth. This is the closest we have here. No one drinks it warm. But it'll do the same."

I was grateful for it. "Thanks."

"You're welcome. Here is the thing about what you said —it's wrong." He sat back down next to me. "You make it sound like a business transaction. You expect to like someone enough to decide to spend your life together?

Where is the love in that? Earthlings talk about love. I've heard them."

I set down my fork. "I've never had the luxury of love. It's not real to me or even something I remotely understand. And where is love in your arrangement? You say I'm your mate because you smelled me and somehow the animal inside of you decided it was so? You can't possibly claim to love me. You don't even know me, you may not like me."

He leaned on his elbow. "Love comes later after the recognition of the mating. It builds. It happens. I will love you. I'm already enthralled."

Now there was a word I didn't hear flung around very often. Enthralled. "I'm afraid that in this case, what you're feeling is going to have to be one-sided, and it is my hope that you'll get over it. I'm not right for you. I'm not built for love." I'd always known these things about myself. It hurt to say it, but sometimes truth hurt. It was still worth saying. "And I don't like sex, I don't want to have it. So you're better off with someone else. Tell your animal half, or however that works, to find someone else."

I couldn't believe I'd said that, but as it was not the craziest thing I'd said since I'd come here, I had to attribute it to some sort of trauma caused by the missile attack since I couldn't figure out any other reasons. I would have sworn I felt fine about it, but clearly, it had thrown me off-kilter. I was just going to have to go with it until I could get it under control and hope I didn't screw up my whole life in the meantime.

He reached over, running a hand down the exposed skin of my arm. "You think you don't like sex?" His eyes turned red, and I gasped. What did it mean when they did that? "You'll like sex with me, I can promise you that. I would never stop giving you pleasure until you came apart in my arms. But you are, as you've pointed out, not one of us. I like that about you. I like that you are so different than everyone else I have ever known. Within moments of meeting you, I knew that about you. And so I will wait until you are more certain, until you are not questioning every word that comes out of your mouth, every move you make as though it might make the world explode. Then I will own you, Tiffany. Not alone, of course. I've always known I would share my one and only with my brothers. That is how our Pride would work. But I will own you with them. And you will own us in return. Then you will know who you were always meant to be."

He petted my arm gently up and down as he spoke to me.

It was hard to concentrate with the warmth his touch provoked inside of me. Was I touch starved? Was that a thing? I'd never liked it when others wanted to hold my hand or hug me. There was my space, and the rest of the world had to stay out of it. Maybe I needed more of this. It was the only explanation I could come up with that didn't involve wanting to have sex with William when I knew for a fact that I'd hate every second of that and wish it were over before it started.

"I don't believe in things like 'supposed to' when it comes to outcomes of my life. There is only what happens and how you react to it. The universe is chaos. What you're saying implies some kind of destiny, some kind of reason why I landed here. If you're attracted to me, then I suppose I should say thank you and ask you to keep that to yourself."

His smirk was stupid sexy. I hated that I liked it. "You're attracted to me too."

"If you tell me you can smell it, I might end up hating

you for it." I should not have said that to the leader of this planet. It was like I had no control of my inner dialogue.

William leaned so close to me, I could practically feel his breath on my face. "Like honey."

The door to the house opened and closed, which was great because it snapped me out of whatever the hell was happening. I jumped out of my seat and backed up from him just as Casper arrived in the kitchen. His smile was huge as he regarded the two of us. "How are things in here?"

William didn't take his gaze off me when he answered. "Good." Finally, he regarded his brother. My heart raced so fast that I had to grip the wall next to me to calm it down. This wasn't good. Not at all. I was completely off-kilter. What would have happened if Casper hadn't come home? "Did you find anything?"

"We did, actually. That's why I came back to get the two of you." He walked farther into the room. Casper was darker haired than William. I hadn't noticed that the night before. His face was slightly rounder, and his hair curled around his ears. He had the sharpest cheekbones of the three of them and bright eyes that danced when he looked at me.

I was becoming some kind of ridiculous poet. My inner dialogue was going to make me sick.

"What did you find?" I steeled my back and walked forward. I'd be better at managing myself with two of them here. William did crazy things to me, and it would be easier to ignore with Casper as a buffer.

"Evidence of a missile launch. Maybe. Come on. I'll show you."

William didn't move so much as stretch out his legs. "Now just consider this, Tiffany. If you had managed to shoot me to death yesterday, you wouldn't know now about the honey."

Anger made me grit my teeth. "That's not appropriate to say to me, and I'm not going to listen to it anymore."

Casper rocked back on his feet. "Really, William? I thought we talked about this."

"Things changed." He rose slowly. There was a lazy easiness about the way he moved, like he was being deceptive in how he never seemed to rush. As though he might lull me into thinking he wasn't fast when I was absolutely certain he could lethally be that way.

"I'm sorry I fired." I could start there. "It wasn't okay. I'm grateful it didn't work because it would have caused an international incident."

He grabbed my arm and hauled me to him. "You should always shoot if someone makes you uncomfortable or scared. Shoot. Kill. You have no Lion to shift into, so you find your inner feline and you scratch out the eyes of those that would hurt you. And we'll see about getting you something that isn't the equivalent of a tinker toy."

I opened and closed my mouth. A tinker toy? "I killed someone once with that weapon. I wouldn't call it a...a toy."

In a quick move, he ran his fingers over my left cheekbone. It would have been easy to lean into him, and I couldn't believe the thought even occurred to me. The last time I'd even attempted to get help from anyone had been the day my father had told me he wasn't bringing me with him. I'd learned my lesson that I only had myself to rely on.

"I'm sorry that happened to you, but life is hard, isn't it? You have the heart of a Lion. That is why you came to us."

This was too much. With my heart threatening to explode from just too much of this, I backed up and nearly collided with Casper. How had he gotten behind me without me noticing him there? I had to make a note. These guys could move quietly.

"Tiffany," he extended his hand. "Come with me. I'll show you what we found."

That seemed like a great idea. A reset. Missiles. And some fresh air. Had William drugged my egg? I didn't think that was possible, but something was making me respond in ways that I just didn't otherwise.

"I'm afraid I'm not myself right now. I need a moment."

Casper nodded. "Take a moment while we walk. We all have moments where we find different parts of ourselves."

That wasn't what I'd said, but I didn't have the where-withal to argue the point with him right at that second. "A moment usually means I need a second by myself."

"I won't talk to you. You can pretend you're alone. Or you could stay here with William while I go back and then come with him. I'm afraid I can't let you go through the streets alone. It's not safe. You have no weapons that would work and no ability to shift against those that might threaten you."

Now we were back on ground that I could feel solidly beneath my feet. He indicated the door, and I followed him outside, looking over my shoulder at William, who leaned against the wall watching us as though he hadn't just thrown my entire morning into a tailspin.

"Why would they attack me?"

The sun hit me as I exited their home, and I squinted against it. The people who had invaded my privacy to pack my bags for me hadn't thought to pack me sunglasses or a hat. The rest of my stuff had been correct, probably selected from their observations of me over the years. The Union knew everything, including where I was at all times if they chose to find out. The tracker in my arm would always tell them where I was, even after my death.

"You're new. This is territory. What that means is that it

is run by an—I'm going to use the word Alpha, although that better applies to the Wolves, we're told Earthlings understand it—an Alpha Lion. He has his family here. Everyone who lives here, except for my brothers and me, do so under his protection. They are essentially all his family. To come here, you have to have permission to do business here ahead of time. At any time if he doesn't like you, he can kick you out. And his people will forcibly remove those who don't belong."

Now was the time for me to finally grasp how things worked here. It was important I understand. If I were going to find the missiles, I had to know who ran what. I was like a babe in the woods on this assignment. I had to prove myself, and that was that. I also had to avoid the advances of three very attractive men who were preoccupied with thinking I belonged to them.

Somehow, that had thrown me off. That had to be the answer. I was lonely, and they were playing on my weakness that maybe they could even smell. I couldn't also not consider the fact that they were making up this whole mating thing to mess with me. Why hadn't I thought about that earlier than this walk?

I forced myself back into the moment. "So every area has a person in charge of a particular Pride, that's correct?"

He nodded, gently bumping into my arm. "If you were just talking about the females. They're a Pride. I know we used that word last night when describing things. But only because, again, we believe humans from Earth understand it that way. Truth is, it only applies to females. The men are a coalition, together they're really just his family. His people. His group. I don't know that we have a word for it because we all just understand." He knocked me again. It was playful. Was he flirting with me? I ignored it. Ignore and pivot.

That was how I handled these guys, even if they called me on it.

I continued. "But you three are in charge of all of them?"

"For now. The way it works is that there are young males living in these groups who someday will need their own people to rule. Much younger than I am. And some day, they'll be in charge. They'll run things for everyone until they pick a group to take over for themselves."

A lot of that was what I'd understood from the little studying I'd done, only it was different too. But that begged the question, particularly since William had said he traveled when he was thirty and it was a long time ago. He didn't look much older than that. "How old are you?"

"I'm almost a hundred years old. William is one hundred and five. Oscar is one hundred and three."

Wow. Aging was very different here. "I...I never would have guessed that."

He bumped me again, just a little bit. "We age differently than you do, that is for sure. You're very young aren't you, beautiful?" He winced. "I'm sorry. I know you don't like the endearments. I'm working on not doing it."

Ignore. Pivot. And pretend I didn't like that he just called me beautiful. Okay. Sure. "I'm twenty-eight years old. I probably won't live to be one hundred years old. So maybe depending on your lifespan, we're still on the same track, so to speak. Although you obviously have twice the life experience."

He furrowed his brow. "You've been more places than I've been. I've never left here. Never wanted to."

"Will did?" I'd shortened the name before I thought about it, but Casper didn't flinch at it.

He nodded. "That's right. He had things he wanted to

see. And then he came back, and we started prepping for this."

There was a ton to ask about that, but in the meantime, we'd arrived at a market that was filled with people. As the three guys I was staying with were the only people I'd seen so far, it had felt a little bit like we were alone on the planet. But not now. The market was filled.

Smells hit my senses at the same time I digested the enormous use of color everywhere compared to the drab, quiet landscape past the mid-sized buildings all around us. People were selling clothes, food, and things that looked like they'd be great for use in construction. Children ran around, women talked, men laughed.

Like Casper and his brothers, the men were huge. I looked at the groupings of them for a second before I turned my gaze to the women. Every one of the dozens or so that I saw were gorgeous. They were in bright greens, reds, and yellow colors. One of them was entirely in purple. I'd never seen such a vibrant, gorgeous group of people in one location.

And I quickly felt small and drably coiffed. I looked business-like and uninteresting in comparison.

"Ah," Casper said quietly. "There are the three you were going to meet today. I explained to them things had changed, but I'll introduce you." He touched the small of my back. "This way."

I didn't know why I needed to meet them, per se, if I wasn't going to be working with them, but it was better to have more people to ask for help than not. Casper ended up bringing me through a crowd of women all who hushed when we passed them and then whispered after we did. They might as well have not bothered to whisper since it was perfectly obvious that I was the one they were talking about.

Plus, they could certainly smell me and know I was human and not from here. Since they got so few visitors, it was probably what they were talking about. Not my expensive yet bland looking business attire I'd dressed in for the day.

"Marta, Vera, Angela, this is Tiffany Keyes. You were going to meet with her today, but obviously, that has changed."

They all stared at me for a long moment before dropping their gazes to the ground.

"Please let us know if we can assist you, ma'am." The one I was pretty sure was Marta answered me. She had long blonde hair that fell almost to her feet. It was stick straight. She had it pulled away from her face with a neon green headband that showed her long face with angled nose and bright green eyes that practically matched the headband.

Why was she looking at the ground? Should I do that when I met people? "I'm sorry that I messed with our schedule. It wasn't intentional."

She looked up for a second and then back down. "You don't need to apologize to us. Not ever. But we will see you again. It is our intention to follow where your mates go next. So, we will have ample time to work on projects."

I almost groaned aloud. Mates. So that rumor had already been spread. I shot Casper a look, but he didn't seem at all fazed by it. Clearly, my look sending needed work. Instead, I turned back to the women, who immediately dropped their gazes again.

"It was nice meeting you. I hope that we can work together to solve this quickly if the need arises. The Union will be so grateful."

Behind me, with most of the crowd having gone either silent or into a low buzz, so that when someone loudly gasped, I turned around to see who it was.

A young man stood there. He'd been holding a bag that looked like it was made from fishing wire but had big bricks inside of it. He dropped the bag.

"A human." His voice shook but changed as he spoke, lowering. "A real life human. I heard...but it's true."

"Ah." I didn't know what I would have said, because in the seconds that he took to say those words, his whole body changed. First, his eyes turned red, but unlike the other times I'd seen that happen, they didn't immediately change back. Instead, his body glowed gold for half a second before his whole appearance changed. One second, he was on the skinny side, a tall, lanky-looking teenager, and the next, he was a huge Lion. A roar sounded into the square.

Someone groaned but most people shouted. I screamed before I covered my mouth. Sure, I'd thought I'd understood what this was here, but I hadn't really. How could anyone if they hadn't actually witnessed it with their own eyes?

The kid lunged at me. In a second, I was flung to the left, where I might have fallen over if Will hadn't been there to catch me in an instant. Where had he come from?

A second Lion—it took me a moment to realize it was Casper—flung the teenager forward, pinning him to the ground with a louder, more intense roar. I didn't speak Lion, but I knew which one of those roars I'd listen to if I had to choose. Casper was bigger—huge actually—than the teenage Lion. He was broad, muscled, and his coat a golden shade with a long mane that made him look regal.

His second roar blasted my ears, and I jumped in Will's arms. He wrapped them stronger around me. "You're not in danger from Casper. That stupid cub, well, that's a different sort of problem. He isn't in control of his beast. They're going to fight, and it's going to be bloody. Not for Casper."

Will had uttered that statement when Casper tore into the other Lion's side. I wasn't a fainter and I didn't do so this time, but boy could I actually understand why people did.

This place wasn't just different than anywhere else I'd ever been—it was lethal in a way I'd never seen before.

5

Casper tore at the teenager, who fell several times to the ground, still trying to rise before he was finally set down again, bloody and in the middle of the street.

Barely able to think let alone speak, I still somehow found a way to get my words out. "Is he going to kill him?"

"No, he's teaching him a lesson that should have already been taught. Long ago." William ran a strong hand up and down my side. I would regret clinging to him later. I knew that already, even as I was unable to stop myself from doing so. Not speaking to me this time, Will looked over at Marta and the other women. "Has Boris lost control here?"

"He's getting older. Maybe." She answered him without taking her eyes off Casper and what he was doing to the teenager.

"I'll consider it," William said in response. I didn't track their conversation, but I couldn't focus on that because the teenager shifted back. He was naked, bloodied, and bruised, lying on his side. A second later, Casper did the same.

Unlike the younger man, he wasn't the least bit beat up. He was, however, totally naked.

"Do not shift back and heal," he yelled at the teenager. "If you do, I will find you and make it hurt worse."

The kid did some semblance of nodding before Casper rounded on a man in the crowd. "I want Boris now." His voice still had that low Lion sound, and his eyes were red. I caught my breath. It was like he really wasn't shifted back, even though he was back in his human form. "She okay?"

Will nodded. "I got this. You get that."

Casper took off, following after the stranger he'd yelled at.

Maybe it was the kid rolling on the ground that made me regain my composure, but I pulled out of Will's arms, straightening my shirt and steeling my back. "You're just going to leave him like that?" "He went after my mate. He gets to roll on the ground for a while. It's not a surprise that he lost control of his Lion. Not even a little bit. Impossible to be totally in sync with it until you're about twenty. He's only fifteen years old or so, would be my guess. There's a scent to teenagers that they lose when they are finally about to gain control of themselves. He doesn't have it yet." William walked toward him and stared down at him on the ground. "But since he's a full-sized Lion now with the full capability to hurt someone unsuspecting or weaker than he is, he isn't supposed to be in public. That is the universal rule. He sticks to certain places that are assigned to him where we know he couldn't accidentally kill someone." Will knelt over. "And if he's the kind of asshat who disobeys that, then he is due to have his ass kicked until he remembers some sense."

The kid groaned. "I'm so sorry, I didn't mean to. I've never smelled a human before." He took a deep breath, and his eyes reddened again.

"Do it, and he'll kill you." It was Oscar's voice calling from across the square that answered him. "And if for some reason my brother shows enormous restraint, which he is not known for, I will kill you. And I won't even have to shift to do it. So suck that Lion back down where it belongs and lie there in agony."

Although his body visibly vibrated on the street, the teenager seemed to manage to hold back his Lion. He cried out for help, but no one came to him. Banged his fists on the ground, and still, he was left entirely alone.

I stepped toward William. It was risky, but I did it anyway. My life was all about taking chances. "Aren't they supposed to be his family? Why aren't they helping him?"

"Sometimes, you help family by letting them take their punishments." He didn't turn to look at me, keeping his gaze on the young man's. "And I outrank everyone here. If any of them tried to take me, I'd put them down. He threatened you. He gets to spend some time on that ground thinking about controlling his Lion and not disobeying his orders to stay where he can keep everyone safe from himself."

The kid cried out again, this time his body violently shaking with him. "He doesn't make us. He doesn't make us stay in the zones anymore. Says that is stupid."

"Stupid?" Oscar hadn't moved. "Kids die because they're attacked by teenagers. Kids fucking die."

I didn't know what prompted me to do what I did, considering it had nothing to do with me, what went on here. I was a visitor and hopefully not a long-term one. But there was a kid in pain on the ground. And I'd seen this scene in different versions my whole young life—someone needing just a tiny bit of kindness when they were down and no one giving it. I'd certainly never done so. I'd kept my head down and counted the moments until I got out of wherever I'd been. I was good at running.

But I wasn't a kid anymore.

I stepped next to the young Lion shifter. No one could say I didn't know what I was getting into. I'd just seen the size of him, this young kid could be a deadly animal who wanted to kill me because I smelled wrong to him.

And he had no control of himself.

Only right now, he looked like a million different young guys I couldn't remember the names of who were probably dead before they got to be twenty years old.

"Tiffany." William warned me with just my name, and I ignored him.

Instead, I knelt down and took the kid's hand. "Hi. What's your name?"

His eyes turned red again, and then he sucked it back down. "I'm Edgar."

An old-fashioned Earth name. I'd only seen it written, never heard it actually spoken before. "Hi, Edgar, my name is Tiffany. I'm sorry that you were surprised by my presence, that it threw you off. You don't really want to hurt me, right?"

There was such utter silence around us that every twitch, every bang this kid made sounded like a bomb going off. I wasn't sure that anyone else was even breathing.

He shook his head, his hair rubbing against the ground. "I don't want to hurt you."

"That's good. I'm just a stranger to you. That's all. I'm not a threat. I come from somewhere else, but I don't mean anyone here any harm, I assure you."

That was when Casper came back with whom I could only assume was Boris. He was an older man. Big, of course, all the men here were, but gray-haired with a gray beard. He looked visibly older than the Lions I'd been spending time with.

He was muscular, but somehow less than the three who were currently leaders. In fact, if my own information was to be believed, he was someone they might kill and take over his group. Then they'd be the leaders of this place until someone came and took it from them.

"What is happening?" Boris rushed over.

"He tried to attack my true mate." William bent over to place a hand on the small of my back, and I let go of Edgar's hand, rising to my feet when I did. "And it's within my right to demand that he be put down."

Boris actually paled. "William...I had..."

"You don't enforce the rules. Rules that have been put in place for generations to not let something like this happen. Edgar says that you think they're stupid." Oscar growled as he spoke to Boris, yet his eyes remained their dark brown, not turning red. How did all of this work? "Again, we could enforce putting you down right here while we also took out Edgar."

The older Lion spoke through clenched teeth. "What is it that you want?"

Casper got really into his face. "I want you to apologize to my mate. And then I want you to take your teenager and put him where he belongs. I want this place run up to the very few codes you are expected to abide by. But you are on notice. You are now on the list."

I wasn't going to be able to do anything about this mate thing. The more they said it, the more that others were just going to believe it was true. For the moment, it wasn't important. There was going to be more violence, and I was going to be right in the middle of it.

"I'm okay." I felt the need to point that out. "So, really no harm done. Unless there is something about this I don't understand. Did it harm you, Casper, to shift like that? Or were you hurt during the fight?"

William answered for him, his hand still on my back. "No, shifting doesn't hurt us. It's just another part of our life. Like breathing, once we can control it. And my brother wasn't hurt. But he could have been. There is always a chance that someone can be hurt in a fight." He stared down at the kid on the ground. "No matter how unlikely."

"I'm just trying to point out that no one was hurt except the kid who brought this onto himself. And he's paying for it."

Boris held up his hands in front of him. "I will fix this. Don't put me on the list."

I didn't know what the list they were talking about was, but it was clear Boris didn't want to be on it.

Casper poked him in the chest. It wasn't a gentle move. "We'd take you right now if we didn't have business to take care of first. Handle your people, or we'll handle them for you."

The older man nodded, fast, before he grabbed Edgar off the ground and pulled him away from where we all stood. I watched them until they disappeared from my view. Even after they were gone, no one spoke. There was hardly movement around us at all.

That had to be because of William, Casper, and Oscar. The power structure around here was clear. They were in charge and clearly intimidating enough that they got what they wanted. And right now, they must be giving out some kind of smell or signal that said everyone here should shut the fuck up.

They weren't moving. Did that mean that no one else

could? Oscar dropped the stance first. Walking over to me, he put out his hand. "Come."

Before I could overthink the order, I did as he indicated and laced our fingers together. I wasn't bound by the same rules as everyone else here, but that didn't mean I was going to be an idiot about this. I needed them to complete my mission. If that meant I played ball and went along with the mate thing in public and caused them no issues, then so be it.

Oscar pulled me along gently. With my much shorter legs, I had to hurry to keep up with him. After a moment, he must have realized, because he slowed down to a pace that was a little more conducive to keeping up with.

"Where are we going?" I kept my voice low, although I didn't know if that was necessary. How well could they hear? If they could scent emotions and somehow gleam my innermost thoughts that way, could they also hear me as well? How kind had mutations and evolution been to this planet? And maybe we should be fucking grateful they mostly stayed to themselves and left us alone. If they wanted to, they could really destroy the rest of the galaxy.

Hear better. Scent better. Shift into creatures that could kill us with a swipe of their hands. And they were technologically savvy. They'd figured out how to make our weapons basically useless here. For all that, they also seemed to live somewhat more simply than we did. The market we'd been in, with people talking and gathering? We had nothing like that at home. Big cities. People in and out. No one spoke to one another. It was like that on most planets. The Union delivered goods, controlled trade, and handled what people could buy and not buy. The truth of things was that some places were just more equal than others.

But not here.

With these people who could become Lions.

"Here." Oscar opened the door, and I followed him inside. He closed it behind him. There was a hum inside that I hadn't heard other places, but I was familiar with. It was the sound of electronics. There were a lot of them in here. Different than what they'd had in the house.

"What is this place?"

He didn't answer me so much as back me into the wall. His arms came around on both sides of me, his body held off of mine with enough distance that I wasn't threatened but knew that he meant to somewhat invade my space.

"You're okay." He said it as a statement, not a question. "When I arrived, it was just in time to see that stupid son-of-a-bitch go at you as a Lion."

I breathed, not at all sure how to handle this. People didn't get that upset over me. Over the potential things that might happen to me. Oscar breathed hard like he had run a race.

I touched his chest. There really was nowhere else for me to put my hands, and maybe it was instinct, but he seemed as though he needed me to touch him right now. "I'm okay."

I answered like he'd asked, even though he hadn't. Maybe he needed the confirmation. I had no idea. "Oscar. He was just a teenager. He fucked up. Never smelled a human before. Didn't you ever fuck up when you were young?"

A smile twitched on his mouth before it faded. "I did. Not like that. But I fucked up. Sure. And you didn't want to fuck up with William back then. He was such a task master. You'd think he was already a hundred. One foot out of line and it was...well, it wasn't pretty back then."

I shouldn't care about their personal histories, shouldn't need to hear this narrative from him, and yet I wanted to. Who were these three guys who were both man and animal? How had they gotten to this place where I found them now?

I only knew my own history. I never asked anyone about their lives. Why bother? Everyone was transient to me. Brief interactions. Temporary relationships that didn't matter one bit. Yet...I wanted to know.

"Why William? Where were your parents?" How did familial relationships work here?

He smiled. "Our mother wasn't true mated to our fathers. Most of the time, the relationships can work regardless. You find a reason to pick a partner to be with. In her case, she picked my fathers." So that was how it worked. They just put a s on the word, made it plural. Maybe they didn't know which one of them was the actual biological dad. Maybe it didn't matter. "In their case, it didn't work. Lots of fighting. Lots of accusations of things. Maybe some of them were real. Maybe she was carrying on with members of their group that weren't her husbands. I don't know. All I know is that..." His voice faded off.

I took a deep breath. "You don't have to tell me. I don't need to be able to smell your emotions to know that I've touched on something you'd rather not talk about."

He furrowed his brow. "No, you're my mate. You should know what everyone else on the planet knows about us."

I shook my head. "Not your mate. Don't want to argue. Everyone on the planet? That seems excessive."

"When you take on the leadership role, everyone knows everything about you. That's how it works. We have no secrets. Well...we do. But people don't know that. Anyway, my mother was leaving. Taking us. She was going to go back to her Pride. Casper and I were too young to shift on command. She had to drive."

I'd yet to see a car here, but I tucked that information away. They did have such things as vehicles.

"My fathers got wind of it when she was leaving. They caught up to us only a short distance from our home. They got into such a fight. Yelling. Everyone threatening to shift."

My heart clenched. I knew enough of the universe to know that wherever this was going, it wasn't going to end with roses, chocolates, and a happy ending. "It was...loud. Then our strongest Lion arrived. He was in charge of all of us. Like Boris here. He..." He cleared his throat. "His name was Mistral. Old then, but still strong. He was so embarrassed by the whole thing. It had brought a lot of attention, what was happening. Made him look bad. He killed all of them."

My mouth fell open. "Your Alpha...or whatever you call him...killed all of your parents?"

He nodded. "Yes. Then he took us and raised us himself. Until he was overthrown ten years later. William was...very concerned that we never step out of line. He didn't want us to end the way of our parents. Our family was already embarrassed, already shamed. He was afraid if we didn't hold ourselves to the highest standards, always, that we'd never be here. In charge. Our fathers were not...strong. They were weak Lions. They were never going to be in charge. That's okay. It's honorable to live to make your group stronger, to be part of it. Ninety-nine percent of Lions aren't going to be leaders. But we knew we were meant to. Pretty much from moment one. So, yes, I stepped out of line on occasion, and my brother...he put a stop to that. I'm grateful to him."

There was no doubt that Oscar had just skipped over a

ton of things. How it had been for them when they'd had to live with the man who'd murdered his parents. I couldn't fathom it, and I'd seen a lot of shit in my life. I mean...what the fuck. Yet, in his retelling of the events, Oscar had acted like that was perfectly fine. It absolutely wasn't. And the violence of the whole thing. These guys had witnessed their fathers and mother die at the hand of the person who had then raised them? How strong had that Lion been?

I wasn't a hugger. In fact, I couldn't remember a single time in my life ever being hugged or receiving one. It was a foreign concept to me. But maybe it was having seen it so many times in my life that I knew what to do. Or hell, maybe it was Oscar and the fact that we were practically hugging anyway. I behaved the most unprofessionally I ever had right in that moment, and that included having tried to shoot Will the day before.

I threw my arms around Oscar's neck. "I'm so sorry that happened."

His own came around me. "It's okay, Tiffany. It was a long time ago. So long, I almost never think about it. My parents are distant in my memories. At the end of the day, it made us determined."

He smelled like cinnamon. I wondered where that scent came from. For a second, I closed my eyes and breathed him in. These guys were going to be dangerous to me. What was I even doing?

I let go of him and stepped back, ducking under his arms to get some space from him. I pulled on my shirt to straighten it and smoothed my pants. I really needed that vacation that had been cut short. My head was in a bad, discombobulated place. This was clearly what happened when I didn't get the requisite time off.

"So, what would William do when you stepped out of

line?" I had to remember that this was information gathering. They were violent raised in violence. Their culture was more overt with it than my own, but the truth was, everywhere I went, someone was looking to hurt someone else, to take from the weak, destroy those beneath them. His parents had been killed by the person who should have been there to protect them. William, Casper, and Oscar were not charged with being everyone's leader. Just how violent did they get?

"Ugh." He smiled broadly. "So many chores. Endless scrubbing. And all because I was late for curfew. I didn't even get in trouble with Rick, the pack leader. That was his name. Anyway, Will was so pissed."

That was how Will handled things when he was mad? Chores?

He tilted his head. "This way. I want to show you what I found."

That was right. Oscar could remember why we'd come here. I needed to. Missiles. Yes, I was here to find out who was shooting at Union ships. End of story.

I cleared my throat, suddenly feeling parched. The sooner I got this done, the sooner I could report back and reclaim what was left of my good sense and sanity. They should put a sign up on this planet that says *do not enter, you will become a sappy emotional mess.* I shook my head. I needed to focus.

"Why do you have your equipment here and not at home?"

I gave myself the chance to look around. There was nothing here except the desks and chairs around the computers. This was like an office disguised as a house on the outside. Maybe like the men themselves. They looked like humans, but on the inside, they were something else.

Or maybe I was misreading this. Maybe they weren't hiding it.

"We have no home. We're homeless for now. Soon, we'll pick off our list of groups that need their leader or leaders replaced. We'll challenge them and make it our home when we win. But for now, we live in places that are set up for us on the lands of others. We have no idea what's in there. What devices they may have put in there to monitor us. So, when we go places, I pay off someone who needs it badly, and I set us up a lair, if you will, where I can set up the things I don't want others monitoring. That's why it's here. This place belongs to a man who is away on a long trip visiting his daughter. He needed money for her. We'll be gone before he gets back. No one will know what we did in here."

I scratched my head. "Can't everyone hear us in here?"

"Nope." He held up a device. "You have to be invited in here to hear it. I've seen to it. There are devices to stop this from working. But we take precautions. And if they're spying on us in the house we stay in, then so be it. They hear nothing we don't want them to hear."

They never had an ounce of privacy, and while I was with them, it seemed neither did I. It was best to remember that. Anyone could be listening.

6

"**S**it." He motioned toward one of the chairs. "Let me show you what I've found."

I nodded. "Good idea. Just give me a second. I won't be able to read it without the special glasses that translate like our ear speakers do." I touched my lobe, feeling the telltale presence of a translator I'd gotten the second I'd joined the Union. Some people got them as toddlers, but you had to be rich to get that. People from my zone on Earth had no need for them, and they didn't spend the credits to give them to us.

It had shocked me the first time it worked. There had been a captain from an outer rim planet flying the ship I was on. When I'd boarded, I hadn't been able to understand a word they said. All of a sudden, that was no problem. And what was even stranger was that I could understand it like the words coincided with their spoken words. Their mouths worked correctly. It was an automatic translation in my brain that did something to my synapsis. I didn't get the science, I was just glad it worked.

Reading was another matter altogether. I grabbed the

glasses they'd given me when I got promoted enough to do this job and placed them on my eyes. Now I'd be able to read the words here without trouble. But it wasn't simultaneous. I'd watch the glasses do the translating as I read. One second, the words would look like foreign symbols, the next, the language of my birth. Unless there were words it couldn't translate. Then I'd have to ask for help.

Although you could never be sure people were going to tell you the truth. They could tell me something read as blue when it really read as orange.

All of it was hard. The glasses made it a little bit easier.

I turned back to his screen and sat down. Sure enough, words started to translate, most of it military jargon, not my strongest forte. "Tell me what I'm looking at."

He claimed Lions never lied. I could understand enough that I'd see if that were true.

"These lines are the missiles we control. See, no shots for years and years. We don't fire at space, we want space to leave us alone." He smirked at me. "Since we're so isolationist."

"Why do you find that word so amusing? You all harp on it." I looked up from where I'd been studying. He was right —no missiles fired. And yet I knew there had been. I'd been shot at by one.

He touched the top of my head. "It was just funny. We've been called many things. Isolationist was a new one for us. I guess it's just one of those things that rings funny."

"Maybe the humor is lost in translation." Some things still were. Humor could be one of those things for sure.

He put his hand around my shoulder, bending over to look at the screen with me. "So we're sure that we didn't fire. Except we know it happened to you. That means that someone is firing under our radar. Very concerning, but unfortunately, not impossible. We had years that we battled the Wolves and the Bears. There are sites that aren't as monitored as they should be where someone could conceivably fire an unregistered missile. If they are well versed in deception, they could hide it from this computer. I could do it. So they could too. The question is who and why. I know where the where would be, so to speak."

That cinnamon smell again. "I don't hug. I mean, what I did to you before, I don't hug." I pointed at the screen. "Can you tell definitively that happened?"

He nodded. "One blip. See? If you flip over to the lower radar—"

His description was cut off as the door opened and closed, Casper and William entering.

"Fucking bullshit. That's what it is." William sighed. Despite the seriousness of his statement, he didn't seem angry, more like put out. How did I know that? I didn't know him well enough to be thinking things like that. Maybe he was very calm when he was angry.

"Hey," Oscar said to his brothers, not removing his arm where it was. If anything, he tightened his embrace. "Just going over some things here."

Casper walked right past us, patting his brother on the arm and doing the same to my shoulder. Okay. We had all moved into a touching zone. I should really get Oscar off of me. Only I sort of liked it. The same way I'd sort of liked the hug and the standing. And...the way Casper brushed into me outside. And...the way William almost burned my eggs.

So. Much. Trouble.

"I see the blip." I forced the conversation back to the missiles. "So now what?"

"Well, now I set up a program to monitor those blips,

and we all head north to the unmonitored missile silos and we figure out who is doing this. And why."

William threw himself down on the floor in a dramatic fashion. "Knox's territory. Of course it has to be Knox."

I threw him a look over my shoulder. He had his arm strewn over his eyes like he couldn't stand to look up at the ceiling. "Not a fan?"

"Grumpy old ass." Casper swung around in his seat. "I've been doing research on how matings used to be with humans. Not much information out there. Like it was all shredded on purpose."

I rose, this time giving myself some real space from Oscar. I needed to breathe. My body tensed. Too much touching. "I'm not your mate. Can we just stop with that? I mean...whatever you're smelling...scenting...whatever...it isn't that."

William removed his arm from his eyes. "Are you hungry?"

"Are you just going to ignore I said that?"

He pointed at me. "Diverting, pivoting. I'm learning from you."

His grin told me he was enjoying this. Fine. He wanted to play? I could do it too. "When do we leave?"

"Tomorrow." William sat up. "No need to rush. If they're still there, they're there. If they're not, one day doesn't affect anything. Besides, we don't want to tip them off that we're on to them. Patience goes a long way in conquering one's enemies. We have to wait. Watch and see what they do tonight."

Casper rose and walked over to me. Without a word, he brushed his thumb down the side of my cheek. "You're so beautiful."

I sucked in my breath. People just didn't speak to me like

that. I had no idea what to do with that. His smile was slow as he watched my reaction. "Maybe you just don't like the term 'mate.' What do you use in your world? Wife?"

"No, that is not better." I moved quickly away from him. "Might be worse. Besides, women from the zone where I'm from are very rarely anyone's wives. Never mind. I don't want to talk about that." Why had I said it? It was like I had no filter over my mouth. "Tell me, ah, how the taking over someone's group goes? What do you do with the old leader?"

"We'll have to kill him," Will answered from the floor. "Or them. But most of the time, the fact that they have become weak means they've gotten old and lost their co-leaders. It's just one of them left."

Right back to the violence. "Isn't there an easier way to do that? Some kind of deal to be made?"

I wished I hadn't spoken. I was a visitor. In and out. It wasn't for me to say a word about what they did or didn't do.

"Would you give it up?" William asked, this time rising to his full height. "The territory you'd once had to kill to take? At least once. There are lots of reasons to kill once you have the place too. All that death, sacrifice. Ownership. Would you give it up just because three younger Lions showed up and asked for it? If they said please?"

I shook my head. "No, I suppose not."

"Your Union doesn't ask when they take things, when they conquer." Oscar spoke as he typed on the keyboard. I pulled my glasses off my face. I didn't need them anymore.

"The Union is a unifying organization, democratically appointed to make order in a universe that had none. Before the Union, there was chaos."

All three of them started to laugh. I sighed. There was the humor issue again. This time, I knew I hadn't said anything funny. When discussing the Union, really nothing was funny. "I didn't say that to be amusing. It is what happened."

"The victors always get to determine what history says about them. I'd argue the Union has done more harm than good. Why should all of these planets need Union help to determine their destinies?"

An old argument, and one I had an answer for easily at the tip of my tongue. "Because before the Union created order, entire planets were dying from lack of resources and the unfair distribution of things like oil, gold, and water on planets that were hastily terraformed and not properly thought out in a time when such things should never have been happening. The Union brought order to chaos and saw to it that everyone had enough."

Will blinked. "Like you did? As a child?"

And there was the rub. He was absolutely right—nothing was evenly done, nothing was fair. The old adage about survival of the most adaptable and fittest still hung true, and some people were higher up on valuation charts than others. That was just how it was and how it would always be.

"Think about how much worse things would be without them. Think about the nations that would be starving."

He rolled his eyes. "Or maybe they'd have sorted things out. How will we ever know? The Union runs all their lives."

There wasn't any arguing about this. Not really. I'd heard it all before. I had my canned answers, and he wasn't entirely wrong, either. But I'd never admit it. They had a tag in my shoulder where they could find me anytime they wanted. I'd known when I signed on that they owned me, and I'd gone in with both my eyes open. They used me, and I did the same for them.

I wanted what they were giving me. The life I'd have after.

So I would say as I should, end of story. Maybe they could smell the lie on me. That was fine. In this case, I'd live with it. They could understand that sometimes, I lied. I called bullshit on them not doing it. All Terrans lied. They just did. End of story.

"What now?" I looked between them. "We have an entire day ahead of us before we leave tomorrow. We could leave now."

Casper stretched his arms over his head, and before I could stop myself, I let my gaze caress over his abs as his shirt momentarily exposed them. I quickly looked away. Yes, I liked to watch men. That was all it was. If he actually tried anything with me, I'd dislike the whole process.

If he or his brothers noticed, no one said anything. Instead, he tilted his head. "I want Oscar to take over the research I'm doing. He's better than me at it. Will needs to finish up some things, so you and me... I'm going to show you around."

Show me around? "That's not an effective use of my time."

"It is." He rose and took my hand. "Don't you think you should see more of this place so that you can, I don't know, adequately understand it? You should see it. Right?"

He had a point. A remote one, but I'd give it to them. They didn't want to go until tomorrow. There was little I could do about that. They were my hosts. I was here by invitation, and they could throw me off their planet, which would be a big old F on my record. Of course, they might not do that because they seemed to have some idea of me being their true mate.

That was its own set of trouble. But I couldn't deal with

that if they were going to be unreasonable. We all had to get along until I found the missile and dealt with the perpetrators.

So I followed Casper from the house back onto the street. It was quiet on the street. The crowds that were there before were gone now. Drama over, everyone back to what you were doing earlier. Nothing to see here.

Casper bumped me like he'd been doing earlier. I smiled at him. "That's something you do. Bumping me."

He smirked. "We go a lot by scent around here. Things almost aren't unless we can smell them. We have trouble with addressing things as real if we can't smell them. Intellectually, I get it, but it is a real issue for me. For most of us. Can't smell you, you don't exist. Sort of. Anyway, I want my scent on you. Right now, you mostly smell like Oscar. And that is fine. He's family. It's a good one to have on you. But I want to be there too. Will is there. A little bit. But you're mostly Oscar. Well, and you, of course. You smell like yourself."

I swallowed. That had not been at all what I'd been expecting to hear when I'd asked that question. "I smell like Oscar?"

"You do."

I'd noted his scent myself. "That kind of cinnamon scent he has."

"I suppose that is accurate. We don't identify scents by what they smell like. Everything is just unique. But I can see how Oscar is somehow close to cinnamon."

I was never going to really understand all of this stuff. Not at all. I couldn't. I didn't have a Lion inside of me. It must be like living a dual life that somehow was also just one. I shook my head. Nope. I couldn't even get close to understanding it.

"So you couldn't compare how I smell to something else." I was glad I wore deodorant. How bad must someone with body odor seem to these guys?

He leaned over to breathe me in, his nose pressed against my neck. "You smell like Tiffany. The girl who landed here a day early and who, in the span of one gust of wind, completely altered my existence. In the best possible way."

It didn't make sense to me, and I suspected it never would. "You smell me, and it just makes you feel something. Something is better in the world because of how I smell?"

"Correct." He took my hand in his, pulling me against him as we walked together toward wherever he was taking me. The landscape didn't change based on where we were. There still seemed to be low rising buildings and not much else but flat land around us. Plenty of vegetation, but not much else.

"Is the whole planet like this or just this area? Do you have sweeping canyons and big holes in the ground and mountainous regions?"

He smiled at me. "There are places on this planet that are quite different than here. But I'll be honest, this kind of terrain is the most sought after for us. We just prefer it. Wide open spaces where we can see for miles and miles. It's what we want if we can find it. Where we're going tomorrow is on the coast, that will be different than here." He squeezed my hand. "Do you have a preference for landscape?"

I sighed. "You know it doesn't really matter what I like." He opened his mouth to argue, so I kept speaking. We didn't need to go round and round on a subject we weren't going to agree on. There was nothing more tedious. I was leaving when my job was over. He'd figure it out then, if not before, that something had gone askew here. True mates didn't sound like they left. Not if they completed each other or something like that. "But I've always had an affinity for the ocean. I've never gotten to live near one. We were several hours away from one growing up, but my dad loved to surf and the few times I saw him, once I was old enough to be taught to swim or stay away from the edge safely, he took me with him."

Casper made a face. "I think we are having a word not translate. Happens sometimes, right? Rarer and rarer, but it happens. I don't know the word 'surf.'"

I could hear him say it just as clearly as I'd said it myself, but it was obviously not one he knew. "Do you guys ever build boards to use on the ocean? To stand up on and ride a wave with?"

I could probably have done a better job of describing it, but that should make itself clear enough if they had such a thing. I'd never discussed surfing on any planet other than Earth. I'd seen the ocean on other planets. But I'd never gotten on a board and tried waves anywhere but the one I was born on.

He put his hands on his hips and stared at me, his mouth falling open. "Why would you do that?"

"That's hard to explain. If you don't feel like you must or that you want to, then it really isn't for you, so to speak. No one does that here?"

Casper shook his head slowly. "No. We avoid the ocean, except for things we have to do. We have boats, of course. We fish. But...no, we avoid touching the ocean at all costs."

I smiled at him. "See? We could never work out. I can't live here at all if we can't touch the ocean. Is it poisonous or something to you? To us?" If he couldn't be in it, then I probably couldn't either. Mutations aside, most things that affected one Terran affected all of us. Viruses could travel via spaceship from planet to planet, and everyone caught them. Medicine had to be shared via the Union. It was amazing the shifter planets did without the help. But my mind was wandering, and I had things to focus on here.

He tugged on a piece of my hair. "It's not poisonous. It's just...wet." I laughed, unable to help myself, which made him smirk at me. "Looks like we're getting through the sense of humor problem. I knew you'd get to see how incredibly funny I was eventually. You did that fast. But in all seriousness, it's wet and dangerous. Why would you want to go in there?"

How to explain it? "Maybe the danger of it is part of the appeal. I don't know. It's just something I love. Do you hate all water? Do you not like hot baths?" How far down the no water rabbit hole did these Lion shifters go?

"I love a hot bath. I think you'd agree that the ocean is different. I have put my feet in it, when I was young. It's cold."

Now it was my turn to smirk. "Okay, I see how this is going. You're a Lion shifter. You can actually become a giant predator, shift into a Cat with huge scary teeth and claws. But you are a wimp. I get it. Scared of the cold water."

His laugh surprised me. "So you do have claws. Even if you can't shift into them. You just swipe out of your mouth instead. Sure. I'll own it. When it comes to the freezing cold ocean, I am a wimp. Fine."

That word translated fine. Surfboard, no. Wimp, yes. Good to know. We walked along after that, his hand back in mine, the sun shining down on us. It was midday by the time we left the town. I looked back over my shoulder. "Are we going someplace in particular?"

I had food in the pack I carried, but I didn't have it with

me at the moment. That had been a dumb move. Just another example of how my mind wasn't working properly. I didn't just leave my stuff, technically Union stuff, places. If anyone found out... I sighed. Maybe this time, I'd get along with it.

"Something is concerning you."

It was going to take some getting used to that they just seemed to know things based on what I smelled like. If I ever did this again, I'd need something to block that ability from them. Maybe there were pills that could be developed that would alter our scents from their noses. I'd have to suggest it at the next meeting.

Maybe I could get promoted for doing so.

I side-eyed Casper. It didn't sit well in my stomach, the idea of giving the Union an edge over him. They'd been nice to me. It wasn't my intention to make things harder on everyone here. Not when we had almost no reason to ever be here.

"I was just thinking that I'm going to get hungry. How often do you guys eat?"

His smile was huge. "We eat as much as possible. I'd eat all day if I could. We burn through a lot of calories, so we tend to eat large meals maybe four times a day. But I'm game for whenever you're hungry. And there will be food outside of where we're going. You'll see."

"I don't have any currency with me. The Union pays for all my meals. I realize that William treated me this morning, but I don't expect—"

He interrupted me by placing his hands on my cheeks. "I don't accept that you're not ours. I understand that it is going to be different for you. It has to be. You're not built exactly the same way that we are. Oscar is looking into how it worked in the past. We will figure it out. In the meantime, there are certain things that I'll insist on. All of us will. And feeding you without you thinking you need to handle yourself in that way is one of them."

I stepped back. The touching my cheeks was too much. In my whole life, I'd never had anyone do that before, and I didn't want to like it now. No, I wasn't the kind of person that happened to. I was leaving here, and I might miss it if I let it continue to happen. I hadn't been here very long, and already, I knew that.

Clearly, I'd spent too much time without really getting to know people and it was catching up with me. Or some such thing.

"Fine." I swallowed. "Thank you. I'll accept your hospitality with my thanks."

Casper's hands fell to his side. "You're welcome, Tiffany. Come on."

I followed.

7

I followed him for a moment before he took my hand again, the way it had been before. Casper didn't fluster very long. That was an important thing for me to remember. He'd clearly been thrown when I'd stepped out of his hold, but then he'd moved on fast. His good humor was back, along with the way he seemed to smile at everything and everybody. The clouds in the sky got a grin from him, the way the trees bent over slightly also. He was generally happy.

Did I know anyone else who was that way?

I couldn't think of one other person, and that was somewhat disturbing.

Eventually, we got where we were going. The landscape suddenly changed. At first, I thought it was forests, but actually, it was caves. Three of them, the last one being the biggest. Around it was another market filled with people selling wares. Some of them artistic, some of them technological. There was also the smell of food in the air. I wasn't sure what it was, but someone was cooking something that made my stomach rumble.

Casper lifted an eyebrow. "Hungry first or into the cave?"

"I've never been in a cave." And the idea of actually doing so was much more interesting than hunger. I'd been a lot more in need of food than I was right now. "I don't get to spend a lot of time outside. Most of the time, it's building to building, meeting to meeting. This is unusual. I'd like to focus on the missiles. But if you have a cave and you are willing to show it to me, then let's do that first."

He nodded, but not like he was surprised, it was more like I'd given him the answer he expected. There was no possible way he'd been able to discern what I'd have chosen ahead of time from how I smelled. Emotions, I understood, but thought processes were a whole other thing.

Casper extended his hand, and we approached the cave together. Could we just walk inside? Was it only going to be just a dark hole? The idea of even seeing such a thing was exciting. My hands tingled as I thought about it. Who knew I had such a desire to do outdoorsy things? Maybe it was just that I didn't get to. The novelty of it.

I took his outstretched offering and followed him inside. I expected darkness, but I didn't get that. No, the same lighting system that had lit up the town was inside these caves. I walked close to one, and it was then I realized that it wasn't a lighting system at all. It was crystals.

"They grow naturally in these caves. Once every ten years, and not before, not even by a day, we harvest them. The whole planet uses them to eliminate lighting pollution."

I sucked in a breath. "Like some sort of illuminating stalagmite."

He tilted his head. "I think we've hit a translation problem again."

That wasn't surprising. There were bound to be a lot of

those moments. There always were. Particularly in contract negotiations. Terms to abide by could get really tricky. We'd probably hit a lot of it when we went to discuss missile parts.

Technical terms were problems. Besides, they didn't have stalagmites here. They had light up crystals. I approached one of the crystals. Up close, it was so beautiful.

"Don't touch it. They're fragile and have to be handled in a very particular way. We have artisans who train for it for years. You'll notice the crystal holders on any street are very sturdy. It would take a real blast to destroy them. But your fingers? They could take out the crystals easily."

I kept my hands in my pockets lest I suddenly forget. Not that it was likely, but whatever was going on with me was so abnormal, I couldn't be sure at this point. "You guys simply leave them alone. Because that is what is best for everyone."

I don't know that I'd adequately be able to explain to him how completely odd that was where I was from. And not just there. But every other planet I'd ever been to. People did what was best for them and no one else. That was why we needed the Union—to keep people in line. With violence if necessary.

I stared at the crystal. It really was amazing. Light that was coming in from small holes at the top of the cave struck them, and then rather than it being sent everywhere, the crystals only allowed the light to shine downward, directly beneath them.

This didn't explain how it worked on the streets. There wasn't light when it was nighttime for it to direct. "At night there isn't light above it."

"Likely it's not displaying the current light right now." Casper walked toward me. "It stores it for long periods of time before it releases it. So currently, it's receiving light it might not show us for years."

Interesting. I stared at the white, almost nothingness of its color compared to the yellow illumination on the floor. "You could live off it if a big cloud came and blocked out the sun."

"I think we'd have other issues. It doesn't heat. But, yes, I guess hypothetically. Do you have some intel we don't have about that happening?"

I looked away to meet his dark gaze. "No, of course not. That's above my pay grade. That scenario was actually a nightmare I used to have as a kid. Sorry. More than you needed to know. What happens to them when they wear out? Or do they never?"

He ran a hand through his hair. "Like everything else in the universe, they have their time here and their time when they're gone. Eventually, they have no more light to show. Then they crack and break. Toward the end of their span, some areas of the world will be practically in darkness at night while they wait for the time to harvest more crystals."

And no one went to just take what they needed ahead of schedule to suit themselves? I might never understand it. Truly.

That just wasn't how things went.

But I stared at the crystal observing light and tried to not feel anything about it at all. It was just another interesting fact on another planet that someday, I could mark on a map for having visited. One after another. I really should start writing them down, since I was starting to forget them. They blended into the same planet.

Although this one, for obvious reasons—namely, three Lion shifters who had hijacked my attention since I'd gotten here—made this one slightly different than the others. And

I would probably never forget how beautiful these crystals were.

They just grew naturally here. In these caves, where it would otherwise be dark and where I never would have imagined something like them could emerge.

I rocked back on my feet. A person passed by us heading deeper into the caves. "What's back there?" I let myself watch where the tall—but they were all tall—stranger walked into the darkness.

Casper nodded in that direction. "More. And then darkness. Pitch. Come on."

I followed as he walked toward where I had indicated. Sure enough, there was another space with more crystals, and then a second where there weren't any. In there, it was so dark. I could hear the stranger breathing as he stood in the dark. Otherwise, it was just Cas and myself in there. Immediately, I turned and walked back to the lit-up area. No, I didn't like that much darkness. It was too...familiar. My heart rate kicked up, and I forced it to slow down as I breathed.

Casper put his hand on my lower back, this time following me when I retreated. "You okay?" "Too much."

He nodded once. "There is a big difference between us, from what I understand. When I can't see, it's okay. I can smell my surroundings. In fact, sometimes I prefer it, because it's comforting to let some of my senses go in favor of others."

"When I lose my ability to see, some of my other senses improve. But not like yours. It felt like I was in a coffin in there."

His face fell. "Tiffany..."

I interrupted him before he said something trite because there really was nothing to say in that moment. I'd brought up a coffin. It was bound to elicit a response I didn't really want to deal with. In fact, it would have been better if I hadn't said anything.

"Lunch?" I changed the subject. "And then we need to talk about missiles."

He nodded. "Yes, I'll feed you. Immediately. Plus, missiles. I mean, I can't think of a more romantic subject in the world than missiles. We should have been talking about it this whole time."

I rolled my eyes. "That is my job. I got fired upon. It is what we're supposed to be talking about."

He made a sort of noncommittal sound that I didn't push him on, and then we were back outside. At least it seemed like that. Once I'd been in that super dark room, I couldn't get out of the caves fast enough. I'd wanted to go, but the reality of it had been something else entirely. Mental note—I didn't like confined, dark places. I didn't like them at all.

But it was bright outside, and the smell of food was comforting, even if I didn't know what exactly I was going to eat. My mouth watered. This was new food, but I already knew that I'd like it. Sometimes, I could just tell from the way I anticipated eating something that I'd already love it.

Whatever was being cooked nearby fell into that category.

We walked through a crowd where people darted out of Casper's way all the way to a grill. A woman with pink hair cooked and dished out food with a fast smile that showed off a gold tooth in her mouth. She was happy in a way that couldn't be faked. I could almost always tell the difference between when someone was putting on a show and when they really felt the happiness they exuded. Maybe because I so rarely did the real thing myself.

But that woman was happy. The real fucking deal.

Casper spoke a few words to her, and she grabbed two plates. They didn't exchange any currency. I wasn't clear on how that worked here. Did he pay her some other way? He came back with the food on a plate. It looked something like grilled steak, but I wasn't sure if it wasn't maybe a poultry.

"What kind of animal is this?"

He shook his head. "I don't think it's an animal they find anywhere but here. But it's like your...beef, is that it? I knew that because we imported cows for a while, but people preferred this taste."

I took a bite. Yes, it was close but saltier. Was that a natural flavor, or did she do something to it that made it saltier? "Did you eat the beef?"

He motioned to the side and brought me over to where we both sat down on a long log that was being used as a bench. A gentle breeze moved my hair off my shoulders, and he watched it as he answered me. "I did. I don't know, for me, it was missing a sort of...zing that this has. What do you think of it?"

"Delicious. Saltier than Earth beef, but not as salty as something I ate on another planet recently."

He took a bite of his food. He had a strong jaw. When he'd swallowed, which I couldn't help but stare at the motion like it was the most fascinating thing I'd ever seen, he answered my statement. "You have to tell me about all the places you've been. I want to hear about all of them."

"I doubt I could even remember all of them." That sounded awful, so I quickly added to it. "They kind of blur together. Besides, you could go if you want to. See for yourself."

Cas shook his head. "If that were what I wanted, I'd have done it years ago. Now that time has passed. I don't want to leave. I like it here. I know myself well enough to know that only home suits for me. But I want to hear you talk about all of it. What was the first place you went?"

"I..."

I didn't get to answer as a roar sounded out. I jumped, turning around to look in the direction of the noise. Cas didn't budge or turn at all to look, his attention remaining on me. "Don't worry about that. He's showing off."

The person he referred to was a young, twenty-something guy—but I couldn't really tell how old he was, since Casper didn't look his age either—who was in his human form but roaring like a lion. His eyes were red, and he was focused on us with what I could only describe as rage.

"You were saying?" Casper asked again. "First place you went when you left Earth."

Nope. I wasn't going to be able to answer that, since the guy was now storming toward us. I jumped to my feet. If I had to run, better I be upright to start. My heart raced. Anger like this was about power, regardless of whether the person was full on human or some kind of shifter. It was the same everywhere, and I had none here. I dropped my plate, my uneaten food hitting the dirt with a slight *oomph*.

Casper sighed but rose, finally, to meet the furious stranger who had just interrupted our lunch. He stepped in front of me. "You're Wesley, right? You're the Alpha's son. We haven't met, but I do know who you are."

"I challenge you. You have humiliated my father." He lunged at Casper, who darted out of the way, making Wesley fall onto the bench where we had just been sitting. Behind me, several of the women laughed and one groaned. I took two steps back. Another thing I'd learned the hard way was that men in a rage had no reason when it came to being made fools of.

He roared again, in his human form, sounding like a lion. Okay. That was a new thing. They didn't actually have to look like animals to sound like them. I rubbed the goosebumps breaking out on my arms.

I was never, ever going to get used to this.

"Take a breath, kid." Casper didn't sound particularly concerned. "You aren't thinking about what you're doing. This isn't your time. You have years before you can challenge me. You're just embarrassing yourself and making my human mate nervous. The second part is what is really bothering me right now."

This time when Wesley spoke, it was with a lower voice. "I could take you. William is the one who fights, not you."

This time, Casper laughed. He threw his head back when he did so, and the women around us all laughed too. This was funny? I didn't understand. But one of those women, the one who had just sold us the food, grabbed my arm and tugged me back.

"Wesley is a blowhard. And he's about to get what's coming to him. Year after year, it's the same testosterone infused nonsense. He's going to learn a lesson his father should have taught him—don't mess with your betters unless you want to get popped in the nose."

Well...that wasn't a lesson I'd ever heard before. People really shouldn't go about popping each other in the nose. But there were lots of traditions on planets and this might be one of them.

I half expected Casper to shift, but he didn't. Instead, he took the younger man by the ear, which made him cry out in pain. I winced.

"Listen to me very closely. I get that you're upset that your father's reign is waning. I had a shitty childhood, but I understand it's very hard when you actually like your parents to see them getting older. So I'm going to give you a pass. We have no intention of taking over here. None. But we are in charge of everything right now. That is both our gift and our curse. Your father is fucking up. If you grow up to be a strong, smart shifter, then you can have my role at some point, and maybe, if you're lucky, take over here as the next Lion in charge. If you don't, then someone may beat you to the job. Then you'll have to figure out what you want to do. I don't envy you that. I don't love it myself. But if you think that only William can fight, then you haven't been paying attention. He strikes faster than I do and leaves his opponents alive more often. If I chose to shift and fight you, you wouldn't see another day. I don't fight unless I intend to kill." Casper let Wes' ear go, and Wes promptly fell to his knees, holding on to his ear. "Take your outrage somewhere where it won't get you killed. Or stay here and know this is the last time you'll ever feel the sun on your face. Pick."

Wes struggled to his feet, and with his hand still cradling his ear, he shot Casper a look that wasn't friendly and took off running. Casper turned to me, his face returning to the jovial man I'd spent the day with.

"Let's get you another plate of food, shall we?" He lifted his eyebrows. "Or we can get something else if you'd like."

I swallowed. "I'm sorry. I'm not hungry. The food was delicious." I smiled at the woman who had held my arm. "But it's time for me to get back to town and for us to talk about what I've come here to do. Past time, actually."

His face fell, but he nodded. "Absolutely, we can do that." He smiled at the crowd. "Ladies, as usual, the food is fantastic. I always love coming here."

Our cook stepped forward. "You could do it. You could take over here and run things. All of you. We're a good group. I'm old enough that I remember how it feels to have strong Alphas in charge. How a place can be when there is order and strength. We'd love that back. This constant downshifting, it's exhausting. Makes it chaotic. Miserable. It's like an infection that gets into all of us day by day."

Cas nodded. "I know. I remember it well. But this isn't our place. I don't know how to explain it, but I can feel that it's not. This isn't home."

She sighed. "I had to try. How bad will it get before it's over? Before some group wants to live here and take over?"

For one moment, Casper's face fell into regret. He ran a hand through his hair. "It will get very dark for a while. But you don't have to stay. You know that. No one ever has to stay where they don't want to be. If it gets too much, leave."

She visibly swallowed. "Maybe others could do that. But this is my home. I feel it...the way that you know it's not yours. I'll be here, always."

That had to be the end of the conversation, because Casper took my hand and led me from the area. This time, the silence between us was strained. I took my hand back. I didn't want to hold his while feeling like this.

"What made you upset?" he asked after a while. "Which part?"

"All of it."

This was a physical world. I knew that, but seeing them have to deal with others twice now by literally putting them on the ground had shaken me. What would happen when they got upset with me? Would I be put on the ground? And even if the three brothers wouldn't because they had a thing for me, would others do that to me in my time here? I had no ability to protect myself. Maybe I needed to call this in and let the Union send much bigger men here to do the job. A large group of them.

Of course, if I did that, I'd lose all my seniority at work.

"Tell me." He bumped me gently. "I can't fix it if I don't know."

"Twice in one day, you guys have had to take down other men who have wanted to hurt you. Twice. I haven't been here a full day, and twice it's happened. What is this place? How violent does it get? I know you want it to seem magical, perfect. Those crystals blew my mind. The colors here. The way people smile. All of it. But I'm here because someone is shooting missiles at space crafts that are passing by, including my own." It looked like I'd finally found my focus again. "So between the violence and the missiles, this is certainly not some kind of utopia. That's good. I don't believe in fairy tales. I never did. I get violence. I get how that works. But I don't like it. End of story. I'm going to focus on what I'm here to do. Because the truth? If I don't find out what's happening with these missiles, I'll be shit out of luck at work. But that's not the worst of it. The worst thing that will happen will be that the Union will send ships here. They can't have their cargo being disrupted. They will send a force or they will send assassins or some other thing. And the parts of your planet that are beautiful, that will be long gone."

He stroked his finger down the side of my cheek. "Just because we have chosen to live a certain way for a while now, that doesn't mean that we can't defend ourselves. We can. If the Union came, we would fight back and we would win."

I sighed. "I'm not going to argue that. Maybe you would. Your tech is amazing, it outdoes ours. But how many of your people would die in the meantime? What I'm saying to you is true. The way you've been living, your way of life? It would be irrevocably changed."

"I'm not going to stop you doing your job. None of us

will. In fact, we're leaving first thing so that you can do it." He sighed. "I'm not inherently violent, nor is this place that way. Most of the time, it's not. I guess...there are aspects of our lives, of being a shifter, that does have its element of blood. But what you're seeing is just a part of it. Part of our life right now is handling young guys who don't know what to do with their instincts. He's always going to hate me a little bit, but maybe someday, he'll be Alpha here and be my equal because I'll be Alpha somewhere else."

"You know this is crazy, right? You think I'm your mate. I can't possibly be your mate. I'm a human, and I don't understand any of this and never really will be able to. Besides, if I hadn't come here, you'd never have met me. Some other girl would be your mate. You need to just let me do my job and stop filling my mind with all of this. It's taking up too much space, and I need to pay attention to other things. To missiles. And answers. I can't be thinking about whatever this is. Do you understand?"

He shook his head slowly. "No. But I understand that it is weighing on you. And that makes it my concern. Let's go back to the home here. Pack up. You can work, straighten out your head because that's what you need. Baby steps. You're here. That's really all that matters."

He'd given me what I wanted, said the right things. And yet it didn't make me feel any freer. Just the opposite, somehow.

8

The house was quiet. Either Will or Oscar had brought my bag back. It sat on one of the couches, closed. If they'd opened and rifled through it, I had no way of knowing. Anything they shouldn't see for security reasons was password protected. Maybe they had a way of breaking Union code, but if I went down this path of thinking, it was going to make me nuts.

Before he left for his room, Casper tugged on the end of my hair. "I liked seeing the crystal caves with you today, through your eyes. I thought you would think it was interesting. If I managed to get you to think it was magical, then I'm even luckier. I'm not violent. You're not at risk around me, ever."

I'd hurt his feelings. The thought made my stomach tighten. That hadn't been my intention. But truth was always better than lying when possible. I'd told him mine in that moment.

"I grew up in a dark, violent place made peaceful only by the presence of authorities who brought their own violence with them. They killed my mother. Well, in some ways, she did it to herself. But, nonetheless. Ultimately, it was people who deal in it that ended her life." I sighed. "I'm not saying that's who you are. I'm just explaining that it is difficult for me to deal with on a regular basis. I like order. I make order out of chaos."

He took my cheek in his hands. "Do you think that your Union—the entity bringing order to chaos, as you put it—isn't violent? They are the most violent thing in the universe as far as I'm concerned."

I swallowed. "I know they are."

"Then how do you tolerate it? How do you reconcile your very understandable aversion to violence with what you do for a living?"

My mouth shook. I could hardly utter the words. I never had, not in all the years that I'd been doing it. Yet I managed to make myself say what I never wanted to say before. "Because as long as I'm well in the center of it, then they could never hurt me."

There. I'd done it. Now he could know just how pathetic the very core of me was. "No one would ever hurt you here. I can promise you that. Not as long as there is breath in any of our bodies."

"You can't make promises like that. They're not real. They're not possible to uphold."

He nodded. "That's true. Things can happen, and we can't control them. Death happens. Violence happens. We know this. Random acts of it. All the time. Like it or not, that is just how these things can go. There is nowhere to escape that."

"Not true." I was in for a penny, in for a pound with this. I didn't even know what that expression meant. Something to do with currency in the old days of Earth. One of my teachers used to say it, and I thought it all the time. "There is a place. There is a planet where I am going to buy some land. Edge of the known galaxy. Almost no one goes there. No profit to be made. No resources to draw people out there to plunder. I will stay there and live peacefully."

He audibly exhaled. "Eventually, everywhere has resources. That place won't stay the way you're imagining it. If it does, there will come a time when what someone wants from there is the people. Or the women."

Casper let that hang out there, and my body went cold. Of course, he was right. I knew those things. I had never seen it myself. The Union didn't take people like that, but others did. And without Union protection, yes, that might very well happen.

I stepped back from him. "Well, that is my plan, anyway." I forced myself to swallow. "You should be glad I'm not your mate. I'm all kinds of fucked up. I think I'd just better stay in my room. Do some more research and see you all tomorrow morning when it's time to go."

He shook his head. "Please don't do that. I shouldn't have said that. Not in a million years. I didn't mean that you were going to have that happen to you. Nothing will ever happen to you."

"Something happens to all of us eventually." I smiled. This conversation had to end before I shared anything else that I needed to keep to myself. "Excuse me."

He took one step in my direction. "I've made you so unhappy, when all I want in the universe is to make you smile. Please come out and eat dinner with us. William likes to cook. It'll probably be delicious and..."

"Thank you." I nodded. "If it's not too much trouble."

Casper put his hand on the wall like he needed to brace himself. "It's never too much trouble."

That was sweet. He worried he'd made me unhappy, but

the truth was that I was pretty sure that the time I spent here with them would mean that I stole away his. The best I could do would be to keep this brief and hope his sadness wasn't permanent. I'd been many things in my life, but the stealer of joy wasn't one I'd been before.

Although I'd showered that morning and didn't really feel dirty, I couldn't get over the need to stand under the spray again, so that was what I did as soon as I was away from Cas. I let the water run over me in the bathroom, my clothes in a pile on the floor—very much not my usual way —just to get as clean as I could possibly be.

But it did nothing to wash away whatever was wrong with me since I'd gotten here. I dressed simply in a pair of black pants and a white T-shirt. I didn't have clothes with a lot of color. Not like the women here. Walking in the sun had put some color in my cheeks, and the sight startled me when I glanced in the mirror. I'd had so much sunblock on when I'd gone surfing, I hadn't gotten any evidence of the sun on my skin. When was the last time I'd ever been outside without it on?

I touched my cheek. It was warm, slightly red. Not a terrible amount, and I didn't look like I'd put on too much makeup. I pulled my wet hair back and braided it quickly again because it had fallen out. I hadn't done so in years, but it felt like a braid kind of a day.

For a moment, I debated whether or not I should put on shoes. But the guys were barefoot in the house. I didn't want to be rude wearing shoes inside. They hadn't said anything, but maybe it was a thing I shouldn't do. I looked down at my toes. It was weird to not have them covered. I wiggled them for a second, wondering when the last time I had ever done so was. Had I ever been the kind of person who just wiggled my toes for the fun of it? Probably not.

I'd been a serious child. What other choice had I been given?

I stepped back outside my room into the hall. None of them were on the floor guarding my door. Maybe that had only been a first night thing, or maybe it was just a night thing. I'd have to ask what the rules were. Did they think I'd try to steal away in the darkness?

The smell of cooking food led me to the kitchen. Sure enough, Will was there standing over the stove. Only this time, he was shirtless. Smoke wafted around him as he fried something on the stovetop. His hair blew back slightly from a wind in the air that was probably to try to mitigate the smoke. He stared into it like the sensation didn't bother him at all. A wooden spoon moved over the food on top of the stove. I breathed it in. This was a lot like blackened fish that I'd had back home.

But none of that mattered because he was shirtless. And...beautiful. I'd never really stared at the male form all that much. Sex had been fast and uninteresting, or sometimes even something to avoid altogether. I'd admired the way that men looked, but none of them had ever looked like Will. I knew the guys were big. They were tall, broad. But I hadn't had a sense of the sheer massive strength that was William. Maybe I should have. This wasn't my first time seeing him without his clothes. He'd been naked when he'd defended me from the juvenile on the street.

I sucked in a breath. That had been what he'd done. He'd defended me. Looked out for me so that I didn't get hurt. I'd gone after Casper for violence when both times, it had been in relation to protection, even when Cas had been saving Wes from himself.

I chewed on my lip. Why hadn't I understood that sooner?

Will looked over his shoulder at me, acknowledging my presence for the first time. He set down his spoon and walked over to me. Whatever he'd left on the stove sizzled.

"You're not going to set the house on fire, right?"

His smile surprised me. Will rarely did, or at least that was true so far. "No. It's good. Besides, there is an automatic system if it were to catch aflame. Just needs some more heat for a while."

"What is it?"

I didn't expect him to lift me up and set me on the counter, and I gasped, grabbing on to his arms until he set me down so I sat on top of it. We were closer this way, our faces only inches apart. His mouth came down on mine.

Shock rocked through me, but only for a second. Then a different sensation took over. Heat. Pure, undiluted heat. It moved over every cell in my body, and I gasped. Will deepened the kiss. Tugging my body toward him so that I was practically off the counter where he'd just braced me, he gave me no choice but to cling to him. And I did just that. I chased his kisses, my mind shutting off all thought of right or wrong. I only wanted what he was giving me. What was more, was I craved his continuing. If he stopped, I might fall apart.

Pleasure coursed through me. I'd been kissed, had kissed, many times. Yet it had never felt like this. I barely breathed. Who needed air when there was Will and his mouth, his lips, the breath from his body, the way the slight cut of his whiskers rubbed against my chin? I moaned, the sound surprising me but only for a second, because then I couldn't think again. I'd never before been so lost in just the ability to feel, not think, and I wasn't sure I'd ever find my way back to myself again. That might be just fine with me.

He ran his tongue over my bottom lip, and I wished my

clothes would just vanish. I wanted to be naked and rubbing against him. He groaned, a low guttural, animalistic sound. I smiled against his mouth. I loved that noise. I was being kissed senseless by a man who was sometimes a Lion. A door slammed, and it was like cold water being thrown over my body.

I pulled backward, the strong light of the room practically assaulting my eyes. I covered them for a second, reality intruding on whatever the fuck that was.

"Sorry to interrupt." Oscar strolled over. "Unless I can join. I like to kiss too."

My cheeks got so hot, I thought they might explode. I couldn't open my eyes back to the world. I had to stay just for a second behind my hand like it was some kind of shield that was going to protect me from dying of embarrassment. Remaining in my dark cocoon, I answered him. "I don't kiss. What I just did, I don't do."

Will kissed my cheek. "You do. Clearly. And really, really well."

I dropped my hands. "I'm not behaving like myself. I'm just not. Something is wrong with me. I need to call my boss and go home." Even if I'd never hear the end of it, ever.

"No," Oscar hopped up on the counter next to me, "you're okay. I realize you have no reason to trust me just yet, but if you can try, I'm here to tell you that you're fine."

I sighed. "I don't kiss people like that. On assignment. I mean... No."

Will pressed his nose against my temple and took a deep breath. "You were just waiting for us. I'm enormously grateful you don't kiss others. But you kiss really," his voice deepened, "really well."

I could argue I hadn't wanted it, hadn't asked for it, except that would be a lie. I had. The second his mouth touched mine, I had wanted it. I couldn't even bring myself to tell him not to do it again. Wow. I must really be hard up. This happened to other people, not me.

Oscar lifted an eyebrow. He was close to my body now. "Kiss?"

William hadn't asked, he'd just taken, and somehow, that had worked for me right then. It might not always. Asking me was a whole different thing. It let my brain consider the alternatives. I could say no. Still, my brain and my body didn't seem to be in connection right now. I nodded before I could even think otherwise.

With Will's nose still pressed against my temple, Oscar leaned over and kissed me. It was different than William. He had taken, and I had followed. Oscar was gentle, soothing, like a warm bath on my senses. I pressed deeper against him, and he smiled before he gave in to what I wanted. My head spun.

He'd no sooner licked the outside of my mouth than I pulled back. "Too much."

It was. The two of them together was going to make me do things I wouldn't like myself for later.

They both nodded, and Oscar jumped off the counter. Before walking past, he squeezed my knee, which sent a thrill up my spine. He headed for the refrigerator where he pulled out a large bottle of clear liquid that I could only assume was water. I watched, transfixed, as he took a long swig of it down his throat.

William sighed. "There could be lots and lots of afternoons like this."

"I can help with dinner." I jumped off the counter. Avoidance. Distraction. Whatever it was, I was doing it like a pro. "How can I help?"

"This isn't dinner." William touched the small of my

back and headed to the stove. "This is a tide-you-over-so-you're-not-starving meal because Casper told me you didn't eat lunch."

Oscar set down his water with a thud. "You didn't eat lunch?"

"It fell on the ground." I looked out the window. The sun was starting to go down in the sky. I'd been in the shower for longer than I realized. "It's not dinner time?"

William shook his head slowly. "We eat late here. I don't want you starving, so consider this a late afternoon snack." He turned off the stove and placed whatever he was cooking down in front of me on the plate. It smelled delicious, and it was a huge amount of food.

I pointed at the plate. "This is a snack?"

"William's version." Oscar handed me the fork-esque thing that I'd had at breakfast. "Let me know if you need a knife, but usually, it just falls apart when you touch it."

They both stared at me, and I tried to stop holding my breath. "Thank you for this. Um, what is it?"

"Fish." Will rocked back on his feet. "Do you not like fish?"

"I like fish." Truthfully, raised as I was, I didn't have the luxury of liking or not liking any kind of food. I ate what I was served. Maybe someday, I'd have the time to develop some sort of palette. When I was on the planet that Casper had now suggested I might be kidnapped from for being female. I rubbed my arms at that thought. There were many, many bad existences in this universe. The Union did offer me some protection because people were afraid of them.

William walked over to stand right next to me. "Whatever bad thing you're thinking about that just made your scent go scared and your face to pale, please tell me what it is so I can find it and eliminate it, if at all possible."

"I'll help." Oscar crossed his arms over the expanse of his chest.

"No, it's nothing you can get rid of. Just something that Casper pointed out to me today." I took a bite of the fish. It was delicious. Only the outside was blackened, the inside was moist and easy to eat. But the fry on the outside was spicy. My eyes watered up. "Sorry," I coughed. "Can I have some water?"

Oscar darted behind him. "We should have thought of something to drink. I'm so sorry."

It was in front of me in no time, and I drank it down fast. It was cool, and it tasted really nice on my abused tongue. When I could finally talk again, I smiled. "That's okay. I could have gotten up and gotten my own. You aren't here to wait on me. I'm abusing your hospitality. On some jobs, I sleep in a tent outside."

William picked up my plate and dumped it in the garbage. "I forgot. Earthborn humans don't like things as spicy as we do. This is my mistake. Don't move."

I hadn't planned on going anywhere. I guessed I could go back to my room. But Will dug through the fridge before making me a plate full of some kind of cheese and what looked like fruit. "That will be safe. I'll be right back."

He rushed from the kitchen and out the front door. I looked over at Oscar. "Something I said?"

His smile was huge. "You befuddled my big brother. Hard to do. No, he wants to feed you. And he must have realized that the things he has to feed you will not work. Too spicy."

I took a bite of the cheese, and it didn't threaten to burn my tongue from my mouth. "It really was tasty on the inside."

"We'll adjust." He slid onto the stool next to me. "It's so nice having you here."

"You guys can't be eating bland food while you feed me. I can really figure things out. You are going so far and beyond what is necessary."

Oscar shook his head before he sat, seemingly content just to watch me eat. "We are so incredibly happy to adjust in any ways we can. This is a small thing."

I ate, and we stayed in silence. It should have been awkward, the way he watched me chew and swallow, but I held his gaze and didn't look away, even when I felt the blush start in my cheeks. If he wanted to look at me while I consumed food...then I wanted to let him. What was this strange game we were playing?

"Tell me a story. From your life," I asked him before I could overthink it. "Something about you."

He took my empty plate and placed it in the sink. "For a little while, I thought I'd be a healer."

"What happened to that dream?"

Oscar walked back over and picked me up off the stool. In a quick movement, he carried me over to the couch. "I decided I liked leading too much." He scooted over next to me. He smelled clean. Had he also showered while I had?

A thought dawned on me. "Is there a limit on water? I think I was in the shower a long time."

He slowly shook his head. "Nope. There is plenty. That probably wasn't a really interesting story. I'm not sure I'm a very exciting person. William and Casper tend to do bigger, more dangerous things. And I'm..."

I smiled at him. "The voice of reason?"

"Maybe. That sounds like an accurate description. I keep them out of their own ways. They're happy, easy going people. Until they're not." He took my hand in his. "And don't get me wrong, I can get angry, I can get...involved. But I'm more likely to suggest talking it out."

"Tell me another story."

He ran his thumb over the top of my hand. "What if you tell me a story?"

"I don't know if I have any."

Oscar's laugh could have lit up the universe right there for its warmth.

"We're really interesting people, aren't we?" I asked.

"Obviously, neither one of us can tell stories." He rubbed his eyes. "Okay, I can do better than I wanted to be a healer but I wasn't. I got lost when I was about ten years old. Feels like a million years ago. Now, most Lion shifters would never admit such a thing, and if you tell William or Casper about this, I'll never hear the end of it. See, we have great noses, and we don't get lost. We cover huge amounts of territory and always find our way home."

This was what I'd wanted. To hear a little bit about their world so that I could digest it, understand what it was like here from his perspective. "Is there something wrong with your nose?"

"No." This time his smile was rueful. "It works perfectly. But I got caught in a scent. If I'd had decent parents, I'd never have been out so far by myself. I was left on my own. I went farther and farther, crossed water —which was a problem I would learn to adapt to as I got older—and I got lost. It was so many hours until I could find my way home. When I got there, only William noticed I'd been gone. He was quasi frantic about it. And I felt badly that I'd worried him. So I lied. I made up a whole story about chasing a deer." I wasn't sure if it really was a deer or just how my translator converted it, but the image worked for me. "Then he was mad that I was inconsiderate rather than an idiot who got lost."

I actually could understand completely how he felt. "I didn't have anyone who would have looked for me either. My father...he had another family and only visited a few times a year for a scattering of hours. I was like a bonus child to him. He didn't send us much in the way of credits, and I was...probably someone he would have preferred to forget about most of the time. And my mother...she was unwell. I had to take care of her most of the time. I took a bus to the beach once, and no one knew I'd gone. I never did it again. I was hungry and cold by the time I got home."

His hand stiffened in mine. "I guess at least I had William."

"Well, if I hadn't been alone and left to my own devices and then utterly lost in the world, I never would have found my way here to see who was shooting missiles at the Union."

"Then I guess I'm grateful for it." He leaned forward. "Kiss?"

I should say no. But it was clear I was going to have a hard time ever denying Oscar anything. "Just one."

Our lips met.

9

I pulled back after just one kiss. "We can't keep doing this. I'm leaving. I know you think otherwise, but this is just another job for me. And I could get into a lot of trouble for this."

He took my hand back in his own. "You're running this show, Tiffany. Not us. I understand perhaps it's overwhelming because there are three of us, but if you find yourself having feelings...maybe try to feel them. You aren't the only one for whom this is new. We have never been through this experience either. And there are bound to be changes on all sides. Outside of the obvious toning down of the heat in the food."

It wasn't the heat in the food I was concerned with. It was the heat in other places. But what other changes did he mean? I opened my mouth to ask him when the door slammed open. Casper came in holding a bunch of logs in his arms. He kicked the door behind him closed. "Going to be cold tonight. Obviously, we have heat, but I thought this might be nice."

Did he mean to light a fire? "I've never seen one in a fire-place. Is that something regularly done here?"

I scooted off the couch to where he was walking over to place it in what I had assumed was just decorative. Did it actually work? Such an old-fashioned thing to do. Like out of some kind of movie. And yet also how I identified wealth and prestige. People who could sit and stare at fire they had built out of choice and not out of some kind of need to survive.

Casper smiled at me. If he was mad at our earlier inter-action, I didn't see it in his gaze right now. He was smiling at me, even in his dark eyes. "Note to self, Tiffany likes fires in the fireplace."

"Well, maybe I do. I've never encountered one. I've been by a campfire. Twice. But never this."

Oscar walked behind me, placing his hand on the lower part of my back. "We still haven't fed you."

Casper almost dropped the log but righted it at the last minute before he placed it into the fireplace. He rounded on his brother. "I thought you were going to feed her. Sorry, that's rude. I do have manners. I thought they were going to feed you."

The last bit was addressed to me and made me smile. "They tried."

"Too spicy. Will just ran out to get other things, but she's probably waiting till dinner now. She had cheese and fruit. So I guess we did feed her something. I just don't count that as a meal."

I waved my hand. "It's plenty for me. Seriously, that might be considered a feast. Can we talk about the missiles?"

Casper shook his head, finally squatting down to arrange the logs however he wanted them in the fireplace.

His shirt came up in back, and I tried not to look. I was becoming an ogler. A person who ogled. A full-time ogle beast.

Hell. What was the matter with me? I was starting to find myself amusing too. I wasn't, usually. There was really nothing about my internal dialogue that I generally found all that interesting. Huh.

"That can't be enough." Oscar added paper to the logs. "Get her something else."

"No." I couldn't stress that enough. "I'm good. That could be my dinner. I don't need more food right now."

Oscar yawned. "We're eating again in four hours. Now would probably be the time we'd take a nap."

A nap? I looked at them to make sure they weren't kidding, but neither of them smiled, and it was clear that they meant it. "Don't you go to bed soon?"

"We take a nap about now and then get up for dinner. And then the night starts. Only one of us sleeps at night. Or only one of us now. It was two of us until yesterday but we're not complaining. Then, morning comes, and it starts at dawn."

I blinked. This was going to make my head hurt. I'd been lots of places, seen lots of sleep cycles, but never one like this. "What do you do when you're not sleeping? I know one of you sat outside my room last night. Did you think I was going to do something or run away or..." I couldn't come up with a third option, so I left it like that.

Oscar shook his head. "One of us patrols the outside. Makes sure the house is safe at night. The other one stays up to make sure you are fine. And the third one sleeps. Then we rotate around. William watched you last night into this morning. I was outside. And Casper over there slept."

"Not really." Casper shrugged. "I was a little bit too

excited to sleep. Couldn't settle down. My Lion kept wanting to come out and visit her. It took a lot of concerted effort to keep him inside."

Oscar's mouth fell open. "I can't believe you just admitted that."

Casper rolled his eyes. "You have no idea how it was. You got to shift. I bet if you got Will to admit it, he had the same problem. It's not every day we find a mate."

I held up my hand. "Guys. I can't be your mate."

"We know you think that." Oscar yawned. "That's fine."

I was pretty sure I'd just been dismissed. "It's going to make me feel terrible when I leave the three of you thinking I'm your mate and I'm on a ship away from here. I really wish you'd listen to me on that subject."

"Come to think of it," Cas said with a laugh. "It is strange I admitted weakness. There's a symptom."

A symptom of what? He turned back to the fire, starting it. Okay. Enough was enough. "Ignoring what I'm saying to you doesn't change. I can keep redirecting or we can talk about this."

"I really like how you handle arguments with upfront truth." Casper put the gate in front of the fire as it started to blaze. "See how I deflected?"

Now it was my turn to roll my eyes. "Are you listening to me?"

"We're listening," Oscar answered. "We aren't going to get a consensus on this. I don't believe you'll be leaving. I think you are going to rapidly change your mind. You don't think that. Yet. For now, I think the best thing we can do is leave that as a disagreement."

I sighed. This was getting exhausting. "Agreeing to disagree rarely works."

"Why do you care if you're leaving?" Oscar raised one eyebrow. "What difference does it make?"

"I..." Fine. He wanted an answer. I'd give him one. "I like you guys as people."

Casper nodded. "Well, that's good. We like you as a person too."

"Can we at least agree to stop discussing the mating? Like if we're going to leave it, can you not bring it up?"

In unison, they both shook their heads. Well, this was getting us nowhere. Or maybe even backtracking us. "I'm going to leave you guys to your nap."

Oscar walked over and grabbed the pillows off the couch. They were big and soft. He put three down on the ground in front of the couch, at a distance that would be quite a ways from the fire.

"I'm not tired." I stared at the now roaring fire. It was orange and red, seeming to dance within its containment, although I knew it could easily get out of control if it were less monitored and not so restrained within the fireplace. Still, I kind of loved looking at it.

"Then just lie down with us." Casper nodded toward the big pillows. "You'll be comfortable. If you're not tired, read in front of the fire."

I did have things I needed to catch up on. I could look at my tablet while they napped. It would be nice to have the experience of being in front of the fire. I'd always wanted it.

"Let me get my tablet."

Casper nodded. "Great."

It took me a few seconds to grab the device. By the time I came back, they'd taken the outer body pillows, leaving me the one in the middle. I stepped over Oscar, having to really stretch to do that. It was funny. I'd almost gotten used to how big they were. Almost.

As I settled down on the pillow, they rolled onto their sides, each facing me. It would be awkward if their eyes weren't already closing. "How long do you guys usually sleep?"

Without opening his lids, Casper answered. "Probably about four hours."

I gaped. That meant we were going to be eating dinner really, really late. Had they eaten after I'd gone to bed? This was all really confusing to me. For two of them, this four-hour nap was going to be all they got for the day?

"Do you do this often? Lie down in front of the fire and go to bed?"

"No." This time it was Oscar who answered. "Usually, we go to bed in our own rooms. Or one of us on the couch."

"And is everyone doing this right about now? Like the whole planet just lies down and takes a nap?"

Casper scooted closer to me, placing his hand on my hip. "It's not four o'clock everywhere. But roughly around four in different time zones, yes, people are sleeping."

I was going to stop talking now. The years in the orphanage had taught me that there was nothing quite as annoying as someone speaking when you were trying to sleep. Where was Will? If everyone just went to sleep, shouldn't he be back?

I looked down at my tablet. But the fire was crackling and pretty, which made me set it down on my chest. I wanted to watch it. Why wouldn't I just take a moment? There was nothing pressing on me right then. It would be another day or so before I would get a communication from the captain about the missile.

I looked over at Casper. Unlike Oscar, I wasn't convinced he'd knocked right out. "Cas?" I whispered. If he were already asleep, he wouldn't hear me. If he were awake, he would. His eyes opened slowly, lazily, like he had all the time in the world to answer me.

"Tiffany?" My name was like a prayer on his tongue. He said it with the kind of reverence others used in church.

"I owe you an apology."

He ran his forefinger down the slope of my nose. "For what?"

"Earlier. I accused you of things. And it occurred to me that today, both instances of violence were to protect me. That was a shitty, shitty thing for me to do."

He scooted closer. "I said some things too. We are going to disagree. Probably a lot. I like that, actually. I've been thinking about things all day I never would have considered. I don't know if you were right or not. But it made me think. Thank you for that. And I didn't mean that you would be taken away. I'm sorry that I..."

I shook my head. "My turn to apologize. Not yours. Forgive me?"

He laughed, a low sound. "I think you're going to find that you never have to apologize to me."

"I will always say I'm sorry when I'm wrong."

He kissed me. I caught my breath. It was a brief embrace, and he pulled back. "Perfect."

"What?" My mind was whirling. I couldn't follow what he said.

"It was a perfect first kiss. Just what I wanted for us. Never say sorry. Not to me. Close your eyes. You need to sleep."

I shook my head. "I'm not tired."

"Don't get mad." He kissed both my cheeks. "But you are tired. Bone-tired. Maybe the most tired I've ever known a person to be. Close your eyes."

I knew he was wrong. I wouldn't sleep. Only seconds later, my eyes were closing. Then there was just nothing.

I roused slightly with a noise behind me. Oscar hadn't moved, still holding me the way he had been, but Casper's head was on my stomach, his body curled into me. I hadn't even noticed. Quickly, I realized what had awoken me. Will was back. He laid a pillow on the floor by my head, lying down to be like the top of the T to the vertical line we were in.

He shook his head before he placed his hand on my hair. "Too soon. Go back to sleep. Tried not to wake you."

Okay. My tired brain took that news in. "Was worried about you."

The fire burned, illuminating his face in shadows, but I didn't miss the red appearing in his gaze for a second. Something about what I'd said triggered his Lion. "Don't worry about me, beautiful. I am a survivor. Always have been, and it is my job to care for you."

I rolled my eyes. I wasn't doing the mate argument again. He grinned at me, like he could track my thoughts, and lay down, his head near my own. "Let's rest a while yet."

They were all here. I wasn't a napper—this whole day would go in the record book for being strange. But it was warm, probably because of the close contact the guys were giving me, and despite my raging thoughts, my mind let itself shut off again. I slept.

~

"I DIDN'T KNOW it would feel like this." A hushed voice reached my ears, rousing me from the deep sleep I'd fallen into. My eyes didn't want to open, and I almost let myself fall back into the dark, comforting nothingness where I'd been for however long.

Which one of them had said that? I wasn't awake enough to tell.

"How could we?" That was Oscar who answered. Hearing that, his absence next to me resonated. It was colder where he had been. "No one true mates. And now I feel badly for every other person on this planet who isn't us, because everyone should know what this feels like. Best sleep I've ever had. Just this whole sensation of finally having the person who belongs to me right where she belongs. Everything about her..."

"I know." It was William who spoke, who had said the first statement too. "It's like...such a sense of at last and rightness. I can't imagine how I made it a day without her."

No one had ever spoken about me that way before in my life. No one had wanted me. Not my parents. Not my co-workers. Not even the few acquaintances I made here and there who were temporary, situational friends. I caught my breath and let my eyes open slowly. Casper still slept, hard. His breathing was deep and even, his head where it had been earlier. My head swam. I'd fallen into the kind of sleep where I could have made it through the whole night without moving. I put my hands into Casper's hair, running them through it gently. Why? I wasn't sure, but we were lying there together, his head on my stomach, and it seemed like the thing to do.

Nothing really made sense yet. It felt like floating—like reality had the sense of the fantasy right now. This might not really be happening at all. I could be asleep still. In fact, if I closed my eyes... Casper let out a sigh in his sleep that moved right through me. To places not usually affected by such sound. My nipples ached. I wanted...something.

Oscar walked over and knelt next to me where he had been sleeping earlier. "Hey, you're awake."

"Sort of." I smiled at him. "Thinking I may go back to my bedroom and just go back to sleep."

He frowned at me. "We need to eat dinner. And then there are some things you can see."

"I can't wake up. And dinner? I can't fathom it right now." My stomach was turned off. I didn't want food. No. No way.

Casper groaned, his eyes opening. "What time is it?"

Oscar rolled his eyes. "Past the time for you to be up."

"So comfortable." He sighed again. "Keep doing that, Tiff. Don't ever stop."

I stilled my hands from their petting him. Yes, he liked it, obviously. I did too. But I should absolutely not be doing that right now. It wasn't okay. None of this was. My heart rate kicked up.

"Note to self—don't point out things she's doing when she's doing them." Casper lifted his head. "I really, really like that."

I took a deep breath and put my hands back in his hair. The damage was done. I was completely getting fired after this trip and probably deserved to be.

Oscar leaned over and kissed my temple as Casper made that sighing noise again. "I'm going back to bed. Right here. I'm never getting up."

William strode over. "You're both getting up." He smiled down at me, a looming figure who was going to order me out of this comfortable nap. William extended his hand. "Casper, let our mate get up."

He groaned. "You aren't in charge, you know that, right?"

"I do." William nodded, his hand still extended. "But I'm cooking dinner, and I have a beverage she might like to have waiting for her. You can keep her pinned to the floor or you can move. Up to you."

Casper scooted off. "Emotionally blackmailing me by pointing out she might be hungry or thirsty was a dirty game."

As he rose, he stretched his arms over his head, his shirt coming up. I forced my gaze away. I was constantly staring at them. I took Will's outstretched offering and let him help me up. The room tilted slightly. "This isn't going to work. I have to go back to bed. Really, I can do without food. I'm not sure my digestion will be great if I eat this late."

"Only if you try to go to bed right after." Will put his arm around me, and I leaned against him. "And you're not going to do that. It was so strange for me on Earth. You all lie down for eight hours straight and don't enjoy the night at all."

I sat down at the counter. Now I could smell what he was cooking. It was a mild scent, obviously not over spiced, somehow reminiscent of tomatoes but maybe sweeter. Casper walked past, knocking into my chair in that affectionate way that he did. "I'm going to shower. Be right back."

Oscar took the seat next to me as Will put a hot beverage in front of me. "Is this caffeinated?"

"Yes, but lightly. Not like your coffee or tea. Just a touch to wake you up." He picked up and sipped a similar mug. "I need it after the late afternoon nap too."

It was a smooth swallow. Not bitter, more like flavored warm water, but it did have the slightest jolt. "Last night, when I arrived and everything was quiet here, was everyone sleeping?"

"Yep." Oscar nodded. "They were. Except us because we had an alarm go off that an unauthorized ship was landing. That made it our problem. We skipped our nap." He nuzzled against my shoulder. "And grateful we did."

The drink was helping. My eyes were widening and my thoughts clearer. So I was fully aware that I liked what Oscar was doing. That I was in a semi-state of arousal that probably all three of them could scent, which was making me want to run and hide. But conversely, not one of them was saying a word about it, so if they could pretend, then I supposed I could too.

"What are we doing after we eat?" My stomach rumbled. Okay, maybe I was hungry.

"Hard to explain. You'll have to see." Will looked over his shoulder to wink at me. "Almost ready."

"So everyone takes a nap around four-ish. That was," I looked at the clock, "six hours ago, which honestly was a full night sleep for me, so I may not need to go back to bed at all." Oscar shook his head, and I ignored it. Who got more than six to eight regularly? "And the sleep rotation, should I do that, is that one of you will prowl around outside, one will sit outside my door, and one will sleep in his room."

William set the plate down in front of me. "Correct."

He served Oscar and then handed a plate to Casper as he strode back into the room, his hair wet and smelling warm with the faint amount of the scent of soap surrounding him. My head swam. Again. Fuck.

"Is that how it works for everyone? Like say if a woman has five mates, how does that work?"

"They work that out for themselves." Casper took a bite. "Oh, this is good. Well done, Will. But someone will... Did you say prowl?" He grinned at me. "Someone will make sure the inside and bedroom is safe. That's the idea."

Oscar hadn't eaten yet. He watched me as he sipped his warm drink. "Usually the one, or maybe in larger groups, many, that sleep, sleep with their mate. We're just not to that point yet. Seeing as you aren't at all sure yet that you want this."

I ignored the dig. If they'd asked me before I'd been really awake, I'd have told them I wanted it. All of it. That was a problem. A big one.

"I don't need you guys to sit up with me watching the bedroom. In fact, I think that idea is a little irksome. I might not be able to sleep in the future knowing that is happening. And besides, that makes little sense to me. Can't your females shift? That means they're Lions. Why do they need you to stare at their bedroom doors or protect them? Is it so dangerous here? What does a lone female do?"

William pointed at my food as he took a bite of his own. "Eat that. I'll answer."

I complied. It did smell great. It was a pasta dish. Full of flavor but not too much. I closed my eyes. "This is good."

"Think I'm figuring it out. What you can eat, what you can't. I'm on it now, Tiff." I opened my lids, and he finally answered my questions. "I think what you're asking me has to do with gender equality. Here is the deal. Women run businesses here, they hold any job they want. They can be the bosses of males, they can do anything they want. But the truth is that biologically when I shift, I'm bigger than she is. It would take a lot of women together to take me down in a shifted state. I have to be, naturally, the protector. She could put up a good fight, but unless she had like five other women with her, she's not winning that encounter. It's not any more dangerous here than anywhere else, but there are always men who might do the wrong thing. That's true on Earth too. So lone females do tend to live with other females just in case. That's one of the reasons for a strong Alpha Lion. Such things are less likely to occur when everyone knows that the guy in charge, the strongest one there, will destroy you if you were to step out of line that way."

They had to be talking about rape, kidnapping. Casper nudged my chair, a reminder that we'd had this conversation earlier. Yes, I was fully aware.

"It's like we have three lives. One that's very similar to yours. This year is odd for us because we're playing these roles. But Oscar is a programmer. He makes technology we hide away and use that the Union doesn't know about. Casper's a teacher. A good one. The young Lions out of their mind calm down with him. It's pivotal. Only a few people can do what he can. And I deal with the crystal production and distribution for about half the planet. If you want light at night, you had to talk to me."

Similar to jobs on Earth for sure. "And your second life?"

"Lions. Sometimes we're fully animals. My human brain goes somewhere when I'm an animal. I know certain things, but I can't articulate them. I know these two. I know you. I know what I want to be doing, what the right thing is. But there are simple things. There is territory. There is food. There is thirst. There is family. There is fight. There is death. There is being the strongest. Those sorts of things."

I'd never really understand that, holding only one form myself. But that was interesting. He wasn't really the Will he was now when he walked on four legs. I'd remember that.

I lifted three fingers. "And the third?"

"We are both at the same time. There is being a shifter. Human. Animal. And both. There is when I can feel my animal in this form. There is when I can feel this person I am when I am running as a Lion. Those moments happen. All of it has its rules, and that's why Cas and others like him are so important. Some of it is natural. Sometimes that can go askew."

Cas looked at me. "Does any of that make sense?"

"Some of it." And I was starting to understand how little I would ever really grasp the fullness of any of it. They were complicated. I was too, but I'd never touch the zone where they lived daily. I just had my one form, one brain, my own issues that only belonged to me. For once, I was grateful for that.

I took another bite. Meeting Will's eyes, I forced a smile. "Thank you for dinner."

Oscar finally took a bite of his. "Don't thank us for food."

"I told her that. But she seems compelled." Casper's smile was sardonic. "And we have to get used to human ways. We might change her a bit, and she is going to alter us. It's going to be brilliant. I know it."

I wasn't at all so sure.

10

William placed a new glass in my hand. I stared at the clear liquid. "I'm awake."

"Good." His smile moved right through me. It was like he was undressing me with his eyes. "This has a little alcohol in it."

"I hardly ever drink." I sniffed it. Part of my issue was I generally just didn't like the taste. If anything were too bitter, I couldn't tolerate it, and too sweet made me gag. It didn't smell like anything. I took a sip. It wasn't bad at all. A little bit like a not-too-sweet lemonade. I could taste the alcohol, but it didn't overwhelm me.

"It's not bad." Still, it probably wasn't a good idea to drink when I wasn't sure of anything.

Casper walked over, kissing my cheek. "Don't worry. You're safe with us."

I was and I wasn't. Truth was, I didn't trust myself all that well with them. They might not do anything. I couldn't be sure they wouldn't.

Laughter and music came in through the windows. "What is happening out there?"

"Nighttime." Casper walked past me. "William's going to shift. I'm sleeping later. And Casper will be watching to make sure you're okay."

I shook my head. "Can we discuss this arrangement?"

"What don't you like about it?"

I waved my hand in the air. "How do you think you could sleep knowing someone was sitting outside your door staring at your room? It's...weird. Almost borderline creepy. And I don't want it."

They looked at each other. Casper rocked back on his feet. "What if I sat in here? Just close enough to hear if something bad happened?"

What bad did they think was going to happen? "I... That is fine."

They were compromising. I could do the same. William winked at me. "See you later, gorgeous. I'm never far from you."

He took off out the front door, which opened the second he touched it without his having to use the handle—a technology I hadn't seen activated at this house before—and shifted mid-stride onto the porch. With a fling of his intimidating head, he turned around and looked at me. For one long second, I held eye contact with a ginormous Lion. He put his head back and roared. I swallowed and failed to hold my ground, taking two steps back, which meant I banged into Casper. He put his arms around me and his chin on my shoulder.

"You're safe. He'd never hurt you."

Having had the three sides of the shifter explained to me, I wasn't sure I could believe that. "How do you know? If he's in the stage where he is totally lost to the Lion, then how do you know that Lion wouldn't hurt me?"

William ran into the night.

Casper sighed in my ear. "Because the Lion is the reason we knew you were our mate. So it stands to reason the Lion feels the same way we do, or differently, but equally as important. The Lion doesn't kill its mate."

I really was never going to understand this completely. But I knew myself well enough to know that didn't mean I would stop asking. "Was he in zone two, the one where he's lost to the Lion, or zone three, the one where he's both?"

Oscar nodded toward the door. "His eyes weren't red. He was lost to the Lion. There is a tell, it's that."

I'd seen their eyes turn red several times now. First time being when they'd come out of the darkness toward me when I'd gotten off the ship. Which reminded me as I walked out the door to ask one more thing. "Why didn't any of this happen last night? It was quiet. I didn't hear music or laughter. Or anything."

"It was raining last night. As you may recall, we're not big fans of the rain."

The site in front of me caused me to catch my breath. People were everywhere. The night was lit up thanks to the crystals, and yet I could see the sky perfectly. It was like the stars had come down to join the party, to partake of the fun. People were dancing, and in the distance, Lions were on a hill, staring down at the scene. One in particular held my attention. He wasn't looking at us, but I was pretty certain it was William. Maybe it had to do with the stripes in his mane. I might be off or just imagining it was him.

"Come?" Casper held out his hand, and I paused before I took it.

"Can I stay here? I...I don't want to go."

His face fell. "The Lions aren't going to charge the crowd. They're the same men you saw earlier on the street. If you see females, it's the same women. You're safe."

"That isn't it." Although I could understand his thinking it was, considering the conversation we'd been having. "Never mind. Let's go."

They stared at each other, but no one questioned me, which was good because I didn't want to explain why I avoided fairs and other crowded entertainment situations like the plague. This was a happy night, and I wasn't going to be Tiffany, the girl who always brought down the mood. Casper took my hand in his, and I let him lead me to the gathering in the center of the nearby square.

Why did I care what any of them thought? I certainly wouldn't have yesterday. I didn't give a shit what anyone thought of me, except that suddenly, I did. What had changed and why? I was Tiffany who got shit done.

That was all. I pushed forward, determined to meet my goal. I didn't do...this.

Yet, as I wandered with Casper holding my hand and Oscar with his hand on my back, I didn't really care that none of my current behaviors made the least amount of sense.

"Casper," a woman shouted, running toward us. She was tall, like everyone here, with long dark hair, and big brown eyes. Her face was long and her body lean. She was stunning. "Tell me it's not true."

He didn't drop my hand, which meant I got to feel it tense in mine. I didn't know what was happening, and that meant I needed to be free to run if things got violent, since I couldn't protect myself here. I pulled my hand free as Oscar put his arm around me.

"This is Tiffany. She's ours." Oscar spoke quickly. "And she and I are going to go dance while you handle this, Cas. Good to see you, Drew."

My heart clenched as not a second later, Drew let out a

loud yell of no, her eyes turned red, and she sunk to her knees. I'd never been in love, but I wasn't stupid. I could certainly tell the signs. Drew was in love with Casper.

"A human!" She pounded on the ground. "We were so close. So close."

For his part, Casper knelt in front of her. "Drew. Please."

I didn't hear what he was going to say because a crowd had formed to watch the scene. A crowd we were quickly making our way through to get away from it. "Oscar." I finally found my words and made him stop. "This is ridiculous. He should be with her." It hurt me, right in the center of my chest to say those words. "I'm not one of you. And I've told you, I'm..."

He didn't let me finish, taking me onto a dance floor that had been set up next to one of the stops. It was low, slow music, and he drew me to him, his body pressed close to my own. We swayed. "Don't say you're leaving. I know you think that. It hurts me to consider the idea. Just for now, dance with me and don't...do that."

I sighed. "But you have to see, he's hurting her. Probably hurting him too. He's in love with her, and he thinks he has to do something he absolutely doesn't have to. They're in love."

Oscar frowned. "Trust me, he is not now nor has he ever been in love with Drew. She might have convinced herself she'd be with him—with us, I suppose, since we come as a trio. But he was the only one she could stand. And Will and I were never going to go for it. They weren't having sex. You haven't ended a relationship. Casper was nice to her. He's nice to everyone. It's rare when he can say a really shitty thing and be forgiven for it. When he doesn't just have to alternate between being kind and killing someone. When he can actually be himself."

I opened and closed my mouth. "Oscar, I don't want to fuck up your lives. I'm not just some weak human woman who happened to come here. I'm tough. That's why they sent me. I get my way. I win. I kill people when I have to."

He whispered in my ear. "You think I don't know that? You pulled the trigger on William yesterday. If we weren't protected from that laser, he'd be dead. I'm glad you're strong. We all have to be. That's how life works. You're not fucking up our lives. You're completing them."

I wasn't doing that. I wasn't a person who could ever imagine doing such a thing. I was...broken. But I closed my eyes and let Oscar lead me around the dance floor on a foreign planet to a song I'd never heard before. There were some bands who sought to spread their music everywhere. They'd set out with that in mind. But almost none of them made it off Earth or past the Mars colonies, and I'd never heard of a foreign band selling music on Earth, ever. It wasn't likely I'd know this music. It was next to impossible.

But I liked this slow dance. "I've never done this before."

"Danced?" he whispered in my ear. "Well, I'm honored to be your first. I love that, actually. I'm not sure how that's possible. Men probably line up to dance with you. If everyone couldn't smell that you were ours, the men would be lining up now."

I rolled my eyes. "My life hasn't lent itself to being a lot of places where dancing took place."

"Well, on one hand, I'm grateful because you and I have now shared your first dance. On the other, it really makes me fucking pissed that you haven't lived a life where you could have danced before."

That was ridiculously...sweet. He leaned down and kissed me on the lips. It was gentle, and I closed my eyes, letting him warm the part of me that had gotten cold worrying about all the things I couldn't ever do anything about.

There was just the music and Oscar. We swayed together like we'd been doing it for years, and not like it was my first dance ever and I was having it with a man I already knew I'd have to hurt. And what was more was that I was going to feel so much pain doing it.

I pulled back as the music changed. "Oscar, what am I going to do with all of you?"

His smile shocked me. "That is the universal question of everyone who meets us."

"Tiffany." Casper touched my arm. "I'm so sorry that happened. I never made her promises. I wouldn't do that. I don't make promises I can't keep. I'm sorry she had ideas, but they weren't put there by me. That had to be awkward for you. And I'm sorry."

I touched his side. "Casper, I'm not upset. Other than worrying that I'm keeping you from someone like her. You know how I feel about this. I don't want to keep reiterating it. The whole agree to disagree, but you have to understand how I'm feeling about this."

He searched my gaze and then nodded. What internal dialogue was he having? What had he seen that made him do that? "I understand your concern. That's my problem. Okay? If I'm so wrong. If we all are, then I accept that and I'm responsible for my own pain. Not you."

I opened and closed my mouth. "Okay." There really wasn't anything else to say. If he wanted to accept that if—when—it happened it was on him, then it really let me off the hook. Only, I was sure it wouldn't work that way in the end.

"Can we get out of here? I hate crowds." That hadn't changed. Not even with the kissing and dancing. I'd never be okay with choosing to spend time in large groups like this. They might all charge and trample us to death. That was unlikely, but it was what it always felt like. In the distance, a Lion roared. I shot my attention toward the sound.

"Someone found prey." Oscar smiled. "Nothing to worry about."

"You speak Lion even when you aren't currently one?" I forced myself to smile.

Casper took my hand. "No, we just know the general tone of things after years of listening to it. You want to go back? We can do that. Come on. I'm sorry. I thought you'd like this."

I never talked about why, and I wasn't about to right now. I just wanted to get out of there. Too many people meant too many problems. Too many chances for things to blow up in our faces. I had to find the missiles and get out of here before this place and these people made me forget that everything in life ended—usually badly.

Even on planets where they danced every night. "This wasn't happening last night. I would have heard it."

"No, it was raining and a strange unauthorized ship had landed. Everyone was indoors. More the rain than the ship." Oscar smiled.

When we finally made it back to the house we were staying at, I had calmed. It wasn't likely everything would explode here. It was quieter. I could hear the music in the distance, but it wasn't on top of me. There was a comfortable outdoor couch on the porch, and I sank down on it.

"Thanks."

I looked down at the floor of the porch and then out into the darkness. They were staring at me. I didn't have to even see it to know. Their eyes on me... I could tell they were there like warmth moving over my skin. Whatever they were thinking, it wasn't hostile or angry with me. How did I know that? Damn. I didn't know. Maybe I was really starting to imagine things.

Oscar came over and sat down next to me. He put his arm around my shoulder, which was incredibly nice. I closed my eyes. I could get used to this, and that was a big problem.

"It's okay. You're allowed to like being close," he whispered in my ear.

I opened my lids. "Am I?" I wasn't at all sure that was the case.

Casper crossed past us into the house and returned a second later with a blanket that he wrapped around me before he sat down on the other side of me. "It gets cold here at night."

"We're lucky we're here during the warm season. Three months from now, we couldn't sit out here."

A thought dawned on me. "What does everyone do at night when it gets really cold?" I suspected I knew the answer.

"We shift and all of us run around as Lions." Casper tugged on the end of my hair. "We don't feel the cold the same way with all that fur."

That was what I'd thought. "And now that you have me, you can't do that, right? Because two of you have to sit around here instead of being out there. You are now going to be trapped inside during winter months two out of every three days." I just wanted to make sure they really knew what they thought they wanted to commit to here. They could still change their minds. Everyone did when it came to me.

Casper rubbed the back of my head. "I'd rather sit here

with you or be inside with you than out there running as a Lion. I can guarantee Will is hating life right now because he'd rather be here. I couldn't have imagined that I'd feel this way. But I do. We all do. This is how it's supposed to be."

I put my head on Oscar's shoulder. It was right there and inviting. The crystals made it bright enough that I could see the nighttime around us, but not so bright it felt like daylight. A Lion would appear in my scope of vision sometimes and disappear after. I couldn't tell one from the other. They might all be Will over and over. I had no idea.

The music played in the distance with laughter and happiness evident in the sounds reaching us. I didn't realize I was going to fall asleep. I just did.

THE CROWD MOVED AROUND US, angry, yelling. I held my mother's hand as tightly as I could. The truth was she would lose me if I didn't hang on. She might not even notice she had. In my twelve years, I'd had to find my way home alone more times than I could count. One time, I'd had a silent panic at my desk at school because it occurred to me she might move while I was at school. I could come home, and she would be gone. Then what would I do? My father wouldn't take me. I'd stopped even asking. I knew the answer. No, Tiff. No. No. No.

But the crowd, the people she worked with, were drunk, angry, and gathered right now, and for some reason, she wanted to be in the center of it, even though she wasn't working today. We could have stayed home.

But the authorities were here to take a head count. They did this every so often to be sure that no one had moved from where they'd been assigned. I didn't understand what the big deal was. We knew they did this. It was expected.

Every time, people got seriously mad. Every time. Why my mother had to participate in getting angry and drunk this time, I didn't know. I wanted to go home. My feet hurt. I hadn't slept much. And this just...sucked.

My mother dropped my hand, and before I could grab her again, she rushed forward with the crowd. I fell to the ground with an *oomph*. People ran at me, jumping over my body. No, someone was going to step on me. I rolled left and covered my head before a large man almost stomped down on me. Somehow, I managed to get to my feet, stumbling twice before I managed it.

"Mom," I shouted. "Mom."

I didn't see her anywhere. The telltale sounds of lasers being fired caught my attention. I'd heard it one too many times for comfort. If one of them caught me, it would hurt like hell. They didn't kill us unless they had to make some kind of statement. We were low wage labor. No one wanted these jobs. As my mother often said, they kept us miserable, breeding, and breathing so that we kept doing what they wanted.

I darted backward, running in the opposite direction of the crowd. I didn't want to be near those lasers.

This would be over soon. It always was. I made it to the edge, standing against a pillar that should keep people away from me. They wouldn't want to run into the pillar. My body hurt, and my heart raced.

I could have been really hurt. Scanning the crowd, I looked for my mother. She had to be somewhere. Chewing on my lip, I looked and looked. Nowhere. Where was my mother?

Then I spotted her. She was being loaded into a truck. I

gasped and ran forward. Where were they taking her? No, what was happening? The crowd was in my way. I couldn't get there.

Panic hit me hard. It was very, very bad when they took us away. Why had they grabbed her? What had she done?

I woke, fast, my heart racing like it had that day. I sat up straight. I was in bed. Not on the porch. Someone had brought me in here and taken off my shoes. I had one blanket draped over me. But that wasn't what had me continuing to panic.

The whole room was shaking. Hard. Back and forth, back and forth, with a loud rumble accompanying the shake.

What was happening? I screamed. Loud.

11

The door flew open, and Casper—followed immediately by Oscar—came in. The room shook around them, but they seemed relatively unbothered by it as they both ran to my side.

"It's an earthquake. You have them on Earth, right?" Casper smoothed my hair off my face as the room didn't quit its rocking.

"I do, but I've never been in one before." He had spoken in normal tones, but I shouted back at him, even though it was obvious he could hear me.

He nodded. "It'll slow soon. This is a small one, actually."

It was? How much worse would they get? "Should we get in a doorway or something?"

"No. The house is designed to ride it out. Everything here on our planet is. Sometimes, rural areas can take a pounding, but you are fine here."

He looked over at Oscar. "I'm going back to my spot."

His brother nodded, lying down next to me on the bed

so that his body was right there but not actually touching me. "I'll just stay until it settles."

Casper closed the door with a clink, leaving us alone in the shaking darkness. Until seconds later, the shaking stopped. I took a long breath, trying to steady my heart. "I'm not usually such a coward."

"I imagine if I went to Earth tomorrow, there would be things there that would startle the fuck out of me."

Laughing, I threw my head back. I liked that description. "But it's been my job to be okay on other planets. This isn't different. I'm just somehow...different."

"Don't worry about that. You woke up to the house shaking. It would make most people scream. Trust me on that. Even brave people. It doesn't mean whatever you think it means."

My head hurt, and I really felt like someone had taken all the life out of me and sucked it away. Maybe that was why I started talking. Or maybe I didn't need a reason. Maybe I just did.

"My mother took me places that were dangerous. She didn't care if people were on drugs or drunk, ready to fight and get into trouble. Everyone was angry that day. I'm not even sure what they were doing there or screaming about." I could understand that they were angry in general. I'd hated the way we lived too. "I was twelve. The only kid there."

He pushed my hair off my face, moving closer. His gaze met mine. They hadn't closed the windows when they'd put me in here, leaving them as I'd had them last night. With the crystals lighting up outside, I could see him just fine, even in the darkness.

I had his attention, his gaze never straying from my face. I swallowed. It was intimidating to be the center of anyone's thoughts. At least for me.

"Expressing anger is healthy." His voice was low. "But maybe not smart to bring your child if they're at risk."

That was all true. "My mother was never happy. I can't remember her being that way even once. I didn't make her happy. That was for sure. At some point, I stopped trying and just tried to be small, unobtrusive, and when needed, helpful to her. I can't really remember why she decided I should come with her. What conversation, if any, we'd had. But there I was. The crowds got violent." I swallowed. I'd never spoken these words aloud to anyone. "And I lost her. Or she lost me. We lost each other. I wasn't a baby. I should have held on to her."

Oscar continued to stroke my head. Slowly. "You were twelve. I think you can forgive yourself for whatever you're blaming yourself for. Whether it's losing your mom in a crowd or her not being happy or you not making her happy. Or all of it."

I groaned. "In this case, it's losing her. She ran up with the crowd to the Union authorities, and I was almost trampled because I fell."

He winced. "That is on her, not you. Whether she liked you or not—and that is just a terrible thing to even think about—she was responsible for the welfare of her child."

I wished that were the end of it. "Yes, well, I got up. Ran back. That's probably why I don't like crowds. I'm always concerned I'm about to be stomped to death. But that wasn't the worst."

His eyes widened. "What happened next?"

"Most of the time, these things broke up, they got the crowds to go home, but they always made an example of some people. As though that might stop others from rioting. It never worked, but they regularly did it."

He nodded, understanding crossing his gaze. "You? Or your mom?"

"My mom." I supposed it could have been me. It wasn't as though the Union had much use for children other than as future consumers or workers. "They took her away. And injected her with a torture medicine. Something they do to make people pay. Maybe she was rude. Or mean. Or just... they wanted to. I never knew. She came home, and two days later, she was dead."

He sat up. "A torture medicine? Maybe the translator isn't working. What does that mean?"

"It injects a kind of a poison into them, I guess." The truth was, I had no idea really how it worked, medically. "And it tortures them. Saves a person having to do it. More efficient. It comes in waves. You're in horrible, could kill you pain, and then it wanes. You start to feel better. And then it comes again. On and off, on and off. Some people live through it. We don't know how long it lasts. It's individual. So it might be one week for you, three to me. Who knows? If you make it through, you live. She didn't. I tried to take care of her but..." This part was maybe the hardest. "I failed."

He pulled me up against him. "You were twelve. You understand that, right? In no world should that have fallen to you."

"But it did." I didn't realize I was crying until he wiped a tear from my face. "And I always wondered if maybe she sort of gave up. And that makes me...mean."

Oscar shook his head. We were both on our knees now, facing each other. "It's not mean to say the truth to ourselves, to admit things, even if they're hard. You don't have to sugarcoat things. In fact, you shouldn't, at least to yourself. What happened then?"

Then? I blinked. "I tried to clean up."

"No, I mean to you. Although that is awful."

Oh, right. "At some point, they came and took her body. And...I went to live in an orphanage. I had no family that would claim me. My father wasn't interested. He came and visited me there once like that was a normal thing to do. Said he was a friend of the family. And I was so glad for his stupid visit. Then he stopped because he died too. I just thought he'd stopped. I studied. I got out. I went to work for the organization that killed my mom because that was the only means to get the fuck out of there." I sighed. "So as you can see, I'm really a very cold, dead inside person. Sorry you got stuck with me as your mate."

He hugged me so close, my head against his shoulder, that I wasn't sure I could breathe. Or that I even needed to. No one had ever hugged me like this before, and maybe it meant that I could subside on the strength and oxygen that he had while we were like this. It certainly felt that way.

"You're not dead inside. Don't ever think that again. People do all kinds of things to survive. That is what you did. You lived. You got out. No one took care of you, and you did all those things. It got you here. I don't think there is a person alive on any planet who couldn't understand how you had no choices and no protection. Yet you did it anyway."

I pulled back to look at him. "No one wanted me."

"We want you."

I kissed him. Straight on the mouth, hard. Wrapping my arms around his neck, I tried to show him in that kiss everything those three words meant to me. He might never really understand it. He kissed me back, the ferocity of his response showing me that he did get it, he did comprehend what I was trying to say to him without words.

We met mouth-to-mouth. I didn't know how long we did

that, on our knees practically clawing at each other's clothed bodies, while our lips made love to each other. I grabbed at his shirt. I didn't know who this version of me was, but wherever this side of me had come from, I was good with her right now. I kissed his neck, every bit of open skin I could find, until I had to tug his shirt over his head.

Of course, he was built like a stone statue. I ran my hands over him, feeling every well-defined ab. "You're beautiful."

"That's my line."

He pushed me down on the bed, his eyes moving over me. "You are too dressed." He lifted an eyebrow. "Unless you want to stop."

I shook my head. "Shut up with that nonsense."

His smile was huge. "Shutting up."

I'd been so afraid, and now it was like I felt like I could fly. I'd pulled his shirt off, and he did the same for me.

"That's better," he whispered. "Do you like this bra?"

I blinked. "What?"

"I asked if you liked this bra?" he repeated himself. The question I couldn't really understand right in this moment.

Clearing my throat, I wrapped my arms around his neck. "You want to talk about fashion right now?"

He rolled his eyes. "Not at all." Instead, he ripped the garment right off my body. I gasped. Yes, I'd forgotten that he was that strong. He was. No regular human male could do what he did. And right then, it was so...fucking hot. "I'll get you a new one if you like it."

The way Oscar stared at my breasts, it was as though he'd just been given the best gift he'd ever seen. Like something out of a movie. I had never been looked at like that before. My breasts were fine. I supposed they'd best be called proportional for my tiny size. Depending on the outfit, I didn't always have to wear a bra. And if Oscar were just going to rip them off of me, then maybe I wouldn't at all. It would save a little fuss. "In a hurry?"

"No, I just don't like things that get in the way of where I want to be." He leaned down and kissed my neck. Shivers traveled down my body. I hadn't known that was a spot I liked. In fact, I usually didn't care for any of this. But oh when he touched me there... The best possible shivers. I giggled, not a sound I'd ever made before.

Oscar lifted his head and smiled at me. "How about the other side?"

He kissed the opposite part of my neck, the same spot there. This time, I sighed. Moisture pooled in my core, and he hadn't even touched me yet. "I really, really want this."

With a piece of hair falling over one of his eyes, he nodded. "Trust me to take care of you, Tiffany. I want this as much as you do. But we aren't going to rush. Even if I did destroy your bra. What can I say? You bring out the animal in me."

He kissed me then, gently on my mouth, pulling back before I could deepen the kiss. "Put your hands on that headboard and hold them steady. Don't let go till I tell you to."

I pouted. "But I want to touch you too."

"You will. Just not yet. Because when you put your hands on me, I can't think straight, and I intend to keep my head intact for just a little bit longer."

He kissed my chin, and I did as he asked. Oscar was so sweet. Really incredible that way. He shouldn't be, but he somehow managed to come across as gentle, even though in a heartbeat, he could shift into a Lion. He traveled down my body with his mouth, and I quickly forgot my reservations about how strong he was. That strong Lion shifter wanted to worship me with his lips, and I'd be crazy to say no. My body buzzed. I'd never felt like this before.

How had I ever lived without this? With my hands staying where he wanted them, I could only observe and feel. It was strange to not be participating as he planted kisses everywhere he could reach. Warmth flooded me. It was like he was leaving permanent pieces of heat wherever his mouth touched. Eventually, he got to my belly button, and I giggled. I couldn't help it. It turned out I was ticklish. He lifted his head to regard me and smirked.

"Something funny?"

I shook my head. "It tickles."

"Tickles?" He scrunched up his nose. "I don't think that translates."

Interesting. They weren't ticklish. Okay. I'd dwell on that later. "Doesn't matter. Just that if you touch me in some places, I am going to laugh, like a reaction I can't help."

"I love the tiny differences between us. I love how you are so unique to me in so many ways. Like a gift I get to keep unwrapping."

I raised an eyebrow. "Can I let go of this bedpost?"

He shook his head slowly. "Not quite yet."

With a yank, he pulled my pants off and discarded them on the floor. At least he hadn't ripped them. "I do need those. I'm glad they're in one piece."

He smiled. "One piece of ripped clothing a night. I'll keep myself to that."

This was so bizarre. "This is insane."

"In the best possible way." He went back to kissing me over my stomach, stopping at my panties. With his teeth, he bit down on the panties and dragged them down my legs, dropping them on the floor. As his gaze roamed over me, he flared his nostrils. "You are so fucking beautiful."

Okay. Enough was enough. "Oscar, I'm letting go of this headboard."

He smiled. "If that's what you want, that's what I want."

I dropped my hands and darted forward, my arms coming around him to embrace him. I was totally naked, and he had his pants on. That seemed completely out of whack to me.

Raising an eyebrow, I stared at him. "Now this seems rather unfair."

He shook his head. "Seems pretty awesome where I am, but if you insist." He yanked his pants off with a tear, throwing them who knew where in the room.

"You are dangerous to clothes."

"Apparently, when it comes to you, I am." His mouth met mine again, and I got lost in the moment. Maybe it was because we were both completely naked and clinging to each other. I'd never felt like this before. Not this intensity, not this sense of just needing this. Sex had been dull. This was the most exciting thing I'd ever done in terms of intimacy, and despite the nakedness, we hadn't really traveled down to each other's most private of parts yet.

I reached for him. If I was giving in to this suddenly bold version of myself, then I was going to go for it and worry about the whys tomorrow. There was just Oscar right now.

He was big in my hand. Huge actually. I looked down to where I cupped him to confirm what I felt. Yes, his cock was huge. I squeezed him gently, and he closed his eyes.

"Wow." Indeed, yes that. I smiled. Who wouldn't like eliciting such a response from the person she'd decided to go to bed with?

Following my lead, he pressed his finger against my clit. I jolted and caught my breath. Yes, more of that. A lot more of that.

"So responsive," he whispered in my ear, even as he grew impossibly bigger in my hand. I stroked, he did the same. It was almost like we found the same rhythm we might have had with him inside of me.

I moaned, closing my eyes as I rocked against his hand. He stopped his movements and just let me. Somehow, even though I was lost to the pleasure, lost to the intensity, I still stroked his cock. If anything, the closer I came to completion, the harder I gripped him.

"Love that," his whisper was low. "Come for me, beautiful."

I wanted to. "I never have. I don't know if I can. Maybe I can't."

He leaned over to kiss my neck, right at the spot where my neck met my shoulder. It was warm, gentle. "You can. Take it from me. I'm giving it to you. Just reach out, and it's yours. You're so fucking beautiful."

Pleasure pounded on me. All I had to was reach out and take what he gave me. And that was what I did. Right there, on the bed, with Oscar letting me grind against his fingers, I came for the very first time in my life.

I cried out, falling onto Oscar's chest when I did. He held me by my shoulders, kissing my neck over and over while he did. "Good girl. You just gave me your first one. Thank you for that. Thank you. So beautiful."

The room spun, and I held on to him, my body continuing to vibrate, even without the stimulation. I'd come up so high, I couldn't find my way back to normal. I might never want to. I lifted my head to stare at him. He was still hard.

I stroked him, balls to tip. He'd made me come. I was going to do the same thing to him. I wanted it. Badly.

He shook his head. "Can't. I appreciate the effort, and that feels great. So good. You can do it forever. But that's the thing about a true mating—I can't come any way but inside of you ever again. Not my hand. Not yours. Has to be inside of your body." He sniffed my neck, a long inhale. "Like my body knows it only wants the real thing from now on."

I stared at him. "Really? Only inside of me from now on for you?"

"And I'm not complaining about it. I'm so grateful just to be here with you."

A thought dawned on me. "What about in my mouth? That's in my body. Could you come in my mouth?"

He blinked. "I don't know. That's not really an option here. I hadn't even considered it."

So the female shifters didn't give blow jobs. That was interesting, but not so much that I cared all that much at that moment. "We'll have to try it. Another time." I backed up against the headboard and crooked my finger. "You're going to be inside of me tonight. The way you were thinking."

He scooted toward me. "Are you sure? There isn't pressure. I wanted to make you come. I had no expectation that I'd be inside of you. I am happy to wait. I'm surrounded by your scent right now. It's heady and perfect."

I kissed his chin. "I know what I want. And right now, that's you between my thighs."

"Well, if that is what my mate wants, that is what she will have." He moved until we were positioned better, his body over mine. His sheer size had never escaped me, but right then, I was hugely aware of him. I swallowed. It hadn't occurred to me that he might be too big for me. This might be more than I could take.

He kissed the end of my nose. "Don't be worried. And no, I couldn't smell your anxiety. I can't scent anything except how much you want me. So fucking hot. It's just the expression on your face. What are you worried about?"

I swallowed. "You're much bigger than me."

His smile was fast. "I'm blushing." He wasn't, really. Or maybe he was. Even with the natural light in the room, I couldn't really tell that. It was hard to picture strong Oscar blushing. He kissed my neck. "All will be well. I promise. We're made for each other."

For now, that sounded great. I'd go with that. Oscar positioned himself so that he could enter me but didn't right away. Instead, he kissed and kissed me until I was dizzy from it. My head seemed to swim, and it was when I was slightly out of it in the best possible way, he pressed gently inside of me. I cried out but not in pain. It was so...beautiful.

I stretched to fit him.

He gasped and closed his eyes, not moving for a long moment. "Oh, Tiffany. This is...this is everything."

I kissed him, hard, his words moving me in a way I couldn't deal with right then. I wrapped my legs around him, drawing him deeper and forcing him to move. He gave in with no issue. We'd found our rhythm with our hands and did again, as though we were long-term lovers who knew each other's bodies. I pulled, he pressed. I clawed at him. No way did I not leave a mark. He pulled me closer so that our chests brushed against each other with every thrust.

Yes. Fuck. I loved this.

"More," I begged him, and he complied. Deeper. Harder. Yes, I took him, and I let him take me. We were joined. And then the world exploded. I didn't know if we had another earthquake or if we made the world shake. I didn't care. All I knew was pleasure shook me to my core.

I held on to Oscar, and for right then, I knew he'd keep us both safe.

I didn't know who this version of me was, but I liked her.

We didn't separate right away. Every so often, he'd jolt inside of me, and pleasure would flare again. We breathed the same air and said nothing of import. Just murmurs that spoke of what we'd just shared.

Eventually, we rolled apart. He drew me against him, kissing me all over my face.

"Tiffany, you are so beautiful." His words were low, and I smiled at him.

"You say the sweetest things. And you are also beautiful."

He groaned. "I'm not. I'm just lucky to even be able to look at you."

That was just silly. I leaned on my elbow and stared at him. He smiled at me, and I couldn't help but notice that his eyes were mostly closed. Oscar was tired. This was supposed to be his night to sleep.

I ran my finger down his nose. "You need to go to bed."

"I don't. I just like being close to you." Still, he scooted nearer, his eyes closing even more.

I dropped my head to the pillow that we were now going to share. Oscar placed his hand on my hip. "You're so soft. I haven't had anything soft in my life."

I knew that feeling well. "Oscar, I swear I think you should sleep. Tonight is your night to sleep."

He made a low sound in his throat. "I will if you will."

"Okay. It's a deal." I closed my eyes, listening to the sounds in the room. It was quiet in the house, nothing rumbled or shook. Within seconds, he was asleep, his breathing becoming steady and deep. I opened my eyes. The version of myself that I could feel right now loved this. But I knew the other me better, and when she came back in the morning, she was going to have questions about what the hell I had just done and why. Oh, no question, I'd wanted it. I'd never desired anything more than what we'd just shared.

But it was very un...me. What did it mean? I stared at his beautiful face. Right then, I didn't care. I closed my eyes.

12

S leep didn't come immediately for me. It had been
years since my time in the orphanage, but during
those years, I'd discovered, thanks to those being my
insomnia years, that there were all kinds of sleepers. Some
people snored. Some people rolled around—a lot. Others
were still and silent, to the point that you questioned if
they'd quit breathing altogether. Fewer talked in their sleep.
An occasional person would even scream, which was terror
inducing if I did manage to fall asleep. Oscar, he murmured
a little bit. Small words I couldn't make out, or my translator
just didn't know, or maybe they were nonsensical nothings.
In any case, it was sort of adorable.

Yes, I was still in the mushy zone I'd fallen into, and it
didn't seem to be fleeing anywhere so fast. I rubbed the back
of his head gently, feeling his soft hair, and he sighed,
settling down, the low sleep-talking stopping when I did.
Rain pelted the roof. This part of the planet had a lot of it.
Oscar rolled completely onto his back, dragging me with
him when he did. My head came, almost with a hard splat,
which would have happened if I'd been asleep, onto his

chest. He mumbled again and, given that his hold on me could only be called tight, I had no choice but to settle down.

Besides that, his heartbeat helped to soothe me. Slow and steady. Whatever he was dreaming about and mumbling through, he wasn't upset by it. Oscar was calm, easy. That must have been what lulled me to sleep.

I didn't dream.

And when I woke up, it was only because Casper touched my hand. My eyes flew open before I even knew what was going on.

"Hi." His voice was low. "I'm sorry to wake you at all. You look...just beautiful lying there. But it's getting late. Time for you two to rouse so we can hit the road and get to the coast before it's completely dark outside."

I nodded. "Hi." Oscar lay on his side, his arm around my waist, breathing deeply and not disturbed at all by Casper being in here. "Sorry. I don't think we meant...I mean..." Reality dawned on me as I spoke. I'd had sex with Oscar. Really, really good sex. The shame and embarrassment that should have flooded me didn't present. That was...odd. I shook my head. We'd obviously rolled around quite a bit, because I'd been on his chest and now, I was on my side with him spooning me. "Are you going to wake him?"

Cas shook his head slowly. "I think I'll leave that to you. I haven't seen him sleep this deeply, ever. If he's not waking just from us talking, he's pretty out of it. And I'm not sure if he's going to be a bit of a bear over it. You'll be better at rousing him. Sorry you got scared last night. The shakes happen. Everything is built to manage them. It would have scared me too if I didn't know."

I swallowed. "Thanks for running in."

"I'll always be here for you. Always. See you in a little bit." He winked at me and walked quietly out the door.

I turned slightly in Oscar's hold to regard him. It was nice Casper had come in the way he had. If Will had come, he'd just have banged on the wall until everyone was up. I didn't know them that well, but somehow, I was sure of that. How grumpy was Oscar going to be?

I smoothed my finger down the slope of his nose. "Oscar? Time to wake up."

He didn't budge. If he hadn't been audibly breathing, I might have worried about him. I leaned over to kiss both his cheeks. "We've got to get up. They're waiting on us to leave."

When his eyes opened, they were red. The sign that he was both human walking Oscar and Lion walking Oscar. I sucked in my breath. Somehow, I had to stop being so intimidated by this dual nature they had. He was half asleep and in my bed. Even if he were grumpy, he wasn't going to shift and claw my eyes out. I didn't think. Plus, I could see in his gaze, even red as it was, that he was tired. That was all it was. Oscar was bone-weary tired, he'd been sleeping well curled up with me, and I'd kept him up a good portion of when he was supposed to be sleeping. First, because I was scared. And then because I'd jumped him for sex.

"I'm sorry. I'd let you sleep. But I guess the trip is long." I kissed the end of his nose. I'd never woken anyone before that I could remember. My mother had forbidden it when I was a child. The matrons at the orphanage woke us with a bell. We all got up fast. As an adult, I just set an alarm. I was usually up before it.

His eyes lost their red, and only his brown depths stared back at me. His smile was slow and heat inducing. There were other things we could do in this bed if we had the time. Only we didn't.

"Good morning, my mate." That word. It still made my stomach pang, but not because I hated the idea. No, because I wasn't at all sure I could be that for them just logistically. I was still me with my own responsibilities. It was no longer a lack of interest. Although if I were being honest, it was probably never that.

I gently stroked his face, and he closed his eyes again with a sigh. "Good morning. No, don't do that. I need you awake. We both have to get up."

He sighed again, and this time, opened his eyes completely before he stretched his whole body all at once. Then he wrapped me in a huge hug and rolled me over so suddenly, I screeched beneath him. His grin was huge. "Best night of sleep ever. Could have stayed like that all day in bed with you. And I am a high energy person. Just, yes." He kissed me all over my face. "And you smell like me. That's weird for you, right? It's just that I am now in your cells. I can scent it. You are also in mine. It's beautiful. I feel like I could tell the whole world to fuck off right now. I won't. You have work. We have to get you there. But, damn. Yes. Good morning, Tiffany."

I grinned, despite the sort of overwhelming nature of how much he was saying all at once. He went from zero to a lot. "I think I should shower. Not because I'm trying to get you out of my cells or anything. Just because I shower every day."

"Me too. It'll dampen the scent of sex but not where I am not inside of your very being now. That will stay. Oh, fuck, I love this."

I grabbed his arm. "So are you in the cellular makeup of every person you've ever had sex with?"

Was I going to run into shifters—like Drew—who were

walking around marked by the scent of these guys? Even if Cas said they hadn't been that way together.

Oscar shook his head, his eyes widening. "No. That's the true mating part. You can pick up scents during the day from anyone near you. But they go away fast. Like poof. Gone. Not like that." He bent over to smell my neck. "This is like...the best thing ever."

It had clearly made him giddy. "Got it. Sort of." I smiled at him. "It might get old that I can't ever really understand."

"Never." He kissed me then. A real kiss. A kiss a man gave a woman who he wanted to say something to without using words. It was good morning. It was thank you. It was something else so profound that I couldn't even let myself think it.

I kissed him back and then pushed at his chest. "They're waiting on us."

"I know." He let me get up. "See you at breakfast." He winked at me.

I crossed quickly to the bathroom and put on the shower. I'd been doing okay up until that kiss. That had said words that I'd never heard in my whole life. I wasn't ready for that. Why? Because I had no idea what they meant really or how I was supposed to digest them. Maybe that was why he hadn't actually said it. I was already naked, so I just got under the water.

A thought dawned on me. Sure, Oscar had seen me naked. We'd had sex. But Casper had walked right in on us and he'd seen me. I hadn't even given that a thought. I shook my head. Despite whatever this anxiety was creeping up on me, I couldn't help my smile. Last night had been fantastic. My insides tingled thinking about it.

I washed quickly. What did the scent of sex smell like to them?

WILLIAM PUT a creamed egg dish in front of me, and I practically licked the plate. We were alone in the kitchen. Casper and Oscar had gone to get the car.

"You liked that. I'm getting the hang of your tastebuds." He took the plate from me before he bent over and kissed me. It wasn't a gentle morning embrace. So far, there had always been ownership in Will's kisses. This morning, I didn't mind.

He reached behind me and knocked a cup off the counter. I blinked. "Why did you do that?"

"The kiss or the glass?" He kissed me again. "Both things because I wanted to."

I stared at the glass. "I'll pick it up."

"No," he smiled. "I want it on the floor."

We had reached one of those cultural things I might not understand. Or maybe it was a William thing. I didn't get to dwell on it because he kissed me again.

I put my hand on his chest to stop him, and he took the hint. It wasn't that I didn't like it. Just the opposite, in fact. But we were leaving, and I had to keep my head clear. "Was the glass just bothering you?"

"It's a Cat thing, babe. Sometimes, things just belong on the floor."

Well, I supposed that was that. "Were you okay out there last night? With the weather and the shaking ground?"

Something flared in his gaze before he leaned on the counter. "I was fine. I'm always fine. That is something you'll learn about me. They're here."

A car pulled up in front of the house a second later. He had either heard them or smelled them, and I'd guess the latter. My bag was on the couch and I walked over to grab it, but Will was faster. "I'll carry it for you."

"Thanks. And Will? I'm always fine too. But that doesn't mean we really are, right? Sometimes, we're not fine."

He put his arm around me. "I don't get to be not fine. That's not how the universe works for me. I'm better now that you're here though. And Oscar? I've never seen him like he was this morning. You might be magic."

I wasn't that, and because I knew just how not magic-like I truly was, I couldn't help but wonder how long it would be until they knew it too.

There were no cars on the road except ours.

"Why are we the only ones traveling like this?"

Oscar was driving with William up front with him. I sat in the back with Casper, who stretched his long legs out in front of him with no trouble. These vehicles had been designed for bigger people than me. I felt a little bit like a small child allowed to sit at a big dinner table, with my feet dangling over the side of the chair.

I'd seen pictures of that in advertisements. We'd never had a dinner table, and by the time I was at the orphanage, I'd been big enough to sit anywhere I wanted and not be too small for it.

"Most people don't leave." Will turned in his seat to look at me. "Groups stay together. Only Alphas or someone representing them leave often. Or people like us, who are currently without a home or a group, looking to take over one."

I lifted an eyebrow. "Really interesting how you are also in charge of everything. Essentially homeless and the supreme leaders."

"Well." Casper took my hand in his. "It means that we have a broader interest in the whole planet. Alpha Lions tend to just focus on their own people, their own territory, and forget about those who they don't share borders with. It will happen to us too. Particularly now that we've found you. I can already feel my attention becoming really family oriented. Like if it isn't going to affect you, your happiness, and your safety, I care less and less about it."

William made a sound that said he agreed before he settled into talking to Oscar about which roads they'd be taking. It was obvious there was little travel on this planet, because the roads were not wonderfully maintained. Huge potholes were everywhere, and it was a little bit of an adventure for Oscar to drive the car around to avoid them.

I side-eyed Casper. "So if I said that it would make me happier if the roads were better, would you get them fixed?"

His smile was huge. "I love the manipulation, Tiffany, and yes, I would do it." He leaned over to kiss me.

Time passed, and I watched the landscape change. It went from barren to lush, almost like a rain forest, in a matter of hours. Everyone was lost in their thoughts, but Casper never took his hand off my leg. Periodically, he would wink at me.

I almost forgot I had a job to do, thanks to the fascinating scenery and because he was so adorable, I could have spent the whole drive smiling at him. A very un-Tiffany thing to do. I would just have to continue to catalog all the ways I'd lost my mind.

Pulling out my tablet, I was glad to see it hooked up to the Union satellite from the car. It was meant to do it anywhere in the universe, but I'd found that wasn't always the case. Still, the shifter worlds were right along a major shipping lane. Hence my being here in the first place.

A message popped up. The captain had located the

missile. I read the words he sent me cataloging all the information he'd found.

"Now that is interesting," I said aloud, which caught all of their attention at once. I wasn't even sure what Casper had been looking at outside, but his gaze turned right on me, just as William flung his body half around in the seat. Oscar stared at me for a second in the mirror.

I cleared my throat. "Is there any reason the mysterious missile firers would be using missiles built on Planet Wolf?"

"What?" Casper took off his seat belt and scooted next to me.

"Is that safe?" I stared at him. "I mean, shouldn't you be strapped in?"

He waved his hand. "There's no one on the road."

Yes, that was true, but we were bumping around like we were on some sort of dangerous trek into the wilds. Or at least what I imagined that was like. I really had no idea. In any case, the sooner I showed him, the faster he'd get back where he belonged.

I pointed at the screen. He blinked. "Oscar, where are the translating glasses?"

Our driver shrugged. "In the back compartment."

"I have a pair." I grabbed my bag, which was at my feet —no way was it going anywhere I couldn't reach it—and pulled out the ones I'd used. I passed them to Casper. They should work for him too. He blinked and then nodded.

"Yes, you're right. I can see what the captain is saying here. The missiles are traditional markers for the Wolves. Amazing." He pointed at the screen. "The Union actually has correct intel this time."

I rolled my eyes. They could dismiss the Union all they wanted but they—we—had great intelligence for most of the known galaxy. Just not the Shifter planets. Although this time, we did.

"We use different guidance and propellent systems." He shook his head. "Not ours."

I chewed on my lip. "And yet they are absolutely being shot from here. Let me ask you a question. Do you keep old storage from missiles that were sent here and didn't explode? From old battles? Although nothing here is indicating this is ancient tech. No discussion of corrosion and certainly these things are still blowing up. They're not old."

Casper tugged on my hair. He didn't look at me. Was it an unconscious gesture while he read the screen? "We don't have such a stash. Anything that had ever been sent here and not blown up during the shifter wars—as your people call them—would have been safely blown up so as to protect a civilization population."

That made sense. "Then I suppose you have at least two possibilities here. Maybe more. But you've either got Lions shooting Wolf missiles." William, who still faced us, scowled at that as I said it. He might hate my second suggestion more. "Or you've got Wolves here shooting their missiles at Union ships trying to make it seem like you're doing it to start some kind of trouble for you."

Oscar shook his head. "Or a combo. Wolves working with Lions."

"No." Will turned back around. "No Lion would work with a Wolf. They're foul creatures."

I lifted an eyebrow. "Creatures, huh? Seems to me they're pretty similar to you. Terran and animal at the same time. They shift around. Interesting gene mutations." That earned me a groan from Oscar before he grinned and then quickly stopped. "They might not like being called creature any better than you would."

Will waved his hand in the air. "I'm not interested in hearing about the sensitive feelings of Wolves while they are shooting missiles from my planet to bring the Union down here when the one thing that we ever had in common with them, and the Bears for that matter, was the fact that we all hate the fucking Union and everything they stand for."

Well, that was heated. I'd heard it before, and what was more was I didn't disagree with him. They'd killed my mother. But the sad truth was that I was Union. Maybe I'd had no choice. Or maybe I was pathetic for ever giving in to it. Maybe I should have died or lived totally impoverished rather than take the job that got me out of the Dead Zone. But if he hated all things Union, then maybe that meant that he hated me too.

I typed out a quick message to the hated Union, telling them what I'd found, and sent it off.

Casper kicked Will's chair. "Hey, dipshit. Take a breath and think about what you just said, won't you?"

"What?" He stared at Casper. "What's the problem?"

I didn't want anything to do with this. If William had a problem, I wouldn't blame him. I had a problem. And it seemed most of my life, people had a problem with me one way or another. Even my existence was a problem. That was okay. I'd been foolish to fall down the hole I'd been in this morning.

William reached over and grabbed my leg. "Tiff?"

I put my earphones in my ear. "I have some things I need to listen to for work. Every so often, I have to. The president gives a speech. I'm just going to do that."

"Dumbass." Casper kicked Will's chair again. "He didn't mean what it sounded like he said."

I nodded and put on the noise. It would just be better if I zoned out to the weekly address and... Will grabbed my leg one second before he launched himself into the backseat, taking up all the space where Cas should have been sitting. He said something to Casper, who climbed back up front to sit next to Oscar.

William touched my knee again and pointed at his ears. Even the droning voice of the Union president wasn't going to get me out of having to listen to this. I pulled the earphones off.

"Tiff, obviously, I didn't mean that." He held up his hands. "I don't hate you or think of you in any way as Union. You're not that."

I leaned forward. "But I am. I know that makes me small and miserable. But I did it. I am here as a Union representative. I am what you hate."

He leaned over. "You're my mate. You've been forced to do things to survive. I get that. But you are not the personification of the Union to me. Nothing could be further apart than you and the Union to me."

"Will, like it or not, you have to come to terms with who I am. And I'm used to people hating me. You don't lie. So you said what you feel."

My seatbelt was off, and I was suddenly in his arms. "I don't hate you. You're mine. Do you understand? Yes, I don't like the Union. So listen to me closely. You are the most important person ever born in the universe. I wouldn't hurt you for anything in the world. I'm sorry."

Oscar lifted his eyebrows and made eye contact with Casper. Was it unusual for him to apologize?

I sighed. "There's nothing to apologize for. You said what you thought. And...the truth is I don't like what I do very much either. But it is what it is. I don't see that changing and..."

He hugged me tighter. "I would hurt anyone who said

one bad word against you. If we were in our Lion forms, I would tear them to bits. I'm not alone in that. Any of the three of us would. So don't you say one bad word about yourself, Tiff. I won't hear it."

I rubbed my head against his shoulder. "You don't know me well enough to say that. There are going to be lots of things you don't like about me."

"What the fuck?" Oscar yelled out. "Hold on. We're draining power."

Casper leaned over Oscar. "Yes, we are."

"I can read if we're having a power drain without you agreeing." Oscar pulled the car over to the side with a jerk, and I wished Will and I were buckled in. But he took the brunt of the sudden jolt to a stop with his shoulder and didn't even seem to notice, keeping me in his arms the whole time.

He let go of me with one arm but not the other. "What is going on?"

"I don't know." Oscar opened the door. "Something is draining all the power. I checked the car yesterday. Perfect working order."

"Well." Will sat back on his seat. "Let's see what the problem is, shall we?"

We all got out of the car. I looked left and right. "Where are we?"

"In the middle of nowhere." Oscar sighed, cupping my cheek. "I'm sorry, beautiful."

The skies opened up because, of course, it was raining.

13

They worked on the systems for hours. There was no question it had been tampered with. There were holes drilled into it. It quickly became clear that while there was no question Oscar could fix it—he even had the tools—the rain was going to make it impossible to do. He kept trying as we stood outside getting wet. They tried to get me to sit in the car, but that wasn't happening. I had a raincoat in my bag. If they could handle it, I could too.

Four o'clock came and went. No one stopped to nap or even particularly noticed. So it wasn't like there was a turn off switch, even if everyone napped at the same time every day on regular occasions. They continued trying to fill holes and fill up machines with oil. I didn't understand any of it.

But then the sun went down.

The rain started to seep into my coat. I didn't say a word, just passed another gauge to Casper, who used it to help Oscar.

"Okay, enough," Will snapped. "We're done for the night. We can't fix anything until morning."

Oscar lifted his head. "When I find out who did this, they're dead."

"There's no scent. They were careful." Casper slammed the lid closed where he'd been working. "Let's get set up."

I raised my hand. "I have a tent. It's small, but we could stay in it."

"We have a big one," Will supplied.

It took some more time to get out the bags that included the tent. The sun was officially down, and the temperature had dropped significantly. William and Casper set up the tent, which was more complicated than my own that simply blew up until it was formed. But theirs was also much bigger. Oscar walked over and put his arm around me.

"I wish you'd wait in the car."

"I've hit a threshold where when I get out of the rain, I need to stay out of the rain. Going in the car and coming back out, can't do that." It was nonsensical, but right in that moment, that was how I absolutely felt. "I'll get dry and sticky in the car. Then I might actually start to form mold."

He shook his head and kissed my wet temple. It wasn't lost on me that they were all in T-shirts and not at all cold. I shivered, and he stopped to look at me. "You're freezing."

"It's fine."

He spoke in a low voice, like a lion, when he answered me. "It's not."

I'd bet he had red eyes right then, but I wasn't going to turn my head to look at him. I needed to keep straight ahead, or my head might fall off. Now, that was ridiculous. My thoughts were getting muddled. That couldn't be good. What did that mean?

"She's freezing," he called out. "Hurry up."

"It's done. Come on," Casper called, and Oscar picked me up to carry me into the huge tent that was a good distance from the road. How far? I should have known, but right then, I didn't. But I was hustled inside where all four of us could stand upright and still have room. There was light inside too, with a crystal illuminating everything around in a gentle, dusk-like glow.

Will was quickly next to me. "Okay. I'm going to get you warmed, fast. Her body temperature is a good two degrees less than ours, maybe more depending on her personal stats, and she's going to feel the cold a lot faster than we do, even in our human form. I forgot. I'm sorry, sweetheart."

Casper kissed my cheek before he pulled my jacket off me and discarded it to the side. "Out of the wet clothes. I'm on far out patrol tonight. Nothing changed because we're here. I don't like this any more than you do, Will."

Was he talking to me? To Will? It was all sort of confusing, but Casper was soon out the door, presumably to shift and patrol the forest around us. Oscar too, who helped me get out of my shoes before he left. He was going to guard the tent right outside, which left Will and me alone in the huge tent.

I'd object to his stripping me, but I shook too much to care, and soon I was completely naked and then so was he. Although at most times, everything with Will would be sexual—he was gorgeous—right then, I could hardly notice. Instead, he bundled us both into what amounted to their version of a huge sleeping bag and pressed me against his form.

"You're going to warm up, fast. If you don't, I'll shift and then I'll be even warmer."

I snuggled against him. "Sorry about the shaking."

"Don't apologize for things you can't control. I won't let this happen to you again."

I pressed my head against his chest. "This is on me. Not you."

He kissed my temple. "Shush. Your health is my premier concern in life. And I know about humans from Earth. I was there. I know better."

Clarity started to visit my brain again as the warmth came back. "I wasn't thinking clearly. I think the cold muddled me for a bit."

He kissed my forehead. "You're still cold. Your skin hasn't warmed back up yet entirely. Just rest here with me. Let me fix this. And if you start to feel sick after this, we'll get you a healer when we get to the coast."

"I won't suffer in silence. You would probably smell it anyway."

He laughed. "That is true."

"So it occurs to me that whoever damaged the car might have done it so that we'd be in this position—vulnerable on the side of the road. They might be coming to attack or something." I tried to sit up, but his arms around me kept me right where I was. "We need to get ready to fight. Not that I can. I have no working weapon here, and you are all so much bigger than me."

He shifted slightly. "Don't worry. We are not unprepared for that. My brothers are shifted. They're out there patrolling. No one will get past them. And if they do, I'm here. We didn't get to this position by not being able to take care of ourselves, and we can easily take down any enemies. We will keep you safe."

I wasn't actually worried about my own safety. Maybe I should have been. If the car was damaged because I was here investigating things, then I supposed I should be terrified for my life. But I had been in mortal danger a lot. I was still here. No, I was more concerned that if this were a Wolf thing, that they'd be armed with guns that actually could hurt them, even if they were big, powerful Lions.

"They're out there, and you are stuck in here with me because I don't have any sense to know when I'm getting too cold."

He stroked a hand down my back. "I'd hardly call it stuck. Let's see here, lying cuddled up to my mate, who I need to find a way to apologize to so that she actually forgives me, in a sleeping bag where we are both naked, or outside, shifted into a Lion in the rain watching for enemies. Hmm. Which one should I prefer to do?"

We were both naked. I should be embarrassed. I wasn't. Maybe it was time to figure out why. "I don't seem like myself. This thing we're doing? I'd never have been able to handle it a week ago. What happened with Oscar and me last night? Same deal. I can feel myself changing, and I'm not sure why."

The slow strokes on my back didn't falter as he turned his head to look at me. "Oscar found all kinds of information on how it used to be with Lion shifter and human matings. Lots of information in databases people don't look at anymore. The same instincts that hit us, hit the humans, even if you don't consciously smell it. Our need to be close to you? You have the same desire. It happens to you differently. It could be that you just know that you're where you're supposed to be and naturally there are changes, desires, things that will seem different to you based on that."

I stared at him, lifting my head just a little to do so. "In other words, the same shift that makes you want to stay here with me, when you would normally want to be out there prowling around, has hit me to make me...want things I don't usually want."

"Or," that slow, beautiful stroke down my back, "you are

just opening up to wanting things you maybe did want but couldn't allow yourself to before. And that is true for me too. I always wanted this. I just never said it aloud."

I rolled onto my stomach, and he let me. "You went looking for answers. It's why you took to the stars when almost no one from here does."

"I was looking for you. I think I always knew you were there. I just had to find you. Had to try."

"Will," I curled my head against his chest, "I'm not angry with you for what you said. I don't like the Union either. How could I? But I think you've got to stop and consider that the second I signed on, I became them, whether I like it or not. I have worked for their benefit. I have made them money. I have—"

He interrupted me. "Yes, that was what you had to do to get you here. Now, you don't have to do that anymore."

I shook my head. "I don't know if it'll be that easy. They have a tracker in me. I can't just vanish."

He rolled onto his side. "Where is the tracker?"

I put my hand on my shoulder blade. "Somewhere in there."

"We'll get it out."

Will sounded so sure. "Will..."

"When the time comes, we'll get it out."

I sighed. "I only did it because it was a means to the way out. I needed to be able to build a life where no one could hurt me. Where I could be safe. And yes, I had dreams about certain luxuries. Maybe that makes me a bad person. All of it makes me a bad person."

"It doesn't make you a bad person. It makes you a person who was on your own and had to figure things out. Well, you found your way to where you were supposed to go." I was getting warmer, but every once in a while, I'd have a jolt of cold that made me shiver. William drew me back to him. "What were your luxuries? What things did you want? Gold walls? Endless bottles of wine? Ours is a little different but similar to Earth."

I shook my head. "I wanted..."

He waited a second and then answered me. "Yes?"

"I wanted to have as much to eat as I wanted. A full fridge."

William pressed his forehead against mine. "That's not luxury. But, okay. What else?"

"I wanted bright colors. Rugs on the floor. Soft blankets. Pillows that I never used that were just decoration, and a big bathtub that I could fill up whenever I wanted to do nothing but soak in hot water."

He waited again. When I didn't answer, he tilted his head slightly. "Is that all you wanted?"

"That's what I wanted. And to feel safe. And not be at the mercy of anyone."

He ran his hands through my hair. It was so gentle, soothing. I really was starting to feel the heat from his body. "You can have all of that, it's practically nothing. And other things that you don't want yet. You can have all of that here. When we settle and take over wherever we'll be living, you will have all of those desires and ones you haven't even imagined yet."

"The money I earned doesn't work here. All of those credits. It's like I have nothing."

He shook his head, a frown marring his face. "We're very rich, Tiff. All three of us, and what is ours is yours. Take all of it. I don't want a thing other than to care for you."

"That is very sweet." I pushed his hair out of his face. "I told Oscar I wouldn't argue about leaving anymore. And I'm not. Truth is, that it is getting easier to see staying with you.

Like this mating thing has muddled my good sense. But, Will, if something happened to the three of you, what would I do? I'm on a planet of Lion shifters, and I'm not one. I'm safe because I'm with you. I have no working weapons. I'd have to find a way off the planet by myself to a world where I belonged nowhere. Being dependent, even on someone who wants to literally give me everything he owns or could own, it's frightening to me. I've been alone since I was twelve. I've had to learn how to survive like this. I'd make it work. I know, my mind is scattered. I'm here, there, and everywhere in how I'm trying to describe this, but can you understand that even if I give in to this beautiful, warm feeling that being with you brings to me, I can't let that be it?"

I was sure he would argue with me. There were ways these Lion shifters did things. The ways they assumed true matings would go. I was just supposed to want what I should want. Instead, he leaned down. "I do understand. We will figure out something you can do so that you can earn your own money here. And never be entirely dependent on us."

I caught my breath. He'd listened, and he'd actually understood. I didn't know why it brought tears to my eyes. I didn't know why it struck me the way that it did. But I was hardly ever really listened to except when I procured information someone else needed to use. "Thank you."

"You don't ever need to thank me for anything." He sighed. Maybe the warmth was getting to him too. "There are other benefits to our mating. You, for example, are extending your life."

That didn't make any sense. "What?"

"Oscar has spent a lot of time reading sources that no one has read since we became...isolationist...and it seems that humans who true mated our ancestors lived a lot longer than their normal spans. Something about this mating is going to change you at a cellular level. Not as long as we live, but longer than you. Closer to ours, which is good because we are already older than you, so it will level out in the end."

I rolled onto my side, and he did the same until we were looking at each other straight on. "So what you're telling me is that I am going to live a long time but still die before you, so maybe I don't need to worry about suddenly finding myself alone on this planet. You guys are the ones more likely to be left alone here."

"No, I wasn't thinking that. I can't fathom you dying. It is my biggest fear, and I've only known you a few days. It has replaced all other concerns in my life. So no, I wasn't thinking that at all. I was thinking of you living." His eyes widened as he spoke. "And if you were to die, I would not stay here alone. Not a day more than I had to. I would follow you."

This conversation had gotten very dark. "Don't do that. There is a pack of Lions somewhere that will need you to run it, to make their lives better so their youth don't step out and accidentally kill strangers, their people don't starve, and their way of life doesn't fall apart. You have things to do, important things."

He leaned over so that our faces were closer, and almost in unison, we both laid them down on the pillow. "I care less about that than I do about you. How important does your job feel right now?"

That was a good question. I blinked. "I want to make it safe here, no missiles firing, so no one comes to bother you guys in a way where you might be in danger."

"I will secure us a...pack, as you called it. I will make it strong and healthy, so that you have a great life there. Not for the glory. Not for the power. Just for that alone."

My heart beat faster with his words. Was any of this really happening, or had I hit my head and now I was in some kind of delusion that I needed to wake up from? "Favorite thing in the world." I held up my finger. "Don't say me. That is very sweet, and I can almost not...handle it. Other than me. Favorite thing or activity or just favorite."

He chewed on his bottom lip. "A really good meal and a really good booze to go with it. And nothing the next day that is really important so that if I do just a little bit too much of the second one, then I don't have to feel badly for lying around."

"I've had good meals but never a day off to lie around. Not ever. The Union doesn't even let me take my vacations. They pulled me off a surfing trip when I'd been off work for less than twelve hours."

"Truth?" He yawned. "I've had maybe two of those days in my life. But that is why they are my favorite things. Tell me about surfing. You just get on a board and somehow don't fall off when very scary waves throw you around?"

My eyes were getting heavier. "It's not for everyone. You either have the need, the drive, the want of it, or you don't."

"I don't. I've never even heard of anyone doing anything like that here."

I snuggled closer. "That is really too bad. It's the closest thing to freedom I've ever known."

I must have fallen asleep then, because when I woke up, it was still dark, and I knew I hadn't slept very long. The crystal had dimmed the light in our tent even more, or maybe it was something Will had done before he fell asleep. He was pressed next to me, his eyelids closed, his breath light and barely audible in the warmth of the tent. I'd conked out facing him, our heads sharing the pillow, and we were still like that.

In the slightest light, I could make out his features. They were strong, but in sleep, he looked beautiful, gentle even. I'd thought they all looked alike when I'd first met the brothers, but now they were quite different to me, even to the point that I wasn't sure how they looked alike at all. The shades of their brown hair weren't even close. They were all beautiful. And in this moment, Will was all-consuming.

I wouldn't bother him. He needed to sleep. But I could admire him from this close distance. The slope of his nose. The hardness of his body. How strong he was. How he looked at me and seemed to really see me. How he took care of everyone. His natural leadership. The way he tilted his head when he considered things.

Fuck. I really wanted him. Even thinking of him hardened my nipples, and I tried not to squirm. Will's eyes flew open, and he stared at me for a moment before he blinked.

"For me?"

I didn't understand. "What?"

"Is your desire for me?" He took a deep breath, and I caught up. My desire had roused him from sleep.

I put my arms around him. "Of course it's for you."

His gaze met and held my own. "I so want it to be for me. I want to be worthy of it."

I kissed his chin, both sides of his face. "Listen to me, my darling. It is for you. I'm sorry it woke you. I was lying here just thinking of how much I want you. How much I..."

His mouth came down on my own, effectively silencing me. I didn't mind because he also tugged me up against him so our bodies were completely touching. Will claimed my mouth. That was what he always did when he kissed me. He took one and owned it. I loved it. But maybe he had been able to smell that I wanted him this whole time.

And yet...he still questioned me. How could he not

know how much I wanted him? I pulled back to kiss his chin again and then traveled down his body. I wasn't terribly experienced when it came to sex, but instinct led me and what it was telling me right then was that he needed to be kissed everywhere. Just to have me touch him for a change.

"Tiff?" His voice was low.

"Let me." I pushed the sleeping bag back slightly to make more room behind me.

He caught his breath, and I took that as a yes. Maybe no one had ever just wanted to kiss him everywhere before. That thought brought me joy. This would be a new thing for both of us. I could worship his body and he could let me.

Will didn't let people get close enough to hurt him. I'd only known him days, and I could already tell that about him. Vulnerability didn't exist in Will's life. Yet, he let himself be that way with me. I kissed his nipple, and he let out the smallest moan. It moved right through me like he'd put a finger in my pussy. It was really amazing. Just his noises could get me wet.

Continuing down his body, I kissed his hard muscles just to feel them jump under my mouth. His breathing kicked up. I could feel the way he suddenly needed more air. That didn't slow me. I had a goal in mind, but teasing him on my way there as I loved on his body was a temptation I wouldn't avoid. I grinned at him.

"I like it too."

Whatever he would have said, he didn't because I kissed and then tongued his inner thigh. His cock was huge and, from my current view, only getting bigger. I kissed his other thigh.

"I understand you can only come inside my body. Do you suppose that means you could come in my mouth?" I had to lift my head to ask him that question, which meant I got to watch him visibly swallow.

"I...I have no fucking idea." His words were barely a whisper. "That isn't something that women do here."

I raised an eyebrow. If I was going to be this new version of myself thanks to whatever was happening in this mating, then I was just going to go for it in bed. "Their loss."

I put my mouth on him, and he gasped, his hips coming off the bed, arching his back when I did. That brought him quickly and farther down my throat. I moaned, loving this feeling. I'd never noticed there was power in it before. It had always felt more like a task to get through. But Will's cock in my mouth, the way he tasted, the way my nipples hardened the more that I sucked? Yes, I'd take this any day, any time.

Gladly.

14

H e grabbed on to my hair. "You can't imagine how that feels, but you need to let me, you need to let me make you feel good too. I *need* it."

I really didn't want to stop what I was doing. I'd found a rhythm, and he really seemed to like it. His moans were getting louder, and I had to assume he liked it too. But maybe we had a solution to both of those things.

I scooted around. This was daring, and I almost couldn't believe I was going to do it. But if I put my pussy near his mouth, we could both do this together.

He must have liked the idea because the only response I got was that he pulled me slightly closer before his tongue was right where I would have wanted it. I bent over to take him further in my mouth just as the pleasure hit me. I moaned around the head of his cock, and he jolted again. I closed my eyes and forced my brain to turn off.

This was about feeling, not about thinking about it. So I let myself go. I sucked and squirmed. Each movement of his tongue on me was enough to set me over the edge, but my desire to bring him pleasure kept me going longer than I might have been able to hold out otherwise.

Because it felt so amazingly good. In this moment, it wasn't about getting to the end as much as it was enjoying every second of this. We'd never have a first time together again. It should go on as long as it possibly could.

He pulled his tongue out, replacing it with a finger, and I came. He no more than had to touch my clit, and I exploded. Colors crossed over my vision, and I deep throated him in the moment. He hissed but didn't come in my mouth, even as I must have been drenching his.

Will grabbed my hip, stopping me. "Trust me, I want to come. But I'm not going to. I've never felt anything like what you're doing to me. I didn't know I could. I'd let go if it were possible ten times over. But I think I have to be inside of you."

I lifted my head. "It felt good?"

"Good doesn't cover it. Come here. You gifted me with the best moment of my life just now, and if you'll let me inside of you, I'd like to feel you come around me. If you'd like it."

I spun around, which wasn't a graceful thing to do, but I doubted most people would be in this situation. We were face-to-face, and he kissed me, gently this time. "You let me do that, you let me give you pleasure."

I shook my head. "Did you think that I wouldn't?"

"I want to be worthy of you." His voice was low.

"I think it's the opposite way around." Squirming down, I fit his hard cock on the edge of my core and pressed down. I was going to be on top. It just seemed like that was how this should go right now.

He closed his eyes, gripping the sleeping bag. "I'm so close, too close."

"You don't have to hold back." He felt great inside of me. I was still swollen from coming a moment ago, and every rub I made over it jolted me back into the pleasure he'd given me just moments ago. I didn't need more, I'd already had.

He shook his head, his eyes opening. "Yes, I do."

Then he took over. I was on top, but he was in charge of our movements. He grabbed my hips and drove me down on top of him, the movement hitting all my pleasure points—some I hadn't even been aware I had. I thrust up, and he did it again. We both moaned. Eventually, he rolled me over so that he was on top. We were a tangle of legs and arms in that movement, and then he thrust, hard.

I came around him with a shout. My ears rang, my back arched, and he smiled at me a second before he came inside of me. We panted, clinging to each other's bodies. Then he kissed me with so much sweetness, it brought tears to my eyes. I let them travel down my cheeks, and Will kissed them away.

We lay in the darkness together just like that for minutes. Eventually, he pulled out of me and rolled to the side. With a minimum of movements, he pulled me against him and covered us both again in the sleeping bag.

I snuggled down into him.

"Tiff," his voice was low, "you are such a gift to me."

I shook my head. "The more you know me, the less you may think that."

He pressed his mouth to my temple. "I am determined that you will stop thinking like that. A year from now when I say that, your first instinct won't be to say that you're less than wonderful. You will say thank you, yes, I am wonderful."

I laughed. "It's hard for me to imagine that. I...I don't think I'm ever going to tell you that I'm wonderful."

He made a noise that was sort of a groan and then settled down beside me, his head once again sharing the sleeping bag's pillow with me. I ran my hand through his hair. "You should sleep. I won't wake you up again. You haven't had a night's sleep in days, and I woke you up."

"I promise you that there is never going to be a time that I won't want to wake up to you wanting me. That is...that is a dream I didn't expect to experience. Ever. I don't need more sleep. I need you."

But even as he said that, I could see that his eyes were closing. I let my own lids close. He needed me. That was so fucking wonderful.

Sun streamed through the tent when a rustling noise woke me. Casper was shirtless and in a pair of pants he must have shoved on after he shifted back, and he didn't have any shoes on, which couldn't have been comfortable outside. I blinked at him as he approached. William slept, his arm thrown over me in a dead weight, his back to Casper as he approached. He snored lightly.

His brother stared down at him and then winked at me before he actually stepped over his body to sit down next to me on the other side.

"Hi." He kept his voice low. "He is out."

William really was. Oscar had been the day before. These guys were tired. I wouldn't have known it, but sleeping with them made it very clear. They needed rest they weren't getting.

Casper brushed my hair off my face. "Wake him up and come out soon. We got the car ready. Best to get back on the road."

I nodded. "Any trouble last night?"

He shook his head. "No. And I got a scent this morning. There was never going to be real trouble. Drew damaged the car. I'm so sorry. This is my fault." He bent over and kissed my cheek. "So sorry, Tiffany."

I shook my head. "Oh, you don't need to apologize. She's clearly...deranged. Damaged your car to keep you there I bet. Didn't know what she was doing except for trying to hide her scent. It's okay, Casper. Don't beat yourself up over this. You can't help it if you're irresistible."

I'd meant the last bit to be amusing, but his eyes flared red for a second. "She's not the one I want to be irresistible to. My turn to hold you tonight. All I want is to feel your softness all night."

He kissed my cheek again. "Tell my brother he's being lazy and he needs to get his ass up."

Then he rose from where he sat, winked at me, and stepped once more over his sleeping brother to exit the tent. I turned toward William, who seemed like he'd completely slept through the whole encounter. I couldn't imagine people got to step over him sleeping without waking him ever before.

I touched his face. "Will, I need you to wake up."

He made a little sound in the back of his throat that was sort of a groan and then settled back down to snoring again. I shook my head. Well, that hadn't worked. I knew what would wake him. If I got myself all worked up and turned on, he'd be up in a second. But we didn't have time for that. There were missiles to find. Even if my reasons for wanting to find them had changed.

Stroking my finger down the slope of his nose, I kissed both his cheeks. "They've finished fixing the car. We need to get up. I'm sorry to wake you. But I also have to pee."

He lifted his arm off me first and then it looked like he

had to wrench his eyes open. "Fuck. What time is it?" He lifted his head, looking left and right. "Was Cas in here?"

They lived a whole life of identifying scents I'd never really be able to understand. "He was."

"Wow." Will rubbed his eyes. "I was...out."

I shrugged. "I was asleep until he came in. Don't worry. We were up and down last night."

His smile was slow and heat inducing. "Yes, we were." He leaned over to kiss me. "And I think I understand why Oscar slept in the way he did. It's like you gave me something I've never had before. It's like I'm filled with you now in my soul and I feel peaceful. Like I could rest. Even though we were on this sleeping bag instead of a nice comfy bed."

A huff sounded a second before a Lion strode into the tent. I gasped and then maybe yelped before Will grabbed my arm. "It's okay. Don't be scared. It's just Casper. I guess we were taking too long."

I tried to swallow. "I...I can't tell you guys apart. I don't know one Lion from another yet, and it just startles me. He could have been anyone."

"No." Will smiled, getting up and bringing me gently with him until we were both standing. "Because I'd have smelled a strange Lion, and I knew it was Casper. But you need to use your eyes, so let's take a look at him, shall we?"

While he spoke, he dressed himself, putting on clothes. "Do you have any clean ones or do you need to put on yesterday's again?"

I had plenty of clean ones. Keeping my gaze fixed on the Lion that was Casper, because he had a big, mean-looking jaw that was sure to have dangerous teeth inside of it and claws that could rip my skin apart, I rushed to my bag and changed myself.

"Why is he like this right now?" I dressed fast. It was

stupid, but I wanted the layer of clothes between me and certain destruction from the Lion. Maybe they would offer some semblance of protection. A small amount, but some.

Will shook his head. "I don't know. Sometimes, the Lion calls to us. If he's upset about something, his Lion may have taken over to handle it for a bit."

I didn't have a second body to go hide in if I got upset. "Drew is the one who damaged the car."

"Aha." Will walked over and bumped his brother's Lion body, which earned him a low groan of a sound back. "I told you she was a little bit out of her mind, but at least it's not something worse, like someone trying to kill our mate for looking for the missiles. She can be handled for doing that."

Casper lay down on the ground, his eyes not leaving me as I finished dressing. "I told you, not your fault. People do what people do."

"When the three of us are together, in our Lion form, Cas is the biggest of us all. And this red on his mane and on his paws is different than the brown and gray that Oscar and I have. That's how you can tell him. The red."

I saw where he indicated. "Can I...can I touch him?"

"He'd chew off his own paw before he hurt you, so I'd say yes. Come on." He touched his brother on the head, and I swear, Casper shot him a look that told him to fuck off when he did that.

I swallowed. My hand trembled, but I forced myself to touch Casper on the top of his head. One quick pet, and I darted backward. He was soft. But clearly lethal. The Lion that was Cas didn't give me the same attitude he'd given Will and instead walked over to me, lowering his head like he wanted me to do it again.

I steeled my back. "Okay, Casper. You can probably smell my anxiety. It's a natural human thing. We don't touch predators unless we want to lose a hand. But I'm trusting you are you in there and that your Lion likes me too."

"He more than likes you." Will's whisper was low, and I didn't pause to consider what he said. Instead, I stroked Cas' fur again. He lifted his eyes to regard me, and I did it again. And again. He really was soft. Plus, he took up almost all the room in the tent. If I didn't pet him, I didn't really have room to go anywhere else.

Finally, Will patted his brother on the back. "She needs to pee and eat something. Then we have to go. Back it out of here please and meet me by the car. No one is mad at you. Drew will pay for potentially harming our mate. If she gets sick from her chill, it'll be a bigger punishment. Come on."

Casper gently bumped me before he shot his brother another look and exited through the hole in the tent.

"Good job. You really battled back that fear. That's all we can ask of you at this point. I get that us being Lions is not natural to you. Maybe you even forget it for a second. But it is the reality. At some point, and I'm not saying it has to be any time soon, you'll need to be okay with and trust we are still us. Thanks for trying. He didn't come in for that reason. He's probably barely conscious of why he needed to shift. We just do it like breathing because that is what it is for us."

I considered his words while I put on my shoes. "Does anything scare you?" I held up my hand. "And although, again, it's very sweet, don't say losing me. Something that scares you that has nothing to do with me."

He furrowed his brow. "Do you think that I'm making light of your fear?"

"I didn't say that." Although his idea that I just had to get over my concerns was a little disconcerting. "I'm more interested in what frightens you. Does anything? Or does being a

man and a Lion make you feel pretty bulletproof and there-
fore not afraid of anything?"

He visibly swallowed. "I never feel bulletproof. I feel
lucky you had the wrong gun."

Yes, I'd almost shot him. I walked over and placed my
hand over where I would have blown a hole in his stomach.
"I feel lucky too."

"I'm afraid of failure. Of letting everyone down. Of ultimately leading everyone I care about into a dark path we
never come out of."

Well, that was a real fear. A big one. "I don't think you're
capable of that. I've seen you in action the last few days. You
make good choices. You lead everyone, and they follow
because of that reason. Everyone trusts you."

He took my hand in his. "Are lions what frightens you
most in the world? Because there will be a real irony to the
universe if that is the case."

"No. I just have a natural need to run from things that
want to eat me. That isn't my biggest fear." I kissed his chest,
right over his heart. "I don't want to die like my mother did."

Will opened and closed his mouth. "Won't happen."

"Well, I hope not." I leaned up to kiss him. "But fear isn't
always reasonable. I'll work on my natural aversion to being
eaten. How's that?"

He sighed. "Have I pissed you off again?"

Shaking my head slowly, I winked at him. "No. And even
if you did, I'd forgive you. We are in each other's cells now,
right? If I could smell, I'd scent myself on you? I'd know that
we were linked forever. And all the things that it means?"

Will blinked rapidly. "You would. I wish that you could
scent all the things I can about what we are like together. I
wish you could know."

"I wish you could know how blind I am here. How I am

literally dulled in a sense you guys use to navigate your lives. I'll come around to not being afraid. I promise you that. In my own time. Okay?"

He furrowed his brow. "I hadn't really considered how it must feel to be without it on a planet where we use it for everything."

"You probably will consider it though. In time. When I do something wrong, or fuck something up, or don't follow a cue I should have. Or, if this progresses, and we have children..." I could barely speak that word. Kids had never been a possibility really. A far-off maybe of a dream I hadn't considered possible. "And they have that problem. Or they don't, and I can't properly parent them. Or they're embarrassed because their mother just has no idea if the people around her are only telling shades of the truth because she can't scent a lie."

Will's face fell. "Tiffany..."

I put my hand on his mouth. "Nothing to be done about it today. But I'm guessing that whether or not I get a little nervous about touching a full-grown male Lion when I've just had days to get used to the idea, is going to be among the smallest of our problems."

I really did have to pee, and I hurried out to do that.

After finding a spot to pee and clean myself with some wipes I kept in my bag for just this sort of problem, I discovered they'd taken down the tent. Will and Oscar spoke by the car. Will was fully dressed, and Oscar only partially. Casper ran over to touch my arm.

"Sorry if I scared you earlier. I was just feeling really disjointed about the whole idea that there is a woman so worked up over something I did that she damaged a car over it. I really, truly, never made a promise to her in word or deed." He handed me a bar that looked like what I'd call granola back home. "I don't think this is going to be too spicy for you."

I kissed his cheek. "We can't control other people's behavior. I have been making a living trying to keep people in line, and even I have no idea what they'll do and when they'll do it. Don't worry."

His cheeks reddened. From the kiss? I wasn't sure. "I'll work on it. And I heard what you said to Will."

"Yes, I imagine there isn't much in the way of secrets with your Lion ears." I smiled at him. "I need to apologize for hitting him with all that stuff so early in the morning."

He smirked. "It's almost lunch. You guys really did sleep in. And he can handle it. We all can. Even if some things are tougher, I would never want anyone but you. Any cubs we had would only be proud you were their mother. Trust me on that."

"We shouldn't be thinking about kids. I certainly shouldn't be talking about them. It's all hypothetical."

Cas took my arm, and we walked to the car together. "I doubt any of us can help it. This time? When true mates used to meet, they'd go off for a while and emerge months later."

"What were they doing? Procreating?" I had a shot that was going to stop me from doing that for at least six more months. I'd deal with figuring out how to handle that then. Not now.

"Not necessarily. Female shifters don't ovulate very often. Probably because we live so long. But yes, lots of sex. Months and months of sex. That sort of thing naturally lends itself to these kinds of talks. And the kinds of needs we're all having, it certainly could result in a baby."

He opened the door for me. "We ovulate every month.

Well, a lot of us do. I'm on medicine to prevent it. No babies right now."

Casper shut the door. That had probably thrown the three of them off. Unless they could all already scent that. Maybe they had my entire medical history just with one whiff. Why was I feeling so disgruntled all of a sudden? I'd woken up feeling great.

Oscar opened the door and slid in next to me. "Will's driving. Cas is up front. You get me."

I smiled at him. "I'm touchy and in a bad mood."

"Eat that. You're just hungry." He pointed to the granola. "Seriously."

I took a bite. Cas had been right—it wasn't too spicy. In fact, there was the slightest taste of chocolate to it. I ate it fast, and my stomach settled. I hadn't eaten any dinner. He was right—I was probably just hungry. In fact, by the time Will and Cas got in the car, I felt much better.

The rain started to pound on the car, and I didn't even mind. Will met my gaze in the rearview mirror. "We are all making a mental note to keep you fed. You haven't eaten since breakfast yesterday. I'm sorry."

That was right, actually. "It's not your job to remember that. It's mine. And...yeah, I forgot too. Sorry if I laid into you three. Hunger is a trigger in many ways. I've been very hungry in my life. Sometimes, I don't notice it."

"Well," Oscar drew me up against him, "that stops. We can try to eat more on your schedule too. That is certainly a small adjustment we can make." He kissed the top of my head. "See that monkey? Did you see it?"

He pointed out the window, and I looked where he indicated. "No, I totally missed it."

"Keep looking. I saw a ton of them last night. Those fuckers tried to mess with my Lion. If I hadn't been on patrol, I'd have taken a few down for the fun of it. They don't taste great."

Cas turned around. "That's an understatement. They taste awful. And one of them started chucking things at me. I was disgruntled over it." His smile was huge. I watched them back and forth talking about their night outside as Lions. They loved it. That much was clear. The way they could describe the detail, and the way they'd felt.

It was beautiful.

Strange.

And now my reality.

Since I'd accepted this as now being something I was going to do. I was going to quit my job after I found the missiles, and I was going to make this planet my home. Everything I'd warned Will about was true. But somehow, I was going to do it anyway.

15

Ferguson, my boss who I hated and wished I could forget existed, had written me back telling me to keep doing what I was doing. I rolled my eyes. Thanks for nothing, asshole. But that was how it tended to go. All right, well I'd keep up doing what I was doing then. Not that he had any idea what that actually entailed right now.

We arrived on the outskirts of the town right as we came out of the rainforest. I caught my breath. There in the distance was the ocean. I could see it over a cliff as we turned a corner. We were on the coast, but here, that meant big, sweeping, white mountainous precipices that seemed to go down forever.

Will pulled the car into an open area and turned to his brothers. "You need to go tell Knox we're here. We could just show up, but that'll get his back up and we want his cooperation tomorrow looking for the missiles. Go do the respect thing you two do so well."

I smirked. Did Will not do the so-called respect thing all that well? Oscar rolled his eyes but sat up and, after he gave me a sweet kiss on the cheek, exited the car. Casper was grumpier with the way he slammed the door on their way out. I'd never had a sibling, but I imagined this was sometimes how it went. Even when you had to lead a planet together.

They walked from the car toward the town, and I watched them for a moment.

"Come sit up here with me. I miss you."

They made it look easy to do the way they went in and out of the seats, but my legs weren't big enough so it was a challenge for me to do as he said. Of course, I could have gotten out and entered that way. That only dawned on me after I'd done it. It was made harder by me bringing my bag up with me. Truly, I didn't even want to go to the front seat without it. I checked the time on my tablet after I settled. It was almost four o'clock. Nap time had been disregarded yesterday. Were they feeling the effect?

"Tired?"

He shook his head. "I slept like a log next to you. Not tired. But I think Cas is. He always gets a little wound up. His turn to know how nice it is to spend the night next to you tonight."

"I'm sorry I was less than understanding when you were trying to help me this morning."

He shook his head. "I'm sorry I got preachy."

Amazing our translator could get that word out. He really was so handsome. "Maybe we'll be those kinds of true mates who tick each other off occasionally."

Will laughed, which was what I was hoping would happen. "That would keep things interesting. Maybe we'll be that way for a while, but I think ultimately, you and I are going to understand each other completely and we'll be better for—"

I don't know what he would have said because his eyes widened, and in a move I couldn't have replicated, he put his hand through the windshield, breaking it into a thousand or more pieces, before he tossed me through it. I had no time to contemplate what happened as I fell to the ground with an *oomph*, my bag still attached to me.

But my own pain and shock was nothing because the next thing I realized was that a loud crash sounded all around me. The car that I'd been in—that Will was still in—had been hit straight on by a car behind it. We weren't in the way. Screeching, banging metal. Some things were the same on every planet, and as I watched in utter horror, Will and the car went over the cliff.

The car that hit it stopped, and two men got out, running for their lives with no intention to stop. This hadn't been an accident.

I jumped to my feet. I was going to be sore tomorrow, but right now, I couldn't feel a fucking thing except utter horror, with my heart racing faster than it ever had before I cried out in pain. My brain stuttered in disbelief, not wanting to believe the image that my eyes showed me. Will was in that car, and as it went down into the waves below, he couldn't possibly be okay.

Sometimes, you just had to know what to do. I'd had training. Years of it. I grabbed my bag and pulled out what I needed as I simultaneously kicked off my shoes. They'd weigh me down. The Union prepared us for all kinds of things, and getting out of a submerged car was one of them. There were a million things I should consider, but I didn't give them a second thought. Will was not okay. He needed me. My bag fell off the cliff. I registered that distantly, but it didn't matter. No, there was just one thing to do.

I dove.

For a second, I heard someone call to me from behind, but the decision was done before I even launched. I was doing this. Will wasn't going to die. Not while I could save him.

This wasn't the first time I had cliff dived. It was one of those things I'd done over the years to feel something. To feel anything. But this was different. I knew nothing about the water I was diving into.

Still, as my body hit the cold water, I didn't freeze. Pressure hit my ears, and I ignored the sensation. The water was clear, and I could see the car where Will was straight in front of me. The good news was that I was an excellent swimmer. Outside of surfing, swimming was my favorite thing to do. I was strong and capable.

Not to mention determined. I swam down, even as the bubbles around me would have me rising to the surface. I fought. Finally, I reached the car. I'd been barely a minute behind Will, but the vehicle was already filled up with water.

In my hand, I used the weapon I'd brought with me for this purpose. I smashed the window, once, then twice, which let me yank open the door. It was all about altering the pressure so that I could get him.

He was out cold, his head on the steering wheel and obviously not breathing since he was in the water. I'd save him after I got him out. With a yank, I had his body in my arms, and although he was dead weight, I was more than capable of doing this. I kicked. Hard. So fucking hard. So much fucking harder than I ever had before.

We reached the surface and air burned my lungs. People were shouting. I didn't know from where. Right then, I didn't care. With everything to lose, I swam us to a small surface of rocks that would have to do for now.

Terror started to seep in me, but I wouldn't let it visit, not yet. I wasn't done. Truth was, I didn't remember getting Will onto the rocks, but he was there, so somehow in my crazed need to beat death just this one time, I must have done it. He was human right now. Compressions would have to work. I'd been trained to revive someone from drowning, and I got to doing it.

Suddenly and finally, he spit up water, gasping for air. I sat him up. We held eye contact before his rolled to the back of his head. What? What was happening?

Strong hands dragged me backward. It was Casper. And Oscar. They were there. Others I didn't know.

"Please," an older woman said to me. "Good work. You saved him. But he needs me. Please, ma'am, let me save him."

The word healer reached my ears, and I stopped struggling, not something I'd known I was doing. His brothers, my other two mates, stared at me, equal expressions of horror staring back at me.

"There...there..." Why couldn't I talk? That was when I saw them. In the distance. Farther down the rock beach were two men. I'd seen them. They'd tried to kill us. And please, let them not have succeeded with Will. All I could do was point. "They did it."

Casper and Oscar's eyes turned red at the same time.

"Go get them," an older man who I hadn't noticed yelled. "Get them. I will care for your mate and your brother. He will not die. Alora will save his Lion. Go."

Casper grabbed his arm. "Knox, I charge you with their safety. If they are hurt in any way, there will be pain like you can't imagine."

"I think I can imagine. Go."

I pushed at Casper. "Get them. Please."

This couldn't be allowed. They'd get away, and that couldn't happen. There had to be vengeance.

Oscar took off after the two men down the way, who, in turn, shifted into Wolves. *Wolves.* This was about the fucking missiles.

"We need to move him to the house. Come." Alora spoke to the crowd, and as I was powerless, everyone around me moved William from me. I could hardly move, but I tried to follow. A hand pulled me back.

"Young lady." The man they'd called Knox addressed me. "You've saved his life and probably prevented a crisis. Please allow me to help you."

Help me? I blinked at him and then stared down to where his gaze was. I was soaking wet and covered in glass, bleeding in any number of places. Funny. I couldn't feel a thing. Not anything at all.

That was probably bad. "Okay."

He put his arm around me. "You're safe here. All evidence to the contrary. We will get to the bottom of how this happened. And, that thing you just did, that was the bravest thing I've ever seen anyone do. Ever."

Was it? I guess we'd see. If Will lived, it was brave. If he died...well, I didn't know what it would be then.

I STOOD over Will's bed, shaking and bleeding. Once we'd gotten to the house, and distantly, I realized it was quite a house in size and appearance, I'd insisted on staying with him. He was pale, passed out, and maybe I had hurt him. Maybe I had done something wrong.

The older woman, the healer, injected something into his arm, and I jolted. "What are you doing to him? What did you give him?"

"Young lady," Knox said that again, maybe for the fifth time. I didn't care. I wasn't going anywhere.

Alora lifted her gaze to mine. "You saved his life. You did a wonderful job. None of us could believe what we saw you do. Surely, you should both be dead, but here you are and so is he. When we are injured badly or revived from death, the Lion has to be protected. Sometimes, the human part is saved and then the Lion dies, which kills the human anyway. What I gave him should protect his Lion, allow his animal to rest. It will keep them both asleep tonight into lunch time tomorrow. Then he will wake up and be cranky." She stepped toward me. "He'll have to be medicated again. Not the same way, just to control the pain. Male Lions don't do a good job with that kind of pain. They can hurt themselves. It will keep him calmer. But in two days, he'll be back to almost normal, and by the end of this week, he'll be well."

Okay. I nodded. "He isn't going to die?"

Because everyone died on me, and I could see it now. All of it. Will would die, and then Casper and Oscar would die. I would be alone without them. I didn't get to have love like this. I didn't deserve it. I never had.

"He isn't going to die." It was Knox who answered. "He does not smell like death. He smells like he is injured. But young William will survive this, heal, and be well enough to kill me should he choose to challenge me, by the end of the week. Now, you need to be treated."

I sucked in a breath. Will would hate being called young William, but what he'd said was right—yes, my guys might kill this man. I couldn't think about that at all. That was for next, when that came. If it came.

I lifted my chin. "I'm not leaving him."

"Let me ask you, if William were awake, would he want

you standing here freezing cold, wet, and bleeding? Would he be okay with that?"

I stared at Knox, really looking at him for the first time. He was old, that was for sure. His wrinkles had wrinkles. But he had strong, sharp eyes, and he was strong like all the people here seemed to be. I could see he was a leader, it was in his direct gaze. The way he held the attention of the whole room.

And he was correct. "No. He absolutely wouldn't."

Knox nodded. "Then you're going to let Alora's assistant get the glass out of you, then you're going to take a shower and come eat dinner with me."

I rubbed my face. "On my planet, we have a bird that lives in zoos. It's called a parrot. It just keeps repeating itself. Allow me to once again say that I'm not leaving him. So thank you, kindly, for the invitation to dinner, but I can't accept. I'm not leaving him."

The Alpha Lion held up his hand. "Fair enough. We'll eat in the main room."

That was right. This was a suite of rooms. Multiple all connected. At least six of them. And in the center, there was a living area. I hadn't seen a kitchen or dining room, but maybe I'd missed it. I hadn't exactly been focused on that.

"Brother," Alora said. "There is the problem of the Wolves."

His eyes turned red for a second. "Yes, well those boys will find them. They will stop them, as brothers do when one is injured. They will come back to their true mate with answers. There is much to celebrate right now. There is a true mating." He extended his hand. "Come, young lady. You need to be treated."

A thought dawned on me. My bag was gone. It had probably saved me a lot of pain, in retrospect. I'd sort of landed on it. But it had gone right over the side. "I don't have any clothes. Really, I don't have anything. It's all...gone."

It was a good thing I'd decided to quit my job, because the Union was going to kill me for losing my stuff. That tablet was more important to them than I was. I laughed at the thought, which had to make me seem deranged to everyone there, unless they could smell the madness moving in where my nothingness had settled for a little bit.

"We'll take care of that."

That was when I was escorted out. Alora's assistant, a nice woman named Nicole, started picking glass out of my skin. I closed my eyes. This was a first for me. I forced the crazy back where it belonged. I'd stay numb. It was preferable.

And I sat there while Nicole picked glass out one agonizing piece at a time. It was okay. Whatever discomfort I had was because Will had decided to save my life instead of his own. He'd thrown me out of the window instead of doing anything to protect himself. I winced at one particularly big shard in my arm.

Nicole touched my arm. "Is it true that you are true mates?"

I turned my attention to her. "It is." Was that my voice sounding so strained and small? "Or at least they tell me it is. I'm human, not a shifter. As I'm sure you can smell. I'm not able to know these things like you all are."

"I think you're beautiful, and I've always wanted to meet a human. We think, a lot of us, that stopping our relationships with humans is why we're all so alone. That we were meant to be together with the universe."

Will had said something similar, and it seemed it was an opinion that he didn't hold alone. "We don't know anything about humans ever having mated with shifters. It's not something anyone is letting us know."

A niggling thought formed in the back of my mind. Although maybe there were lots of things society should know about these places that they didn't. Maybe that was something to consider when we weren't in such dire straits. If such a time ever came.

She smiled at me. "Maybe after the threat is over, and those Wolves who did this are found and disposed of, you and I could share a meal. With other friends of mine too. The males are wonderful and it seems you have three of our best devoted to you, but you can't really know a place without female friends. Don't you agree?"

I looked up at her, she was taking something out of my cheek now. It would probably scar. A constant reminder of this terrible day that could have been so much worse. "I've never had female friends. Well, I have acquaintances that come and go. My job makes it hard."

Her smile was big. "Then you are overdue. What is your first name? Unless you would like me to call you ma'am, as would be the tradition because of who your mates are."

No, I didn't want to be called ma'am. Not until I was old and gray and maybe not then either. "My name is Tiffany."

"Tiffany." Her smile was big. "Welcome. We are hoping so much that you will stay."

I stared at her for a long moment. "Do you not like Knox?"

"Oh, we love him. He is a wonderful man." She moved to get more glass out of me. "But it is time. He's lost control. This thing with the Wolves couldn't happen in a healthy pack. We will mourn him for years, but everyone knows, even Knox, that it is beyond time for his departure."

This was a strange world in a lot of ways. They loved

Knox, but they were happy, in some ways, to see him die so that their pack could be strong again. Just another thing I was sure I would never understand.

No one had told me which room was my own, so I just picked the one closest to Will. The shower was huge, and I used it, wincing every time it touched one of my wounds. Nicole met me afterward to dress them now that I was clean, which left me just the problem of not really having any clothes. I couldn't go eat dinner with Knox in my bathrobe, which was soft and comfy but still wouldn't do.

Entering the bedroom, however, took care of that problem. Someone had left a lot of folded clothes on the bed for me. Piles of them. I stared down at the collection. Well, Knox had said it would be taken care of, and I guessed that meant it would be, fast. Were these someone else's clothes I was taking?

I'd find out so I could repay them. In the meantime, although it hurt to put the cloth on my body, I ended up wearing a long yellow dress. Out of all the selection, it clung the least and that seemed preferable at the moment. It was sleeveless and touched the tips of my toes. I didn't have shoes either, and it looked like I was going to have to ask for those.

I'd never worn yellow in my life. It was bright, cheery, and just not indicative to how things usually went for me. But the women here wore it, and in this, at least, I'd fit in. As I left the room, my hair still wet, I wondered if this was a calf length or short dress on its owner. On me, it was draped to the floor.

Food was set out on the ground, displayed on two rugs that someone had set down on them. It smelled really good, and my stomach growled. Knox lifted an eyebrow at my appearance, and I nodded to him, but I had to see Will before I could stomach eating.

He was quiet, an IV hooked to his arm as he slept, a pained look on his face. Alora lifted her head when I entered. I'd interrupted her knitting in a chair.

"Your mate is strong. He's doing just what he needs to do right now."

I walked over to him. My mate. How and when had I gotten used to that term? It was like it hadn't been okay, and then suddenly, it was everything. Life was like that. Something wasn't until it just was. Then it was everything.

"Can I touch him?"

She looked up. "It won't bother him. He's not waking up until tomorrow, but we'll watch him just to be sure. You can touch him. I thought you'd be eating."

"I will." I bent over and kissed him lightly on his temple. I just needed a moment. Whispering, which was probably pointless since I had a Lion shifter in the room with me, seemed like the thing to do. "Please don't fight resting and get better. How else are we going to go back to saying the wrong things to each other?"

Someone had picked the glass out of his skin too, so as carefully as I could in case I caught a place that hurt, I smoothed his hair off his face. "Good night."

I stepped back. "Please don't let him die."

She lifted her eyebrows. "You've had a lot of loss. I can scent it on you. I can never promise people won't die, but I can promise that I will do everything I can not to let that happen to him tonight."

That was the best I could ask for and more than I'd ever had with my mother. No one had helped, and I'd let her die because I hadn't had any idea what to do for her.

On quiet feet, I left Will to his dreams and the care of a healer I'd just met but trusted.

Knox gestured to the food in front of him, and I sat across on the rug.

"Young lady, you are going to hurt tomorrow."

I didn't know what any of these foods were or if they were going to beat the shit out of my mouth in spice. "Tiffany, that's my name. I'm Tiffany Keyes. You don't have to keep calling me young lady if you know my name."

His mouth twitched into a smile. "Fair enough. Please, help yourself."

I grabbed a plate and started spooning small amounts of things onto it. "Thanks."

"Tiffany, you are going to be in pain tomorrow."

I set down my plate and started to try things. So far, it was all things my palette could handle. "I'm in pain now."

"You're going to be in worse pain tomorrow. A dive like that? Into that water? You're going to hurt. My healers can help you."

I nodded. I tended not to ask for help. "Thank you. I have a pretty high tolerance for it. Even though I'm a human."

He laughed, throwing his head back. "I think you are probably tougher than we are in a lot of ways. We rely on our Lions to keep us safe, to keep us strong, and for the most part, we do. In our human forms, we tend to be very vulnerable. You've had to learn to keep yourself safe in ways we should know how. I told you. That dive you made over the cliff to save your mate? That was the bravest thing I've ever seen."

There was an orange cheese that was a little bit too spicy, so I set it down and took a sip of the water in front of me. "I'd do it again. In a heartbeat."

"I know. I didn't know what to expect when I heard that they had found a true mate and she was human. But you weren't it. What is your story? How did you come to be this person?"

Now, that was a loaded question.

16

"**M**aybe that's more than you want to know." I tried the next piece of cheese. It was better. Knox watched me eat, occasionally picking at his own food, but he seemed much more inclined to see which pieces I liked and which I didn't than to really eat his meal.

He shook his head. "I wouldn't ask if I didn't want to know."

I lifted my gaze to his own. Maybe it was because I was exhausted, had been through a trauma, or maybe it was something to do with the elderly man himself, but I launched into my story. The whole bit of it. From my birth to now, I told him all the pieces that mattered and maybe some that didn't. By the time I was finished, and I'd hardly taken a breath, he had furrowed his brow and was drinking a dark liquid that he'd had in front of him.

"So you are alone in the universe with only the Union" —the way he said that word, it was clear he felt the same as Will did— "to protect you?"

"They don't really protect me. I protect them. Or I used

to. That's going to have to change." I pulled my knees up to my chin. The dress covered me in ways I could do this and still maintain some semblance of modesty.

He waved his hand. "The point being you have no family."

I shook my head. "None that know about me. My father's real family doesn't know I exist."

"Then you are alone in the universe?"

That was a very dramatic way to think of it. Of course, I had similar thoughts in my darkest of moments. "Right now, I'm sitting here with you so not alone, but sometimes I'm alone. We're all that way on occasion."

He rose, an impressive height when I stood and even bigger now that I was seated on the ground. "Then you will be my family."

I rose, not that it helped much. He might even be taller than Will, who towered over me. "What?"

"You are now my family. A member of my, you'd probably call it, pack. And one of my family. I never had any children. My brothers and I mated—not a true mating, grant you—a lovely woman, but we were never able to have any. They're all gone now. It's just me left here mismanaging this group we once made strong. But no one should be alone. You'll be my family, and we'll see to it that your mates treat you right until you are all settled with each other. And once I am gone, you will still always have family to call on. My sisters. This group. They are now your family."

I couldn't catch my breath, it was like I'd just gotten out of the water again. "That isn't how it works. You can't just be family. You either are or you aren't."

"That is how it can be, Tiffany." He put his hand on my arm. "Because I say that it can be that way."

I shook my head. Why was this making me feel crazed?

"Who are you? People don't just do this. They don't just say...you've been alone, so now you're my family. What is your story?"

I threw his own words back at him to make my point, only it just made him smile instead of angry.

"I was born many days from here. But when my brothers and I—there were four of us—decided to challenge for leadership, it was here that we fell in love. Most Lions don't care for the water. But we found it inspiring every morning. A reminder of how fragile life was and how we had to take every day as a chance to do better. We built this pack to strength. And then time did what it does—it picks everyone off one by one, until there was only me. In that time before this, we did have a mate. Not a true mate, but we were all content together. Now, I'm here waiting for someone to take my pack so that I don't die in my sleep and leave it unprotected until it falls apart, which it is already doing since clearly, some of my people are consorting with Wolves."

My heart rate slowed just a little bit. "I'm sorry you've lost everyone."

That didn't seem enough to say, but I said it anyway. He reached out and touched my arm. "You did too. But now you are found. You're my family, and you belong to them. I imagine the other two will be back soon. I'll see you in the morning."

He walked away, like he hadn't just done something... significant. I rubbed my arms. He'd just made me his family with a declaration. We didn't even know each other. How did he know that he liked me enough to want me around? And...well, I did like him. He was gruff, and he made his points bluntly. But there was something about him that had made me tell him my life story in a way I never had before. Even with the guys, I'd had to drag it out over days.

Knox had led his people for a long time, and now he wanted to sacrifice his life to keep them safe. He could be gone very soon, and yet maybe I'd be lucky to be his family for just that long.

Not sure what to do with myself, I cleaned up the dinner we'd barely touched, throwing some things out and finding a small fridge in the corner that was hidden the way it had been in the first town we'd been in.

I had to learn to look for fridges like that.

With nothing to do, and not even my tablet to distract me, I went back to Will. Alora looked up at me and smiled. "Welcome to the family."

I sank into a chair. "Thanks."

She went back to her knitting. I focused on Will. I'd send him some kind of healing energy. It never worked with my mother and probably wasn't real, but I'd do it anyway. That was at least trying to do something.

I WOKE up in the chair, my head in a weird position and Casper squatting in front of me. "Hey."

"Hi." I sat up, rubbing my neck. Alora stood by Will's bed talking to Oscar, who held his brother's hand for a second before he gently set it down.

"Good." Oscar nodded. "Thank you for caring for him. You can go back to your rooms now. I'll watch him. And if I need you, I'll let you know."

She rose. "It's an honor to help. I'll be back in the morning. He will not wake up happy or even seeming like himself." She addressed that to me. "Male Lion shifters are difficult when they're not feeling well."

Cas rubbed his face. "I don't know if we're so much

worse than females when they're in similar predicaments." He held up his hand. "Never mind. I don't want to argue. I'm sure you're right."

Oscar ran his hands through my hair as Alora left the room. Cas drew me from the chair, and a second later, I was sandwiched between Oscar and him. When they finally spoke, it was Cas who started. "At first, I thought you were both gone, that you were both going over in the car."

His voice shook, and I clung to him because I could feel his pain, feel his terror in how he sounded right then.

Oscar continued for him. "Then you got up and we realized that you were alive, that Will must have saved you, and although we were in utter horror and disbelief that he'd gone over, you were okay because of course you were. Of course he would save you. We'd have done the same."

I shook my head. "He shouldn't have done that. I—"

Cas cut me off. "Yes, he should have. Of course he did. Then you got up. And as we were running for you, you dove off the fucking cliff."

"I had to save him." Didn't they understand?

Oscar ran his hands through my hair. "Of course you did." He reused the phrase. "But I've never been so afraid in my life. Truly."

"Both of us. We thought...we thought you were both gone." His voice hitched again. "Please don't do that again. Please don't ever."

They had to understand. "I'd do it for both of you too. I'd save you. A million times if I had to."

Oscar kissed both my cheeks, then the end of my nose. "Go. With Casper, go to bed. I'll wake you guys in the morning. I'm going to stay here with Will."

I nodded and kissed him lightly on the lips. "Did you guys get them? The Wolves?"

"One of them. He's in a lockup, and we'll be questioning him tomorrow. He's rather beat up right now," Casper answered. "And tomorrow, we will find the other one too. We both wanted to get back here to you and Will."

Casper led me from Oscar. I turned just enough to see him adjusting Will's blankets before he sat down in the chair I'd been sitting in to wait out the night.

"Do you guys not need to patrol here?" I didn't want them to leave, but it dawned on me that we were completely off of routine. I pointed to the room that I'd sort of made mine. The clothes I'd been given were still on the bed, and I picked them up to move them to the chair on the side of the room. They needed to be hung up or put away, but I didn't have the wherewithal to consider that basic organization at the moment.

Casper stared at me from the side of the bed. Like Oscar, he was shirtless. I didn't know where he'd gotten his pants that he wore. These places must store basic sweatpants all over, because I didn't see naked people everywhere. With the shifting back and forth, they had a constant need to keep clothes in random places. That was a funny thought. Someone had to be in charge of those logistics.

He really was so handsome. His chin pointed out in a way that his brothers' didn't. His cheekbones were the highest, and his eyes never missed a thing. They were warm like a hot bath.

"I didn't think. I just knew I could save him and I had to."

He walked toward me. "I had a different thought than Oscar. We haven't talked about it, but I'm sure he had his own worries. I just know it wasn't this one. It occurred to me that you didn't know how I felt about you. That you had no idea all of the things that I feel. Just from me. That you knew from them, but I'd never gotten to tell you or show you. I just waited because I wanted this alone time. Not because it wasn't important."

I gasped. "Casper, I didn't feel like you didn't care. I know that you do." My feelings for him were huge. If anything, he had been the one to wake me to this life we could have. His spending time with me, his bumping me in that way that he did. It made something that I'd never known existed sit up and take notice. It was like he had taken hold of my soul and breathed new life into it.

"Well, I thought you were dead. And I felt that grief for you and Will. With my older brother, I have some thoughts on things I need to say to him. Thanks I need to make. But with you, the trickery of grief told me you didn't know." He fell to his knees in front of me, and I gasped. What was he doing? Casper pressed his head to my stomach and clung to me. "I just got you, and then you were gone. But then you popped up from the water after an impossibly long time. We were trying to get to you, down this stupid rock face that led to the beach. Couldn't move fast enough, and it was steep. I needed two feet. I'd have fallen over as a Lion. You were swimming with Will in your arms. You're so much smaller than us, and you just did that. You just somehow managed all of it. We didn't even get there in time to revive him. You did that too."

"Cas." I needed him to hear me. "We all do what we have to do in the moments that require us to be more than ourselves. I've seen it many places. In desperation, people can do things they might not otherwise do. I'm trained in what I did. Not the diving off the cliff part. That I happen to know how to do because I'm an adventure seeker. But the rest of it, I know how to do. Okay?" I squeezed him back. "Come up here so I can kiss you."

He rose slowly, capturing my cheeks in his hands. "Do

you know how you saved me by just existing? I was miserable, and I thought I would always stay that way. Then it
turned out you were real and you were here. Everything
short-circuited for me, and I am better because you exist. I
want to be that for you. I want to be someone who makes
your life better."

I pulled him to me. His body vibrated. "You do. I'm staying. I'm not going anywhere. It was terrible today, and I'm
glad that it's over."

He kissed me then. A long, hard, hot kiss. Our tongues
danced together, and it was like the numb that had taken
hold earlier burned away in that instant. Fuck, I wanted
him. No, I needed him. Inside of my body. Right then and
there.

I clawed at his pants. "Can we?"

"Yes. Fuck. Yes." He pushed me down on the bed and
came over me. "Are you too hurt for this?"

"Right now, I am not feeling anything except how much
I want you. That's what I want to feel. That's all I want.
Please."

He widened his eyes. "Tiffany, you don't ever have to say
please for me to love you. You always have it."

His words were so sweet, they brought tears to my eyes.
His pants were off fast and my dress over my head. "Where
did you get that?" he asked me as he discarded the dress to
the side.

"I don't have any things. Knox gave it to me. It's yellow." I
spoke the obvious, but I really didn't want to be talking at
all. I kissed his chest, his shoulder. Anywhere I could reach
until he met me with his mouth.

I loved kissing Casper, I loved how quickly I lost all
sense except for him in the universe. He pushed a finger
inside of me and then moaned. He must have liked what

he felt. I reached for his cock. He couldn't come in my hand, but he got impossibly harder. We stroked and kissed just like that until I panted for him. My breasts actually hurt, and in the second I thought that, he took my nipple in his hand and squeezed it like he'd known it needed attention.

Pleasure warred with pain in the best possible way. I arched my back, sucking in all the air I could get, which forced me to let go of his cock. I reached for it again, and he shook his head. "I want to make you do that again."

His mouth came down on my nipple and sucked while his other hand squeezed at the other one. Goosebumps broke out everywhere. I didn't know if I did the same thing I had or if I did anything at all. I was so lost to it and so fucking wet. I just wanted him. All of him.

"Casper. Please."

He let go to whisper in my ear. "No please. Never that. Whatever you want is always yours, Tiffany. Like you are mine."

With those words delivered like a balm to my soul, he pressed himself inside me. Yes, that was what I needed. All of him. Filling me. Pushing me. Hitting every nerve ending inside of me until I was clawing at his back, begging for more, crying out in ways that sounded almost animal-like from me. I was practically keening.

And then I was coming. Hard, fast, in a cry that was like a sigh or a prayer. Casper too. We came together like we were made to do it that way. He closed his eyes, his forehead on my shoulder. We panted, and I held him like I might lose him because I never wanted to. I wanted to hold him forever and ever.

He kissed all over my face. "I love you. I know that it's soon, and we know that you're human and it's too soon for you. But I love you. I do. I've loved you from the first moment."

I took his face in my hands like he'd held mine. "I love you too."

Life was short. I wasn't going to wait to say things.

~

I SWAM *through the water toward the car. He was in the car, and I had to reach him. People shouted my name. I could hear them through the sludge. Bubbles surrounded me, forcing me upward, and I couldn't reach the car. He was in there. He was going to die if I didn't reach him. He might already be, but I had to go up, up again. I wasn't going to make it.*

I woke up gasping for air and sobbing. I couldn't stop. Cas was there in the pitch-black room. He held me against him.

"What is it? Talk to me, Tiffany. What's the matter?" His voice was low as he rocked me against him. Over and over. "Shh. You're okay. What's the matter?"

I shook my head. "I couldn't make it. To the car. Dead. Drowning."

"Oh, but you did make it. You made it. You saved him. You're okay. It's just a dream. It's anxiety. A bad reaction. Of course you're having one."

I sobbed and sobbed, drenching his skin. I cried until I didn't have any more tears, and at that point, I must have passed out again, clinging to his body like the lifeline Casper was.

~

THE SUN STREAMED through the windows and hit my eyes like it wanted to abuse me. My head pounded. This must be what a hangover felt like. I'd never had one, but this had to be it. My whole body hurt to go with it. Every muscle. Every joint. All of it.

Casper had held me the whole night, but right then, he was sitting up, his knees pulled forward, with his hand on my leg. His head was bent, and he was listening to something. To me, it just sounded like whispers, but Cas must have been able to hear what they said, because he frowned before he looked at me.

"Seems that Knox has made you family." He rubbed my knee. "That's a good thing. And he's reminding Oscar to do better with certain things. You need clothes made. You need things. And food that you'll actually eat."

I smiled. "Sounds like him."

"He's leaving now." Cas rolled toward me. "But he's going to be back later." Cas frowned at me. "You're in pain. A lot of it." He jumped off the bed. "I could smell it while you were sleeping, almost woke you to give you something for it, but I thought sleep was probably best for you."

That was awful. "You're supposed to have slept last night. Between my breakdown and now keeping you up because of my pain and..."

"Don't do that." He put on his shirt before he walked over to kiss me. "I was happy to be here with you last night. It was a gift to hold you when you needed it. And you didn't keep me up. I slept really well, actually. Much longer than usual. Your pain that you have because you dove off a cliff to save my brother is not something you should apologize for." He kissed me again. "Stay here. I'm going to get you some pills that will help. The healer should have some."

With a wink, he left me. I sat up, holding my head. Yes,

everything hurt. A lot. I groaned and lay back down. This was going to be one of those days. Maybe several days. I really hated pain.

Oscar came in carrying the pills that Cas had left to get. He handed it to me. "He's talking to Will. Well, no one is talking to Will. Will is yelling and pissed off. Refusing his medications. It's a whole thing."

Really? I couldn't hear any of it. The noise canceling must be really good here to give people some privacy. Still, Cas had been able to hear what was happening outside.

I swung my legs over the bed and rose on wobbly feet. "Little bit beat up."

He grabbed me a robe and wrapped it around me. "I can see that. Amazing you aren't more hurt. It has been made clear to me that we are not doing the best job of caring for you. Granted, up until today, you had clothes of your own, but I assure you that we will do better. Your family is going to make sure of it."

I limped over to the pile of clothes. "He insisted on it. Just pronounced I was family."

"Yes, as he should have. You deserve a family, and Knox is powerful. His people will always be your people. It's a good thing."

I put my hand out to him. "I love you."

His eyes widened. "I love you. Every piece of you. Every cell in your body. All of you. I almost lost you yesterday. Or it seemed that way."

I hugged him tight and then winced. Yes, everything was hurting right now, which reminded me I hadn't taken the pills yet. Limping to the sink in the bathroom, I took them using a cup next to it.

"You get to handle this by just shifting?"

He shook his head, putting his arm back around me

when I came out. "Not always. There are some instances when that is the last thing we should do. Will right now is an example of that. Let's go see him. He's really on a rant wanting to see you."

I leaned on Oscar. "I'm going to be a mess today. But I'll pull it together."

"No rush." He hugged me closer. "I'm more worried about you than anything else right now. The Wolf can wait in his cell, and the other one has nowhere to go. Knox spent the morning interrogating a bunch of his Lions. He's sent the ones he's sure aren't involved in this out to patrol. The guy isn't getting away any time soon."

That reminded me of something. "Why didn't you guys have to do that last night? I never got an answer about that."

"Because this is the main house. They have guards to do that. This is where the Alpha lives. He put us right in his house. Think he's trying to tell us something?"

Indeed...I did.

17

I could hear Will the second I was in the hallway. Yes, he was yelling.

"And if you try to come at me with that needle again, I will break it in half. And you, brother, if you try, I will break your arm."

Oscar rolled his eyes. "He's particularly bad when he's injured. When he was ten, well, it was bad for a week."

We entered the room. Sure enough, he was on the bed, bleary eyed, and I didn't have to be able to scent emotions to know he was all over the place.

"Hey." I let go of Oscar. "What is this scene you're making?"

In the corner were all three healers. They held a needle, and Alora had a scowl on her face. Casper had his arms crossed in front of him, wearing a matching expression to Alora. I forced myself to walk as normally as I could.

William sat up as straight as he could, his expression falling. He held out his hands. "Tiff. They tell me I didn't dream it, you leapt off a cliff to get me. I don't know that part. That's just what Cas told me. But I remember you, when I woke up. You were there. You risked your life to get me."

I waved my hand. "We can talk about what I did and didn't do another time. What we need to talk about is what you're doing right now."

He scowled at me for a second. "I don't want to be knocked out. I don't like it. I've slept. Too long. I don't want that thing."

Certainly, I could understand how he felt. I sat on the corner of his bed and took his hands. "Today's shot isn't going to knock you out. It's to make your pain go away. You might sleep. But that's just so that tomorrow you're back to yourself."

He sniffed the air, his expression falling. "You're in pain. You take the shot."

"She doesn't have a Lion to save," Alora said with a huff. "And she took her pills. Even asked for them."

I ignored her. She was right, but that wasn't helpful. "Will, I hate seeing you in pain, and we need to talk about what to do next. Can you please take your shot so we can do that?"

His face fell. "Sure. For you, Tiff, I'll let them dose me."

Alora rushed forward as though he might change his mind and jammed that needle right into Will's arm. I winced, watching. That would hurt like hell. But he barely seemed to notice.

Having delivered the dose, Alora, Nicole, and the other woman I didn't know hurried out. I didn't blame them. Will was being a bit of a bear. He'd hate that description, but there it was.

I scooted closer to him until we were both stretched out on the bed. "Thank you."

"I really hate feeling out of control."

I kissed his cheek. "We all do. But yesterday you were dead for a while, so just behave, okay?"

He leaned over, which made him groan, and kissed me. "How did you get me out of the car? I'm not clear on details."

Oscar sat down next to me, stretching out like Will and I were. He put his arm over his head. It was a good thing these beds were so big. We could all fit if Cas sat next to Will. But he walked to the window instead, looking out.

He was the one who answered. "She dove headfirst off the cliff into the ocean and then emerged, after way too long, with you in her arms, where she then proceeded to swim you to safety and revive you from death. So...yeah... she's incredible, which we already knew."

I shook my head. "You threw me out the window, Will. When you could have been saving yourself. And since you saved my life, I was then able to save yours. So I guess you could say you actually saved both of us."

William groaned. "That is some mental gymnastics right there. No, I didn't save both of us, and I'm going to have nightmares thinking of you diving off a cliff."

"Well, that's okay because I had a nightmare last night where I didn't save you. Poor Cas had to deal with that. And I can't get the image of you and the car going over the cliff out of my mind."

Oscar held up his hand. "Enough with the cliff. Casper and I saw both of you go over. Trust me, bad image to have."

Cas turned around. "It was my honor to be there for you when you needed me."

"Maybe less said about what happened the better, because every time we bring it up, I have to recall just how much I was sure everything good in life was over." Oscar sat up. "Let's talk about the Wolf locked up and finding his fucking buddy."

I reached around Will to stroke his hair. I hurt, but he was in brutal pain. The medicine hadn't worked for him yet, and it was actually starting to take effect for me. With gentle twirls of my fingers, I petted him. He shifted slightly to lean closer to me.

The ache in my neck was lessening. "So you don't think he can get out of the general area."

Oscar nodded. "Exactly. And we will find out who has been helping him. Knox can do that. Or we can interrogate it out of the Canine's lying ass. I can smell every falsehood coming out of his mouth. Wolves don't have the same desire to tell the truth that we do. They can smell lies, but they do it anyway. It's like saying to the other person that they aren't important enough to tell the truth to."

Casper turned around. "Thank you, Will."

"What?" My injured mate didn't understand that transition any more than I did.

"Thank you. For everything you did. All the years you raised us, took care of us, gave up years of time and dreams to take care of Oscar and me. Thank you. I don't know if I'd have been as self-sacrificing as you in the same situation. You kept our souls alive, and I don't know what it did to you to do that. I should have said it early. Thank you." He hardly took a breath as he delivered that speech.

If it were possible, Will got even more stiff. He blinked rapidly. "To steal a phrase from you, Casper, it was my honor to be there for you when you needed me."

Oscar caught his breath. "I didn't know he was going to do that but that goes twice for me. Seriously, Will, when we almost lost you..."

My oldest mate held up his hand. "Thank you. I know

what it takes to...say what you guys are saying. But, please, no more. I know how you feel about me and what it meant to you. It never occurred to me not to. You're my brothers."

I wiped tears from my eyes. "That was really beautiful."

Will nudged me and then winced. "Can we talk about beating up Wolves? I'm more comfortable on that topic. I haven't even seen a Wolf since we took that one down when we were teenagers. He came here to start shit and got hauled away for it."

Oscar's smile was huge. "That was a good day."

"Well, we have to find the second Wolf. That is first and foremost the thing we need to do." Casper sighed. "And all of Tiffany's notes are gone because they are now in the water. I saw that happen. You kind of kicked it. I can't imagine you did it on purpose."

I shook my head. "It was a total accident, but fortunately, the only casualty from yesterday. Yes, they're gone, but there might be something we can do. Do you have a tablet I can use? Or I mean, I guess we all have to borrow one from Knox."

Oscar nodded. "I can get one."

"Great. Because I can bring back the information. And you guys need to go find that Wolf. I'll deal with the one we have." The pain meds were working now. I could actually sort of squirm without pain. "That is sort of what I do. I have interrogated people before. I'm good at it."

Cas opened and closed his mouth. "Tiffany, I'm...I'm not sure I'm comfortable with that. If something goes wrong with the Wolf, we're not there to help you."

"It won't go wrong." I sighed. "This is what I do. I promise. Send one of Knox's people to stand outside if you're really that worried, but I won't need any help. Let's not delay things. Let's just get this done. I don't think we have time for me to prove I don't need help with this. I dove off a cliff. I can do many things."

A snore caught all our attention. It had been a long second since Will said something, and I guessed the pain medication had made him feel much better. He was out cold, his head on the headboard, actually full-on snoring. I grinned. It might have been my petting his head.

I let go of him and sat up. "Well, that is Will's opinion."

Oscar rubbed his eyes. "Okay, much as I hate the idea, I have to admit this is what you do. We should let you do it. Then we can get this behind us. And talk about what's next."

That was the part where one of them would kill Knox, the old man who wanted to be my family. I couldn't think about that at all. Forcing Wolves to tell me things? That I could do.

"We have to order her some clothes."

My heart pinged. "I can do that. But I don't have any money."

"We're not doing this again." Casper helped me off the bed, which I did gently because I needed to make sure Will was comfortable before I left. He settled down into the pillow, which made him stop snoring. I patted his head. He was going to be so annoyed he'd knocked out.

Oscar retrieved a tablet, and I logged into it, finding the message I'd sent to Ferguson earlier. "Here, take this. It has all the info you might need on the missiles themselves. Oh hold on." I grabbed it back and sent Ferguson a message telling him my tablet was gone but I was still on the move handling the missiles. I quickly handed it back to Oscar.

For now, I had a purple sweater and a short pair of pants to wear, but I was still without shoes. I looked down at myself. Yesterday's dress had been pretty, but this looked like a little girl's outfit. I was so much smaller than everyone else, it really might be children's clothes. The shoes were going to be a problem.

I pointed at my feet. "This is going to be a problem."

"No." Oscar laughed. "We rescued your shoes before we came home. You kicked them off."

He ran into the other room and returned with my shoes. Okay. Well, that had been easy. I hoped the whole day would go like that, but this was me. It rarely did.

"THAT'S AN INTERESTING OUTFIT." The Wolf who looked like a man right now lifted his hand. "Did your mommy dress you, human?"

"Hey," Knox, who had insisted on walking me over to the holding cell, yelled. "You don't talk to her like that. Do you understand, you mangy mutt?"

I put my hand on his arm. Apparently, being his family really meant something to him. That was nice and I wouldn't mind rolling around in the feeling, only it wasn't the time. "I'm okay. Would you please wait outside?" As we'd discussed, but I wouldn't remind him of at the moment.

He shot the prisoner another look but left, closing the door behind him. If I screamed, he'd come and rescue me. Only I highly doubted it was me who was going to be doing the screaming. I steeled my spine. I'd softened over the last few days. Inside, I was melting in a way I hadn't known possible because I hadn't understood I was frozen there. Like I'd been waiting for someone to want me, to choose me, to thaw out.

Now I had that in abundance. Not just with men who wanted to love me, but an elderly gentleman who'd declared I was family.

All of that aside, I could still do my fucking job. Everything that made me, well, me hadn't disappeared. I could feel my old self just fine as I regard this asshole who had tried to kill Will and me from across a table.

The Lions weren't playing around. They'd beaten him up, and he still wore the marks. Maybe he had to shift to heal, or maybe my Cats were better at healing than this Dog. They'd tied his hands up and strapped him to a chair where he'd been all night. I was impressed he hadn't messed himself, at least not yet.

Eventually, he was going to have to pee.

There was a desk between us and a chair that was placed for the interrogator to sit in. Since that was me, I took my seat.

"These aren't my clothes," I told him. "I think it was very nice that the people from Knox's group gave them to me. Since you drowned mine, and I haven't had a chance to wash the ones I still have left." I chewed on my lip. I was tiny and blonde. If the Union had taught me anything at all, it was that I could use my size to my advantage in times like this. Men did tend to underestimate me. When I was interrogating, I liked it that way. I'd just play along. Until I didn't anymore. I couldn't lie. He'd smell that.

But he'd find that out on his own.

"We couldn't believe you did that." His eyes flared Wolf. That was something that was similar to the Lions. Suddenly, they couldn't keep back their other half. The duality of them. It was so interesting. If I were lucky, I'd get a lifetime to study it up close. "I've never seen a human be that brave."

He'd clearly not seen very many humans. We did all sorts of things that were brave. Or at least some humans did. People didn't have to be brave until they had to be.

"Have you spent a lot of time with us? With humans?"

He looked away. "No. We don't let you on our planet. Smartest thing we ever did."

It needed to seem like I wanted to have a conversation. "You and the Lions have that in common. You don't like us."

"We have nothing in common with these furballs." He spit on the ground. Well, that was gross and so unhygienic. Just, yuck.

"You both keep humans off your planet. That you do have in common." I pushed him just a little. "And look, I don't care what you do with humans and your home worlds. I work for the Union, and you're shooting at our ships from this planet, a planet I think you really shouldn't be on, right?"

He growled. "This should be our planet too. This should all be ours. And the Bears too. Wolves will rule all shifters, as it always should have been."

This guy wasn't even making it hard. "Oh, I think I'm understanding the brilliance of this plan." In the sense that there was no brilliance. "You wanted us to think the Cats were shooting at us? So that we'd come down here and take care of the problem for you? Then you'd come here and take over? Something like that?"

He growled. "Little girl, I don't have to tell you anything."

That was fine. I would have been shocked if this really had been a walk in the park. He'd push. So I would too.

I sighed, loudly. On purpose. "Here's the thing—I don't have a gun. So I can't shoot you. They took it from me. I did try to kill someone when I first got here. I might have a problem, I don't know. But I'm sure if I opened the door, I could get a new weapon from the very nice man who likes me and hates you. I don't think anyone on this whole planet would care if I really, really hurt you."

He lunged forward but couldn't move. "Hurt me."

"Oh, I see. That's what you want me to do. I have never dealt with the Wolves at all, so I didn't realize. That was the wrong move." I had him right where I wanted him. He just didn't know that. "That's fine, then. I won't hurt you. Not at all. I'll just have you dropped back home and explain to everyone that you were just too weak to kill a human."

His eyes widened. "Don't do that."

"You got captured. That's pretty bad, right? I mean...you should at least die in glory." I pushed my chair back. "Well, it wasn't nice meeting you. I can't say it was. You tried to kill me. But it was something, that was for sure."

"Wait." His voice actually broke. I felt sort of sorry for him. Not much. A little bit. He was younger than me, or at least he looked that way. He could be much older, only I'd wager whatever his age, he was still considered a juvenile among the Wolves. "Yes, we wanted the Union to pay attention, to take out the Lions. This could help all of us. We could actually make a bargain together. Wouldn't that be something the Union wanted in the end?"

I was quiet for so long, he started to squirm. Or maybe he had to pee. "If the leaders of your planet wanted a relationship with us" —it hurt a little bit to say 'us,' but I was being this version of me right then— "then all they need do is contact us. There would be a deal made in minutes. You couldn't do that, which means you're not really speaking for the leadership. You're not really anything but a usurper, you and whatever group you're with. You don't have any power, and your leaders don't even know you're here."

He visibly swallowed. "There needs to be change."

"I'm sure there does. Everywhere needs change. I've never been anywhere that doesn't, and I've been everywhere." Even here. There was a man standing outside this door who had to die to protect his people, was practically picking out his executioners. And my mates would have to do that job after living a life where they had been forced to live with their parents' executioners. Yep, this place was as fucked up as everywhere else. But it had my mates, and so it was worlds better than anywhere else.

As Cas had pointed out to me, there was nowhere that I was going to find that was really the utopia of my childhood dreams. Something bad always happened everywhere.

I continued, "But this isn't how you do it. It's just not. You have one piece to bargain with here. You can tell me where the missiles are so I can go find them. Your friend is still on the run. They'll find him and tear him up. This is really your last chance."

Of course, I hadn't told him what I'd give him, and if he didn't push me on that, it would be exactly nothing. Just how dumb was he?

His voice shook. "In the old missile silos that are just outside the settlement. They're not visible from here. If we time the launches for the nighttime gatherings, no one sees it."

That made sense. "How much help did you have? How many of Knox's people?"

"Four."

I rose. Well, that was easier than it should have been. I hadn't even had to get a weapon. I turned to the door, and he called out.

"Hold on, I thought we were making a deal."

I shrugged. "So did I, but then you started babbling. Thanks for that."

He howled, and I hurried on my way, closing the door behind me. Knox lifted an eyebrow as the door closed. "That was impressive. I have to find four traitors. I have two of them.

I can guess who the next two are. The next leader will be left with a more cohesive group. These four were always pains in my asses. They probably think there shouldn't be leadership or we should be living with the Wolves. No memory of history, no idea how impossible it is to even deal with the Canines."

I would guess they were saying the same shit on Planet Wolf, but I lived here now. I was going to be team Cat all the way.

He put out his arm. "Who did you shoot?"

"Tiffany." Will wobble-charged toward us at a rather impressive gait for someone who had to be in a huge amount of pain. "Were you in there alone with the prisoner? With that Wolf?" The last word was said with so much disdain, I almost smiled from it. They did really all hate each other. In the meantime, the Union was trudging around ruining lives for countless others. What a fucked-up universe it was.

I patted Knox's arm but went to Will instead. "I got all the info we needed."

He sagged gently next to me. "I woke up. You were all gone. I don't even remember falling asleep. The last thing I could recall was you saying you'd handle it. Apparently, that's how it went?"

"Yes, your brothers were smart enough to trust me. That wasn't even hard. I promise we're okay. No one was hurt over here. Tomorrow, we can end this whole thing by getting rid of the missiles."

The sound of the ocean pressed into my consciousness. I hadn't been paying attention to it since my dive into the water the day before. Almost like my subconscious had deliberately tuned it out. But there it was. Beautiful. Big. Vast. Huge waves. Those were surfing waves.

I blinked. Knox was talking to me. "What should we do with him?"

"That's beyond me. That's Will's call. He's one of the three supreme leaders or whatever we're calling you."

My mate snorted. "What would you do with him if it was your call, little human?"

I supposed if I got to call him supreme leader, he could call me little human. "Send him back with a note to the Wolves that you found this kid wandering around shooting missiles. You caught him and you'd let them handle their problems. It might start a dialogue."

"That's different than my inclination to kill him." Knox looked over his shoulder.

"We'll try it your way, Tiff." Will kissed my cheek. He really needed to go back to bed. He was practically vibrating against me.

"Speaking of my way, what would happen if when the two of you met on the battlefield so to speak, to challenge him, if you do that, if Knox just conceded. Would he have to die? Or could he stay here as some sort of mentor, considering he knows this pack inside and out? He could help with the transition or whatever."

They both stared at me like I'd grown two heads. I started walking toward the house. It seemed I wouldn't get an answer. Maybe it was just something to think about. I really, really liked Knox. Why did he have to go so fast?

18

"You should have seen it." Oscar laughed. "The Wolf actually thought he was going to get away from us by climbing a tree." His laugh was infectious, and I grinned. We were all spread out in the living area of the suite where we resided.

I had my head in Casper's lap, his legs stretched out before him as he leaned against the couch. Oscar was across from us, and Will on the other side of him. It was almost four o'clock. Everyone was going to take a nap, and even though I'd only successfully experienced the ritual once, I could honestly say that I understood it. I was tired and my pain was coming back, but I didn't want more pills. Maybe I could wait it out. Relax through the evening and miraculously develop shifter healing so I'd be fine in the morning.

Probably not, but I could dream about it. During my nap.

"I trust you reminded him that Cats climb better than Dogs." Will smiled, his clenched jaw the only indication he wasn't entirely back to normal.

While we were out, the room had been stocked with

food that Knox had told me he was sure I would like. We'd see. Figuring out how to eat on this planet was going to prove to be the most difficult thing. Maybe I'd develop a taste for spicier foods.

I rose, and Cas whined. "Where are you going?"

"Do you guys want to nap in beds or out here like we did that one time? Because if you want here, then I have to get pillows and blankets."

I'd only meant to gauge their interest, but their smiles were huge and all at the same time, they answered, "Here."

Yes, they'd liked that as much as I had. Not that we couldn't all sleep together in a bed. We could, but there was something sort of nice about being out in the living room. It designated the activity as nap and not bedtime.

I grabbed a bunch of pillows and blankets, dragging them out. Oscar was moving the rugs around when I got back out so that they would act a little bit like mattresses, even though the room already had carpet that made it soft to be against.

After spreading out the pillows so everyone could be comfortable, I was tugged down by Will. "I almost died. I get to have you next to me this time."

"You get to use that once." Oscar held up his hand. "Not for weeks. And she has two sides." He dove down so he was next to me on the other end. I loved how happy Oscar was, how it seemed like it was his default setting.

Casper winked at me. "That's okay. I get to be by her head, I get to listen to her breathe and have our heads pressed together."

"Thank you. For making me feel this way. I never have. Like you always want me to be around, like being with me is what you want more than anything. I know this is new. I know that some of the excitement will probably wear off and there will be things I do that are aggravating, but I want you to know that I've never felt like this. Like I belonged and was wanted. Thank you for that."

They were so quiet, if their eyes hadn't been open, I'd have thought they were asleep. It was Cas who finally spoke. "You make us feel that way too. We have never had a home. Not really. With you, it feels like every day is being surrounded by one. Thank you for being you, Tiffany."

"Come here." Will pulled me tighter. "I did think on the way into the water how lucky I'd been to have had any time with you. That if I hadn't met you, I'd have gone my entire existence and not known what happy really was."

Oscar stroked his finger down my nose. "I didn't know what beautiful was until my eyes saw you."

I almost argued. I didn't think of myself as beautiful or even pretty. I supposed I could best be called cute. Only as Oscar looked at me right then, I realized that he meant every word he said. He did see me that way. I wouldn't take away the incredibleness of his declaration by arguing about it. We'd done what I set out to do. Tomorrow, we were getting rid of the missiles and sending the Wolves away. This nap was celebratory.

"Thank you, guys." That seemed to be enough.

Casper yawned. "You want this place. You like it here. It's feeding your energy. But you don't want Knox to die."

That was all true. "Maybe we should shelve that. I don't want to think about it right before I try to sleep, or I'm not going to sleep."

"Fair enough." He kissed my cheek. "Get some rest."

For once in my life, I was sure that I could.

I didn't dream, and the sounds of music from outside woke me up. Someone had opened the window, and the waves hitting the beach a small distance away coupled with whatever music someone was entertaining with for the evening was what woke me up.

My guys were all up. Will was in the kitchen. He seemed to be moving a lot better than he had before the nap. Cas and Oscar were whispering in the corner. They all turned to look at me when I rose.

"Hey." Will smiled. "I thought maybe we could listen to tonight's fun from up here. Tomorrow night, we can get on a schedule of prowling and sleeping and being up. I think Knox is pretty devoted to keeping you safe. For tonight, we'll trust that."

This. This very moment. This was happy.

I'd no sooner thought it than I wished I hadn't. Did I get to be happy?

~

THE WAVES BANGED against the cliff while we stood in the missile silo. It wasn't a comforting sound. There was weather coming in, and usually, I'd wish I were surfing the big presentation. Only at ten in the morning, I wanted nothing more than to walk back to the apartments and just not start this day.

I had on a pair of translation glasses that Cas had gotten for me so that I could see what Oscar was doing disabling the missiles. He'd done five of them so far. I didn't need to participate, but I liked to know what was happening. Feeling completely unable to function because I couldn't read the words was frustrating. This helped a lot.

Oscar looked up from what he was doing. "You can go wait outside with Will and Knox if you don't like it in here."

I didn't think the problem was the silo. Not that I could really say what the problem was. There was no way that they couldn't all smell that I was disgruntled. Casper knocked into me. "Did you not sleep well? Was Oscar snoring? I didn't hear him. I was conked out."

"I don't snore, dipshit, you do." Oscar didn't look up as he took his brother's jab and shot it back.

We'd all gone to bed together, eventually. Very late, when the music had stopped. I didn't imagine we'd get to do that very much, so actually, I had slept great, snuggled in the bed with them. If anyone snored, I hadn't heard it. We'd all just been together.

But my good mood was gone.

"I'll go outside. I slept great. I'm just...off." Jumpy like something was coming to get me. Maybe I was allergic to happiness.

Knox and William were outside guarding the entrance. We had caught all the people involved in the plot, and the Wolves were on their way home. I rubbed my arms. What was bothering me?

My mate turned and smiled. "Hey, what is going on with you today? Why are you off?"

I threw my hands in the air. "I don't know. Are you feeling better?" Was I worried about him?

"Ninety-eight percent there."

Knox laughed. "Don't tell my sister. She'll make you get back in bed and drug you up."

"I hate that. Seriously. Why do we have to be unconscious?" He shook his head. "She didn't have to be. She got pills and went gallivanting about. The healers thought it was funny to keep me knocked out."

I rolled my eyes. "Maybe it had to do with the severity of your injury."

That was when I heard it—the plane landing. William and Knox must have at the same time because we all looked up together. Realization dawned on me the same time it did Will.

"It's the Union," I told him, but I was sure he already knew. The frown on his now serious face said it all. This was very bad news.

I stepped forward. "Go inside. All of you. I'll handle this. This is for me. Inside."

I might as well have told him to turn blue and grow wings, because he shook his head once like the idea was so ridiculous, he wasn't going to consider it. Okay. Obviously, they weren't going to leave. In fact, the other two bounded outside. Well, I wouldn't want to leave them either.

As the ship landed, Oscar spoke into his wrist. I'd never seen him do that before, but he must have a way of reaching others. Sometimes, I forgot just how much tech they had. They lived really simply most of the time, but they were more advanced than we were.

Or maybe I was part of this here now and not any longer related to that ship coming.

Well...that could be true once I got rid of whoever this was. "Let me handle it. At least stay back. I'll take care of it."

"Did you know they were coming?" Casper asked me, raising his eyebrows. "Or did you just have some kind of feeling?"

I touched his arm. "The second one. Maybe I just subconsciously knew it had been too long since they'd touched base."

I stepped forward pointing my finger at Will. "I'm serious. This will go better if you let me do it."

"It's your job, but now my hackles are raised. This isn't how you pick up an employee or even how they should be entering our air space. If I don't like something, I'm stepping in. And Oscar will be the worst. If they do something inappropriate, he'll rip out their eyes."

I raised an eyebrow at Oscar. "Really?"

"I'm only gentle around you because you're you." He shrugged.

Well...that was something to ponder later.

I walked quickly toward the ship once they were landed. This was a pretty posh one, that meant the person on it was above me in paygrade. This was what I'd been aiming for just a week ago. The right to travel on this kind of ship and have the stuff that came with it. Now? I was sleeping on floors between three guys who had decided that I was everything they wanted in the universe and making jokes with an old man who made me family just because I didn't have one.

They could keep that spaceship. I wanted nothing to do with it.

I walked forward a bit more, and the door opened to let whoever was on it off. After a moment, three guards exited, followed by the last person I ever wanted to see again.

Ferguson.

I steeled my back. The ship was still noisy, but the guys would hear me. "He's my boss, stole the job from me, and I hate him."

I didn't have to turn around to know they now hated him too. It was one of those things I already knew about them. If I hated someone, they would too. As the ship quieted, the sound of the ocean met my ears again, along with Ferguson's glare. Was he mad he'd had to come down here? Why had he bothered?

"I have handled the missiles. It was the Wolves. They've been sent home to be dealt with, and the missiles are now gone. No one will be shooting at cargo ships anymore." I lifted my chin. "And I would have informed you of all of this shortly. Your visit is unnecessary."

He shook his head. "Tiffany Keyes, you have been nothing but a huge problem to me from day one. The trouble was I never had any reason to fire you, no justification. But you have given me one now."

Wow. I hated this man. Hated. Hated. Hated him. "What could that possibly be? And you know what? Never mind. I quit. You can't fire me. I quit."

"Well then, this is much easier. You're under arrest for treason."

I put my hands on my hips and stormed toward him, even as one of my guys roared. The guards took two steps back before they lifted their weapons. I had news for them. They wouldn't work.

"On what fucking grounds are you pulling this bullshit?"

It was funny, in an ironic sort of way. I never heard the tranquilizer gun he fired until after the tranq was embedded in my stomach. I stared down at it, the world immediately turning left and then right like I was on a boat. I grabbed my stomach, hearing the sound of the gun for the first time. My knees gave out.

Lions were roaring.

I'D NEVER BEEN TRANQUED before, but waking up from the experience really fucking sucked. My stomach roiled, and my head pounded. I pulled my knees to my chest and groaned. I was on the floor and not a nice, comfy rug snuggled next to three people who wanted nothing more than to make me happy.

That meant that something really bad had happened.

There was no way I'd be in a small holding cell on a space-ship if they were okay. I didn't care what Ferguson—the worst person I knew, and I knew a lot of bad ones—did to me. But I had to know if my Lions were okay.

I sat up, forcing myself not to puke, and on unsteady feet, walked to the door I knew would be locked. There was protocol for this kind of thing. I knocked on it.

After a few moments, it opened, and sure enough, Ferguson the toad was there. I'd never actually seen a toad. Maybe they got a bad rap. Why did we use them in that expression? Was it an old Earth thing?

"What did you do to them?"

He scratched his head. "If I were you, I'd be more concerned with your own predicament."

"Answer my question." Asshole.

"I don't think I will. I think I'd prefer you not know so that it bothers you. They're obviously people you care about. So, I'll leave you to ponder things. There are, I suppose, three options. The first is that they're dead. My guards took them down before they could do that weird shifting thing. The second is they cut a deal with me. The Union would go back to leaving them alone if they let me take you away. The third is that they are fine and looking for you but will never find you because by the time they have any idea where you are, you'll be in a place they can't follow."

He was making death threats? I blinked. I wouldn't give him the satisfaction or reaction to this nonsense. If they were dead, it was too awful for me to deal with standing in front of Ferguson. They'd never have given me away. They all chose me, they all wanted me. They hadn't lied or fooled me. What we felt for each other was real.

As for the last bit... I sighed. "Ferguson, on what grounds can you possibly accuse me of being treasonous? I am many things, but never that." Unless he'd heard my conversations that I'd had. Even then, I didn't think they could kill me for that. Fire me, yes. Bankrupt me, sure. Not kill me.

"You shared Union protected information with non-Union citizens." I detested how he used that word, 'citizen.' Like it was a real thing. We didn't have the rights of citizens. We were subjects. And maybe not even that.

I put my hands on my hips. I had to get out of this and get back home. Every minute I was on this ship, and I didn't know for how long at this point even, took me farther from my heart. "What the hell are you talking about?"

"You let one of those shifters look at classified letters sent between you and me."

I blinked. "What?"

"We have recordings of him reading it, of his taking information down from it. You know better than anyone, Tiffany, that you aren't allowed to do that. Would you like to see the recording?"

My mouth fell open, and I forced it closed. Shit. Yes, I had done that. With my tablet gone and needing missile information, I'd pulled up the exchanges over a tablet provided by Knox, and I'd handed it to Oscar. Yes, I had completely broken the rules. Not that Oscar gave a shit at all about the bullshit letters I had to send to Ferguson. But he could have accessed other info on there they would not want him to see. Even letting him see the missile info was against the rules, because the Union had seized that missile. That made it ours and our intellectual property.

I rubbed my eyes. "Ferguson, listen. I realize I have been a problem for you. Believe it or not, I didn't want to be. But I'll acknowledge that it's true. I wanted to get through my time and get out. What if you just let me go? I quit. You don't have to see me anymore. I'll disappear from your existence, never to be seen again."

He tapped the wall. "I might consider that if you weren't such a bitch."

That word. It was used to justify so many offenses against women. They got what was coming to them because they were a bitch. Usually said by an insecure man with no balls. But screaming that at him wouldn't be smart right now. I didn't have claws. I had to think my way out of this problem.

"What are you going to do with me? Certainly, we must be able to negotiate. Everything is a negotiation, right?" I was speaking Union language. The big difference between Ferguson and me was that he believed. He was a Union man. A true loyalist. What I'd learned in just my days with the Lions was that I never had been.

He shook his head. "I don't know what I'm going to do with you yet. I have some thoughts, and by tonight, I'll let you know." He looked me up down. "What did you have in mind for negotiation?"

My blood boiled. "Not that."

"Too bad. You might be worth a quick fuck." Ferguson left me in that cell then. Alone with the lone toilet and the knowledge that I was really, really screwed. Just not by him. Not ever. So help me.

I sank to the floor. They weren't dead. They were going to find me, and I was going to be alive for them to do that. I rocked back and forth. I just wanted to go home.

Home to my guys.

～

I WAS FED, but that was it. No one spoke to me. No one ever acknowledged my existence except the bringing and taking away of food. A whole day passed like that. I didn't sleep. I just waited. Doom settled between my shoulder blades.

A constant ache. I tried to tell myself it was okay. The longer I lived, the more chance I had that they would find me. The Union could always find me because of the tracker in my shoulder. I rubbed at it. I'd never been able to feel it, but now it was like a stone on my back. I closed my eyes. Tiredness made me loopy. I needed a nap, but I wouldn't take one until I could have it with the three guys holding my heart.

Who knew I would have so quickly fallen in love with taking a nap? I laughed at the thought.

That was when Ferguson came back. He walked through the door, leaving it open behind him. With an amused grin, he smiled at me. Fuck, I hated him. That wasn't even a strong enough sentiment anymore. Despisable, detestable man.

"I've been doing a lot of reading about you, Tiffany." He shook his head. "You hide quite a past from the Union."

I'd never done such a thing. "That's not true. My past is an open book. I don't like to talk about it, but it's not hidden. Anything you wanted to know couldn't have been very hard for you to find."

"Really? You think you would have gotten this high up in the Union if they knew about your mother?"

I shrugged. Really, I'd never given this any thought. I'd presumed the powers that be knew about her. "What about her?"

"She died because she rose against us."

If he had a point, I wished he'd get to it. My mother had probably committed suicide by Union officers. She'd wanted them to end it in her own way. I'd known she wasn't right and tried to tell my father as much. Not that he'd cared. I certainly wasn't going to get into it with Ferguson. He wouldn't give two shits about her mental health or what living in the Dead Zone does to a person over time. No, he didn't get to know that information.

"I can't seem to bring myself to kill you, but that doesn't mean you won't die."

Suddenly, I was just tired. Done with this whole thing. I couldn't take another minute. "Stop with the bullshit and get to it. What are you doing to me?"

"Your mother died from her dosing because she was weak. Not everyone dies. Some people live through it."

Yes, but the problem was that no one knew how long their individual punishment from the torture drug would last. They didn't...

I gasped. "No."

He pulled out a needle. "Yes."

Fuck no. He was not going to do that to me. That was my deepest fear. I'd even told Will. I jumped up, thoughts of exhaustion fleeing. I didn't have claws, but I had fingernails. I ran at him, with them extended, and managed to get ahold of his face. We wrestled for a second, but he didn't let go of the needle. No, he held that thing like his life depended on it, and soon, I was pulled off of him by the guards he must have stationed in the hall.

I fought. Kicked. Bit. It wasn't pretty, but oh how I tried, screaming at the top of my lungs like a madwoman.

When Ferguson injected me with the drug that killed my mother, I wept, dignity gone. No. No. No. I'd never see them again. People lived, but I'd never met any. Everyone I knew who was dosed with this torture died. It was supposed to be illegal.

"We're one day from Earth. If you live, you can start over there. If you die, well you were a traitor. Not my problem what happens to you." He spit on me. "Were you fucking those Lions?"

I cried into my hands. In all the eventualities I'd ever imagined for myself, this was the one I'd been sure I could prevent. I'd never see the guys, and what time I had left was going to be awful.

He knelt in front of me. "I didn't kill them. They got a lot of my guards. Killed them. We took you and ran. The cost analysis said punishing you was more important."

Even in my hysterics, I knew that was bull crap.

"They'll come looking. And find your dead body. Or not. As you know, there are no grave markers in the Dead Zone."

19

I lay on the floor, feeling the coolness of the fake wood beneath my cheek. I had no choice. There wasn't any furniture in this apartment. I shuddered. I was lucky they'd given me anywhere to stay. Truthfully, I'd expected Ferguson to leave me on the street. But he had bosses to answer to, and saying I resided at this address was cleaner for them than the word 'homeless' strewn across the paper. I knew these things. I used to be him. Although, I'd never ever ever done this to anyone.

That much I could say. I'd never tortured. Killed, yes. Tortured, no. Mostly, I just left people to their own devices, to destroy their own lives, after I left places. So this was probably some kind of punishment for my behavior. I'd worked for the enemy, become the enemy, and now I would die by the enemy. There was kind of a symmetry to it.

I shook, my body vibrating in small shocks that would eventually lead to another seizure. It would be my fourth today. I'd long given up keeping count on how many things happened yesterday. Truth was, I had no idea exactly how long I had been here. As far as I could tell, I was in the throes of the first round of pain, of sickness. I hadn't had my break from it yet. My mother had gone through several rounds before she died. I hummed to myself.

Life was cruel. I'd love to just sleep through the whole fucking thing.

There was a bang, and I winced. The neighbors in this place left me alone. They'd seen that I had no money, all of that being stripped by the Union. All those years of working for no other reason than financial security had blown up in my face. I laughed, then groaned. My humor had really gone dark.

"Tiffany." Strong hands hauled me off the floor. It was Casper. I was in his arms. Unless I was hallucinating. "I've got you. Your scent. What did they do to you? What happened?"

He smelled clean and familiar. It hadn't been that long since I'd seen him, but it seemed a lifetime. I lifted my head, even as my eyes blurred. "What they gave my mom."

Cas nodded. "Well...we're going to fix this."

Will was there too, suddenly in my line of vision. "I'm so sorry this happened. We were dealing with the guns when the coward took off with you. We had to find you. Oscar tapped into the tracking device they used. That's how we knew where you were."

Speaking of him, Oscar put his hand on my back. "I hate to cause you pain, but I want to get it out. Let them think you're here." There was a pinch, but I hardly noticed the removal of the tracker. I had to smell awful. I was covered in filth, and they hardly seemed to be bothered, even though their noses were so much stronger than my own. If I could smell me, they had to be able to.

I shook in Cas' arms. "We have to get her back to the

ship and get the healers on this. Oscar, can you get into their system again and see what the treatment is?"

"On it." Oscar kissed my cheek. "They'll never take you from us again. I promise you that."

I met Will's gaze. "Most people don't live through this."

"You will."

If I could have gotten better from that proclamation alone, I'd have been a lucky woman. I wished that could be the case, even as I seized in Cas' arms.

The next time I woke up, I shivered under three blankets and every muscle in my body hurt like I'd been beaten.

A warm washcloth was on my forehead as Oscar lay next to me, wiping my face with a second one.

"Hi, can you hear me?" He wiped my face slowly. "Or are you still out of it?"

I shook my head. "I can hear you. I'm up."

"Good." He kept wiping. "I missed you. And I'm so sorry this is happening to you."

That was sweet. So ridiculously sweet that tears flooded my eyes. "I'm sorry that I'm doing this to you. You guys flew all the way to Earth to rescue me, and I'm going to die."

He furrowed his brow. "You're not going to die. I refuse to entertain that thought. No." He shook his head. "There weren't any answers in their database, but the healers here are working on ideas. The only thing you have to do is rest and let us take care of you until we get this fixed."

I lifted my arm, and even though my hand shook, I stroked my hand down the side of his face. "Oscar..."

He shook his head. "Don't argue with me on this. You're going to recover, and we're going to spend our lifetime making it up to you."

I closed my eyes. The pain was building inside of me. It started at the base of my spine. "Where are we?"

"On the ship we brought to get you. We have a full crew and the healers. We'll be home in a few days, and then we can make you more comfortable than here." He stopped rubbing my face and instead pulled me against him. "Tiffany, you are my whole world. I will not lose you. We're going to live to be old together, and even then, you'll bury me first."

I hated that idea. "No. I haven't agreed to that. Better if I go first, so I don't have to miss you." I was really feeling the movement of the ship. "Everything is spinning."

He pressed his lips to my shoulder. "Close your eyes and try to sleep. The healers don't want to give you anything to knock you out. We're not clear yet which drugs will interfere with the toxins. As soon as they're clear, we'll give you something for pain, nausea, and to sleep. Whatever you want. And something to clear this up so you don't have to go through it anymore."

"Casper..." I could hardly whisper. "Don't you think if there were a cure, the Union would have it stored in their database?"

His sigh moved through me. "I think our medicine is better than the Union's. I think that the Union is so busy ruining people's lives that they didn't make a cure, but we will."

Sleep swept me under.

I didn't remember getting to the planet, but we were there. And I was puking, a lot. It was the newest part of the toxin. I couldn't keep anything inside of me, which was why a serious-faced Alora had come in and, while I'd been really out of it, put an IV in my arm. It was giving me fluids and nourishment until I could handle food myself.

I'd tried to eat some soup because my stomach had been actually hurting, and now I was paying for that. What was worse was that I was officially so weak, Casper had to sit with me while I did it.

I lifted my head. "Sorry."

He got on his knees to rub my back. "For what?"

"This." That was about all I could manage to say to him right now. If a cure was coming, it wasn't with us yet. The worry lines around my guys' eyes were becoming more pronounced. I didn't think any of them thought this would still be going on as long as it had. I didn't think we were even halfway through the hell that this was yet. Funny, I'd started to think of it as we when I was the one doing it. They were going through their own torture. It was definitely a group activity.

He scowled at me, but there was no heat or anger in his gaze. "Don't apologize. This was done to you. I'm sorry it happened. I'm sorry that we didn't get there faster."

Now it was my turn to scowl. "You can't make the laws of space and time fold differently for you. It took as long as it was going to take. That's not on you."

He sighed and patted his lap, like he wanted me to get it in. I shook my head. "I'm gross, Cas."

"You're not."

I put my head on his shoulder. That was as much as I was going to do right now. "I thought you guys didn't lie."

He squeezed my side. "Tiffany, I don't. I can smell how much pain you're in. I can hear that your body is struggling. I can feel in my heart that you are screaming on the inside. But you are not gross to me. Never that. So take that worry aside and put it away."

I nodded. "Okay."

Time passed like that. My bones hurt, my muscles gave out, and every day, I got weaker. I alternated between sleeping and bouts of horrific wakefulness. Nicole, the healer, came in and messed with my IV, whispering to Will, who was with me, when she did. "This might work."

"It has to." He rubbed his eyes as I watched him through slits of my own.

She nodded at him before she touched my forehead. "I had thought when I read about this that she would get breaks in between episodes, but she really doesn't. Moments of pain in between more awful pain. They have to be punished for hurting her as they have."

He took my hand.

If he said something, I didn't hear it. Instead, I drifted away again. This time, I found myself in the ocean. I didn't have my surfboard, but I was far out to sea—so far out that I could barely see the beach. There were people there, standing on the beach, watching me. Or maybe they were just looking at the ocean. From this far out, it was hard to tell. The sun glared in my eyes, but I was pretty certain it was Will, Casper, and Oscar on the water's edge. Knox was there too. And some others that were blurrier but there.

A boat honked its horn, a loud booming sound that filled the otherwise quiet ocean with uncomfortable noise. There were hardly any waves here. Before that boat showed up, it had been downright serene. No pain. No nausea. No sickness or toxins in my blood slowly killing me over long minutes, hours, days.

I could just float.

But there was that boat. I chewed on my lip. I could get on that boat. There was a ladder, and it was right there for me to climb. Of course, I knew nothing about where the boat would take me. It could go anywhere in the world. Even the universe. I blinked.

I swam toward it, knowing if I climbed up that ladder, that was it. All of this would end. It had just started, and it would be over. I wouldn't have to worry about anything anymore. The boat would simply take me on its journey away from here. There could be wonderful things to see and experiences to have.

But I looked over my shoulder toward the beach. The water was getting cold now, and one way or the other, I was going to have to get out of it. I reached for the ladder and then backed up. No, I didn't want to get on that ladder. Not necessarily ready for the boat. I looked at the shoreline. There they all were, standing there waiting for me.

It was impossibly far without my surfboard. Still, the journey wouldn't get shorter by putting it off. I started to swim for the beach, gliding over the water. Although it had been sunny and serene, the weather changed almost as soon as I headed for the beach. Clouds formed, and rain pelted down on my head. Still, I could see the sun ahead. It was there. The ocean seemed to shake around me. I'd never thought about earthquakes on the ocean, but there it was, shaking me here, there, and everywhere. The waves were huge, threatening to suck me under.

I couldn't give in.

With every ounce of energy I had in the world, I pushed forward. I was almost there.

Almost there...

I sat up, drenched in sweat, with my heart racing so fast, I felt like I'd just run a long race and won. The guys stood at the end of my bed. Will wiped at his eyes. Oscar and Casper were both pale. Will darted forward, grabbing on to my feet, where they were covered at the end of the bed by the blanket. "Tiff?"

"Hi." I sat up, wiping at my face. "That was...that was a weird dream."

"A weird dream?" Oscar walked along one side and Casper the other. "You...you died for a second."

My mouth fell open. "I died?"

"Yes." Will held on to my feet while his shoulders rounded like he was exhausted. "Just a second, but you were gone. We thought...we thought that was it. You were gone from us for always, and we had failed you in every way that mattered."

The door flung open, and three healers darted into the room. Nicole impressively nudged Casper out of the way while she looked at a machine that was next to the bed. "Zero," she said in a whisper, then repeated it louder. "Her toxin level is zero. It worked. The serum I put in worked."

When Casper spoke, it was in a low voice, part animal, part man. "She died for a minute."

"I'm not sure what to say." Nicole winced. "All I can see is that she is without the toxin now."

Alora grabbed my knee. "How do you feel?"

The room shook back and forth, everyone grabbing on to something the second it did. I groaned. "I feel like it's another earthquake."

"We've been getting them all day." Oscar's face was marred with dark circles under his eyes. He was exhausted. Everyone in the room with me was.

"Other than the earthquake?" Alora asked me with a quirk to her mouth as soon as the shaking ceased.

How did I feel? "Tired. Weak. But alert and not in pain. Not nauseous. Just worn out."

"It really is a miracle." She sighed. "Get some rest. Your toxin level is zero. I think it's over." She squeezed Cas' arm when she passed him. "For everyone."

I waited until the healers had left the room to speak again. "There was a boat. I was on the ocean, and all I had to do to get out of the water was get on the boat. I thought about it. I mean, the boat was right there. Climb the ladder, get out of the water, go. It would have been easy. But you were on the beach waiting for me. So I swam for it, even though it was impossibly far."

Will nodded, squeezing my feet. "You swam for it. Thank the universe you did that. Thank you for swimming for the beach."

"Yes," Oscar whispered. "That boat would have taken you where we couldn't follow you just yet. And then what if it was a different boat that showed up for us?"

Cas held up his hand. "No more. She swam for it. That's what matters. There would never be anywhere that Tiffany would go that I wouldn't follow. I would hunt her until she was back in my arms."

I cleared my throat. "Sitting right here."

He blinked. "Sorry, yes." He shook his head. "Might be a little out of it."

I could see that and didn't need their extra sensory abilities to know that. They just looked like hell washed over. I patted the bed. "Come sit down with me, guys."

The bed was huge. We could all fit.

Casper caught Will's gaze and then turned to me. "We sleep in shifts so that one of us is there for you at all times. Well, two of us are. One sleeping. I'm not really comfortable with altering that just yet. I am so glad you are feeling better, that the toxin is zero. But you died less than ten minutes ago. So we're not lying down just yet. Maybe in a few days."

I supposed that made sense. "It doesn't feel real to me that it happened."

Will let out an audible breath. "Don't get on any boats. You are hereby banned from boats."

That wasn't a realistic order, but I'd leave it alone for

now. I was glad to be here. All I'd wanted to do was come home, and somehow, that had happened.

~

WE WERE HAVING at least one earthquake a day. I hated them, but not as much as I did the tension in the room. The constant aching angst caused by the fact that Will, Casper, and Oscar were exhausted. They weren't shifting or doing any of the things I imagined they needed to do to have a normal existence.

And as Knox had visited me daily, I knew he wasn't dead, which meant nothing had progressed on that front either.

I chewed on my lip and regarded them as they argued. They were always doing that right now.

I didn't have all the strength back that I needed, but some of it had returned. I grabbed on to the bedpost just to be sure I was steady and got off the bed. I'd been doing a lot of sleeping, but as far as I could tell, their so-called sleeping in shifts was bullshit. No one but me was getting any rest at all.

Checking the time, it was four in the afternoon. I had started to be able to figure out some symbols and what they meant without needing translating glasses. Numbers were proving easier than letters.

"Who wants to lie down with me?" It had been four days since I'd almost died. Telling me they couldn't take their eyes off of me didn't seem legit anymore, it just seemed like high anxiety and we had to be careful we didn't fall into doing too much of that.

The room shook again. "Or are you going to stand there

and just be angry until one of you passes out from exhaustion?"

Will ran a hand through his hair. "Are we being...mean to each other?"

"Didn't notice?" I grabbed a pillow. "I know this has been too much for you guys. It's been too much for me. But I think the only way we get through this until I'm one hundred percent is to try to do what normal things we can, when we actually can. As it turns out, this involves resting. I can do that."

Casper grabbed all the big pillows, which must have been his version of agreeing. He set them out, and we all lay down. I expected some sort of conversation or sniping at each other, but Will had no sooner put his arm around me than he was absolutely snoring. I smiled. Yep, he was beyond tired at this point.

Oscar settled down on my other side, and his eyes were instantly closed. I met Casper's gaze when he put his head on my pillow to be the top of the T in this nap tonight. "I'm not going anywhere. You're stuck with me."

He put his hand on my hair, running his fingers through it. "Not stuck."

Unlike his brothers, he wasn't so fast to close his eyes, but when he did, it was on a sigh.

I knew how exhausted I'd been taking care of my mom when she'd been dosed. I'd only had days of it. According to Knox, who I had asked, I'd been sick for almost a month. That was a lot of fucking time. It would seem the caregiver often needed care on their own.

Or at least to actually go to sleep for a while.

I lay there listening to them breathe. Eventually, Will stopped snoring. They were quiet. I wasn't at all tired, but didn't dare move. If they woke up, I'd probably have even worse grumpy Lions who hadn't had enough rest.

Now that my head was clear, I could actually think. There had to be ramifications for what the Union had done to me. Sure, it had been Ferguson, but he was their representative. Not to mention, I knew it wasn't only him, not only me this had happened to. They'd killed my mom. The Union destroyed lives.

Something had to be done. But what?

A thought dawned on me. For years, members of the Free Earth coalition had reached out to me and others to try to convince us to go ahead and turn on the Union. We'd been warned that even talking to them would mean instant termination. What I knew now was it would have meant some kind of torture, but the threat of termination had been enough to have me deleting the messages without reading them.

If I got them the information about what the Union had done to me, what it was doing out there in the universe that no one knew about, that organization would be able to do something about it. What had her name been? Cyra something. I would find it, and I would send them my story. Surely that would make a difference.

Although, getting a confession out of Ferguson would go even further. But how... I had no idea where in the universe he'd run off to.

Eventually, music met my ears, and I rose carefully and walked over to the window to listen to it closer.

I couldn't see anything, but I could hear the joy taking place outside. I grinned. Nicole, who had come by every day to gab at me, was probably out there trying to get one of the males she'd known a long time to pay attention to her. They weren't true mates, but she wanted him for a few nights.

Arms came around me, and I knew it was Will without having to look. I could tell them all apart in the dark now too. Just by how they held me, the way that they smelled.

I leaned back. "I thought you might sleep all night."

He kissed my neck. "You'll never know how much I want you. I woke up aching. And I think I'm not alone in that. Can we all have you, Tiff? Can we all have you right now?"

I turned in his arms. "What you're proposing sounds intriguing." I wanted to play with him a little bit. Of course I was going to want that.

Casper and Oscar watched me from their places on the floor. Eyes alert, bodies ready to jump if I said yes. There was so much power in this. I didn't want it anywhere else. Just here. Just now.

"Are you suggesting that your bad moods might have been sexual deprivation?"

"No." Casper rose and came over to us. "It's because we were fucking tired. But we've had a little nap, and we want to love you. All I'd ask is you lie down and let us love on you until you are falling apart in our arms."

Oscar winked at me. "Then we also have a gift for you. It's not contingent on the sex. But we do have one, and we could give it to you...after. Or now, if the sex is a no-go."

I smiled at them slowly. "Use those noses. Am I saying no?"

Will was on me in a fast second.

20

Will pressed me into the pillows beneath me. His gaze was intense. "I want to be clear about something. You are not fully healed and we are not playing around with your health. You aren't to do anything but lie here and let us love on you."

I lifted an eyebrow. "Nothing? I think there are probably things I can still do."

Casper held up his finger, catching my attention. "Will is right—you are going to be loved on and not hurt for it."

I really doubted that making love to them was in any way going to hurt me. But sometimes in life, it was about picking my battles, and since this wasn't one at all, I smiled. "Well, whatever you think."

Lying back and letting them make love to me? Probably wasn't going to be a terrible sacrifice.

I made a show of flipping my hair over my shoulders. I liked being silly like this. It was a whole new side of me. This kept happening. Sides of myself I'd never known before were showing up.

"Have at it, gentlemen." I couldn't help my laugh after

that. "Do your worst. I will restrain myself from touching you."

"Well," Will put my hand on his chest, "you can touch a little bit."

"Ooh, my head is spinning. How on earth...sorry, we're not on Earth...am I supposed to keep up with all of this?"

Casper pinched my side, and I yelped before I giggled. "I think she is teasing us."

"Ya think?" I winked at him, and he kissed my cheek, placing a long kiss there that spoke of heat and upcoming pleasure.

Will tugged on my hair, which brought my attention back to him. He leaned down to kiss my neck, and my teasing stopped. Molten heat filled my body in anticipation of what was about to happen. It also dawned on me that we'd never done anything like this before. I'd had sex with them three times, once each, and not together. Closed doors and separate times had been the name of the game. I lifted my hands over my head, anticipating what he was going to want—my shirt off.

He nodded, and I grinned. We'd had some sort of unspoken conversation, and I'd gotten it right. Will pulled my shirt over my head and discarded it somewhere.

I swallowed. This was becoming very, very real. I was going to have all their eyes on me at the same time. I'd lost a lot of weight in the weeks I'd been sick, and not in a good hey-I-was-exercising-so-I-looked-better kind of a way. No, this had been starvation because I hadn't been able to handle food. And it showed.

Still, as I stared at each of them for a long moment, I didn't see anything but longing. I knew the feeling. I had it myself, all for them.

"What brought this on? The wanting me all at once?"

Oscar leaned over and kissed my chest at the juncture of my neck.

He looked up to speak to me. "We couldn't agree which one of us got to have you first. We thought...let's not decide. Let's all have her the next time."

"With all of us agreeing there would be a next time," Will whispered. "Sometimes, you have to decide things like that to survive the darkest possible thoughts. You push them out with imaginings like this one and hope that someday, you get to have this actual moment."

I kissed him. Then Casper. And then Oscar. It was like a marking, a telling them that they were all desired, all needed. I wanted all of them. Right then.

Will hauled me against him to kiss me hard before he sat me up and then leaned me back, right against Oscar, who was on his knees. In the same position, Casper kneed his way over to my side.

"We're all going to make you feel so good," Cas whispered. "Close your eyes and let us."

It was hard to do that. I hadn't let myself be unaware of my surroundings since I was a little girl. Unless I was battling a Union toxin that threatened to kill me. I swallowed. I still sort of was when I thought about it. The Union had always made it impossible for me to figuratively close my eyes. And fuck that, I was going to win that.

I trusted these men. I trusted their Lions, even if I still found them to be somewhat intimidating. They wanted me. Loved me. And I was going to close my eyes and let them love me.

Closing my eyes meant more to me than they might ever understand, but that was okay because I knew what it represented. Who knew with these guys? Maybe they did know.

They had those noses that could decipher all sorts of things that humans took for granted were private thoughts.

Oscar kissed me on the back of my neck. "Stop thinking so hard."

"That's difficult for me." They had to know that, but I said it anyway.

"I guess we just have to work harder," Cas said in my ear before he licked me. I gasped. "Don't be surprised. We're Cats. We do so love to use our tongues."

That was it. I gave myself over to the moment. I wouldn't try to anticipate what they were going to do. Will backed up. I couldn't see it, but I could feel it. He tugged my pants off. I hadn't bothered to put on panties when I'd dressed earlier. Why bother when I was lounging around in bed all day?

But that decision definitely had their attention. Oscar sucked in a breath. "Look at that pretty pussy, out and ready for some attention."

I was not at all used to him being so openly erotic in how he spoke. My cheeks heated up, and Will laughed. "I think we made her a little embarrassed."

"In the best possible way." Oscar squeezed my sides.

Will ran his hands up my legs, while Oscar started kissing my neck, long deep caresses that made what Will was doing even more sensual. Casper ran his hand up my stomach to my breasts, where he pinched my nipple. I jumped. Maybe I should have guessed what he was going to do, but I hadn't. Stomach to breast, yes that would have made sense.

"I'm going to suck on it now." His voice was barely a whisper. "Just giving you a warning."

I smiled. "Thanks."

"Oh, you want warnings?" Will kept the mood going,

keeping his own voice low. "I'm going to touch you right in your sweet warmth."

That was when Cas bit me. My whole body vibrated before I seemed to lose the ability to sit upright. Yes, I really liked that, and I'd had no idea I would. I'd have a mark for who knew how long, and that was fine with me. Hot even.

But then, oh, Will was touching me right where he said he would. He swirled his finger over my clit. I shuddered. So he did it again. And again. There was so much stimuli, and I couldn't see any of it. Oscar squeezed my ass, and he wasn't gentle about it before he ground his hips into me from behind. That was when Cas bit my nipple. I cried out, and then I was coming hard against Will's hand. I came and came. It had been over a month since I'd had this kind of release. My body let loose all of my pent-up need in that moment.

Coming down from it was hard, and I really needed to open my eyes. "Can I...?" Apparently, I couldn't fully form words.

"Yes, of course." Cas kissed my ear. "Whatever you need. You're so fucking beautiful."

I wrenched my eyes open. There they were, my three, all of them looking at me like Cas' words really were true. They thought I was beautiful, even when I was wrecked from life. I leaned over and kissed Oscar over my shoulder and then turned to Cas, doing the same. They might say I was beautiful, but they were the ones that fit that description.

Then I stared at Will. "Too many clothes. That goes for all of you. Too many clothes."

They scrambled, and I tried to catch my breath. With what I wanted to happen now, I had to pace myself. When he was naked, I climbed on Will's lap. I was wet, I'd just come, but fuck, I was still needy. I straddled him.

"I think you're going to want to put yourself inside of me." My low, sexy voice took me by surprise. But that was becoming something I was almost used to. The way my brain had to catch up to the things that my body already knew had altered in me.

He nodded. Cas and Oscar's gazes bore into my back. They were watching every move I made, and that was so hot. My nipples, which were already hard and aching, grew even more so. Will fitted himself inside of me, and I cried out at the stretch. I was always going to be smaller than they were, and the difference between us was always going to be obvious in these moments. That was okay. I fucking loved it.

Will moved beneath me until that must not have been enough. The position we were in really demanded I do most of the work, but they'd told me not to. He flipped me over so he was on top. I made an *oomph* noise as my back hit the pillow, but right then, it didn't hurt. I couldn't feel pain, I could only feel Will.

I wrapped my legs around him and let him lead me where we needed to go. It didn't take long. I wasn't the only one who hadn't had this in too long. He was lost to me too. Our bodies danced the movements that spoke to us. The way he led, the way I followed, but how he always took his cues from me. That was true in sex and other ways too. I loved these moments. I loved Will being Will. I just...loved him.

He came in a powerful thrust that triggered my own release. I cried out, digging my fingers into his back. Will kissed all over my face. "I love you." His words were low, for my ears only. Could he really tell all the things I thought?

I ran my finger down the slope of his nose, the way I loved to do. "I love you too."

His muscles tensed a moment before he moved off of

me. I would have whined if I hadn't known what was going to happen next.

"You marked her up on her breasts." Will spoke to Cas.

"She loved it," was his only response before he kissed me, taking the place where Will had been.

I kissed him. "Hi."

He winked at me. It was adorable. And then he flipped me over so that I was on my stomach. Wow. Okay. I hadn't seen that coming. "Hold on to that pillow."

This was Cas being in charge. I did as he said, and seconds later, he was inside of me. I'd never had sex like this before. It was such a different angle and so much penetration. Was it too much? No, it wasn't, but it took me a second to realize that. The shock wore off, and the only thing I could feel was him. I couldn't see him, and I missed that, but Cas was not quiet about how he felt.

"Fuck, baby. Fuck. Fuck. I love you. Feel so fucking good."

And it was like we were eye to eye because we were heart-to-heart. I hung on, my orgasm building again. I'd never have believed it was possible that I still could. As a person who used to find this all very blah, it was amazing that I could feel so much, come so hard, need so much. And then I was again. This time it was pleasure that brought Cas' on too. We were both panting when he finally pulled out of me.

Oscar knelt, making eye contact with me from the side of the pillow. "Still got some energy left for me? Or are you exhausted? There's no wrong answer."

I got to my own knees to meet him gaze to gaze. "I always have energy for you. Always."

His smile was huge. "Thank you, beautiful."

He took me in his arms to roll me over. I reached over to

stroke his cock. It was hard and must have ached from need. Oscar hissed and shook his head. "I just need to be inside of you. Too close and no ability to get there without your warmth. That is true for so many things. There's no way to get to happiness without your warmth."

I kissed his chin. "Oh the sweet things you say."

This made him grin. "Just hold on to me, baby. I'll get us both there."

With one push, he was inside of me. I sucked in my breath and knew that he would.

SOMETIME LATER, after I'd showered and hydrated a lot, I was sitting by the window listening to the celebrations outside. "I love how every day here is such a gift that you all just take time to have fun with it. Do you want to go? Tonight? I don't like crowds, but I'll try. For you guys. And you can shift. I'll be fine. You all need to shift."

"Thought we'd stay in tonight." Will smiled.

The three of them were all smiling. After what we'd done, that wasn't surprising, but there was something else happening. That's when it dawned on me. "You have a gift for me."

Oscar pointed at the closet. "Been waiting to show you. You're not quite ready for it yet, but when you are. It's there."

What could that possibly mean? I rose from my seat and walked to the closet door. "I've never had a gift. I know that sounds crazy, but there wasn't money for those kinds of things."

"Then this makes it even more special." Cas nodded. "And we're so happy we thought of it."

I swung open the door and then gasped. There, leaning

up against the wall, was a surfboard. A blue and white one. It was shiny and prettier than any I'd ever owned. Carefully, like it might vanish into thin air, I brought it out to the room. "Oh my... I mean, thank you. How did you find this? And, guys, really? This is incredible. Thank you."

Trying to balance it while I kissed all of them was tricky, but I did it. Happiness flooded my veins. They'd done this. For me. Where? How?

"We gave the specifications to one of the engineers here. They got it done with the help of some masons and artists. Everyone was happy to try. Does it look right to you?"

Tears flooded my eyes. "It does. I love it. Every bit of it."

I hugged the board to my chest. There was nothing in the world they could have given me that I would have loved more. It meant they'd been paying attention to what I loved and they really, truly got me. I just adored it.

"Thank you."

Sometimes words were just not enough.

But they seemed to get it. I was surrounded by their love. And my surfboard.

~

THE DAY WAS FINALLY HERE. I hated to even think about it. But today was the day when Knox wouldn't be leader anymore. That meant he was going to die. I hadn't seen him in almost a week, and I was sure he'd avoided me.

Every Lion in the group was there, and with the exception of Oscar, they were all shifted. He would have to as well. It was the rules. He was putting it off so that he could talk to me and that was sweet, but I almost wished he'd get it over with. Start this mess that everyone seemed to feel just had to happen.

Will would kill Knox, take over this area, and apparently tomorrow, we'd just go on with business. They'd set things in order, establish dominance, and we'd live here until someone came and took it from us. The second they did this, new leaders would be called to take their role. There would be a challenge for those roles, and no one knew who would win. But we'd likely never see them because this would be a healthy area with strong, functioning Alpha Lions. We could go decades upon decades without seeing anything like what happened here.

Nicole bumped me. She was a Lion, but I'd come to be able to identify people more and more.

I patted her head. Even as a Lion, she was always taking care of people. I didn't have girlfriends, but lately, it seemed like I might be getting some.

Oscar put his arm around me. "We don't know what's going to happen."

"What do you mean? We know Knox isn't going to beat Will. That's the way this works. Even if he could, and he's not that strong anymore, Knox would probably throw it because he wants you guys to take this role so much."

Oscar kissed my cheek. "You threw a rather novel idea at them. They listened. I'm not sure they'll do it. I don't know that he's going to concede or if his Lion can even tolerate the idea. But I know he's considered it, and so has Will. But ultimately, it'll come down to their Lions. If it helps, they really did take what you said into consideration. Take that inside if it helps." He kissed my cheek. "See you in a minute."

He shifted. Then it was just me and a lot of Lions. After a few minutes, Knox and Will were alone, facing each other. Knox was bigger but thinner. It was obvious that Will was stronger. He was muscular. Young. And he roared his intent for the world to see. I shivered at the sound. That was power.

Like this, he was lethal. His brothers were back a bit watching. Casper almost looked bored, but it was a fake nonchalance. He would destroy someone if they stepped out of line.

I swallowed. This was when they would strike. When William would kill him.

That very nice man who had embraced me as one of their own right away. I didn't want to be done with him.

Knox lay down on his stomach and rolled over, showing Will his belly. I gasped. I didn't speak Lion, but I knew submission when I saw it. I leaned forward. He was conceding. This was Lion for *I'll give you leadership*.

What was Will going to do?

He walked over slowly and put his gigantic paw right on Knox's stomach. The intent was clear. He could take out Knox if he wanted to. Then he stepped back.

Everyone roared.

Tears flooded my eyes. No one had died. They'd done just what I suggested. Me, a no one from Earth, had just orchestrated this. They'd listened to me. This was the best day ever.

Around me, Lions carried on. It was the best sound in the universe. Like the music we heard every night. They sang.

After a time, Knox shifted. He grabbed a pair of shorts from the pile they kept nearby and approached me. "I didn't know what would happen, but I thought it was worth a try. I think I can still help. If you all want me here."

"I do." I hugged him, tightly.

Even though they were Lions, I could feel my guy's eyes on me as they watched my every move. This was home. The one I'd never had and never could have imagined before now.

EPILOGUE

The wave rushed around me, and I got up on the board. My balance was slightly off, and I corrected. Everything moved fast now. This was the fastest I could go ever, and it was like flying. The waves shifted, and I adjusted just a bit. Yes, I was doing this. Every day, I got a little better at doing this. Every day, I was stronger.

Casper stood on the beach, watching me as I barreled toward the sand. He hated this, but he never looked away. That was what he did for me. What they all did. When William and Oscar were here, they watched too. But they'd had meetings, and they'd been gone for days.

The thought made me almost fall over, but I righted again. The wave slowed, and I dove off. The cool water cleared my head, and I swam for the surface. The water was shallow. A few kicks took me to the edge of the beach where I could feel the rocks beneath my feet.

We didn't have sand like on Earth. Once I got out of the water, I either turned around and went right back or hurried back to the cliffs. The rocks hurt my feet.

Casper ran over, handing me a towel. "Got to cut you off."

"Really?" I'd only had one run. "Why?" I was usually at this for hours. We hadn't figured out what I was going to be doing yet, and for now, this was good for my head. I sorted a lot of things out on the board.

He smiled. "Will and Oscar are back. They have a new gift for you."

"Another one?" I held my board tightly. "I love my gift. I don't need things."

"This one you'll like too." He put his arm around me. "If you can forgive them for...I don't know...not telling you what their business was."

I leaned on his shoulder. "Did they keep something from me?"

"Only so they could get this for you. Go get dressed and meet me outside."

This was downright secretive for Casper. I hurried back home, changed, and ran outside. Casper wasn't alone. Knox was with him. He nodded at me.

"Okay. Someone tell me what is going on."

"This way, babe," Oscar called out. They were by the cell where they kept prisoners.

I stopped moving. "Who's in there?"

Will slowly walked out. "Ferguson."

My mouth fell open. "You're kidding?"

"No, he was our unfinished business. Oscar found him by tapping into their signals, and then we brought him here. He's not going anywhere. He's dying by the end of this. If you want to do it, great. If not, we will. But he dies."

I caught my breath and then steeled my back. Yes, he was going to die. But first things first, he was going to confess. I smiled. I was good at getting people to talk. Then I was going to tell the whole universe what the Union was doing.

I didn't know what would happen. That was someone else's story. I had my Cats. My family. My planet.

But my guys were right—the Fergusons of the world couldn't be allowed to do what they did.

I swung open the door, and he looked up at me. He had two black eyes. They'd not taken him nicely.

"You know what? You screwed up my vacation. And that really used to piss me off. But I should thank you because if you hadn't sent me here, I wouldn't be so happy and content that I could honestly say to you that you lived a terrible life. It will be a short one."

Maybe I had a little Lion inside of me. Or they were just rubbing off on me.

"Confession is good for the soul."

"I love our mate," Casper whispered. "So fucking much."

I put my hands on the table in front of me. "Welcome to Planet Cat, Ferguson."

THANK you so much for reading Planet Cat! Don't worry, I am hard at work on the last book in the series, Planet Wolf. In the meantime, while you wait for Planet Wolf, you might like several other books I have written. If you like books that feature shifters, perhaps take a look at the completed series The Swamp. Start with Hidden: https://www.books2read. com/RRHidden or if you are a fan of books set in the space check out my completed science fiction romance series (12 books, 1 novella) called Wings of Artemis. Start with Kidnapped By Her Husbands: https://www.books2read.com/ RRKidnappedByHerHusbands . For even more information

please visit my website at www.rebeccaroyce.com or my
facebook group Rebecca's Randomness https://www.
facebook.com/groups/RebeccasRandomness

Thanks!-

RR

Turn the page for a complete list of all my books.

ABOUT THE AUTHOR

As a teenager, I would hide in my room to read my favorite romance novels when I was supposed to be doing my homework.

I am the mother of three adorable boys and I am fortunate to be married to my best friend. I live in Austin Texas where I am determined to eat all the barbecue in town.

I am in love with science fiction, fantasy, and the paranormal and try to use all of these elements in my writing. I've been told I'm a little bloodthirsty so I hope that when you read my work you'll enjoy the action packed ride that always ends in romance. I love to write series because I love to see characters develop over time and it always makes me happy to see my favorite characters make guest appearances in other books.

In my world anything is possible, anything can happen, and you should suspect that it will.

I'd love to hear from you! Please visit my website at www.rebeccaroyce.com to sign up for my newsletter and learn about my books!

Here's where you can find me online:

Rebecca's Randomness Reading Group https://www.facebook.com/groups/RebeccasRandomness/

https://www.rebeccaroyce.com

https://www.facebook.com/authorrebeccaroyce/

www.twitter.com/rebeccaroyce

Instagram: rebeccaroyce79
Cheers!!
Rebecca

OTHER BOOKS BY REBECCA ROYCE...

Contemporary Romance

Redheads:

Redhead on the Run https://amzn.to/2Nb3RcH

Redheaded Redemption https://amzn.to/2ZmKbsE

Real Men Love Redheads (coming soon)

Reverse Harem Story (completed series)

Unconventional

Unexpected

Undeniable

Kiss Her Goodbye (completed series)

Hard Truths

Dark Truths

Deadly Truths

Stupid Boys (writing with C.R. Jane)

Stupid Boys

Dumb Girl

Crazy Love (coming soon)

Science Fiction Romance:

Wings of Artemis (completed series)

Kidnapped By Her Husbands https://amzn.to/2BQdUxy

Rescued by Their Wife https://amzn.to/2Rr9as4

Crashing Into Destiny https://amzn.to/2VkyXRL

Meeting Them https://amzn.to/2BLPaXm

Reclaiming Their Love https://amzn.to/2GKAw8E

Loving Them https://amzn.to/2BKDmEK

Ship Called Malice https://amzn.to/2BNputj

Saving Them https://amzn.to/2SsrBtH

Dark Demise https://amzn.to/2VidXv3

Light Unfolding https://amzn.to/2GO6Yqr

Still Waters https://amzn.to/2CFePT8

Rising Tides https://amzn.to/2MCdTlM

Lost Star https://amzn.to/2X8hcZA

Pointed Arrow https://amzn.to/3gK9tYH

Illicit Minds

Illicit Senses

Illicit Connections

Illicit Alliance (coming soon)

Shifter World

Planet Bear

Planet Cat

Planet Wolf (coming soon)

Heart of the Nebula (writing with Heather Long) **completed series**

Queenmaker

Deal Breaker

Throne Taker

Stranded Hearts (writing with Vivien Jackson)

The Girl Who Fell From The Sky

The Girl Who Crossed The Stars (coming soon)

Through the Gates (writing with Skye MacKinnon)

Purgatory City

Infernal Land (coming soon)

Paranormal Romance:

Last Hope (completed series)

Tradition Be Damned

Past Be Damned

Destiny Be Damned

Compassion Be Damned

Future Be Damned

Dragon Wars (completed series)

Forever

Eternal

Always

Evermore

Endless

Wards and Wands (completed series)

Hexed and Vexed

Curse Reversed

Meow, Baby (novella, co-written with Ripley Proserpina)

Tragic Magic

Safe Haven

Everywhere and Nowhere

Dimension X (coming soon)

More coming soon....

Soul Bound

Prisoner of the Dragons

More coming soon....

Shadow Promised

Strange Days

Weird Nights

Bizarre Years

More coming soon...

The Westervelt Wolves (completed series)

Her Wolf

Summer's Wolf

Wolf Reborn

Wolf's Valentine

Wolf's Magic

Alpha Wolf

Angel's Wolf

Darkest Wolf

Lone Wolf

Fallen Alpha

Alpha Rising

Alpha's Strength

Alpha's Sacrifice

Alpha's Truth

Alpha Enticing

Hidden Alpha (coming soon)

Cascade (completed series)

Haunted Redemption

Phoenix Everlasting

Fragility Unearthed

Persuasion Enraptured

The Swamp (completed series)

Hidden

Pursued

Caught

The Coveted (writing with Ripley Proserpina)

Eyes in the Darkness

Voices in the Darkness

Return to the Darkness

Prison Princess (part of the Prison Princess world, writing with CoraLee June)

Young Adult/New Adult Urban Fantasy/Post-Apocalyptic:

The Warrior (completed series)

Initiation

Driven

Subversive

Redemption

Justice

Warrior World (spin off of The Warrior, completed series)

Deacon

Micah

Jason

Fantasy Romance:

The Outsiders

Love Beyond Time

Love Beyond Sanity

Love Beyond Loyalty

Love Beyond Sight

Love Beyond Expectations

Love Beyond Oceans

Love Beyond Flames

Love Beyond Lies

Love Beyond Death (coming soon)

The Storm (writing with Ripley Proserpina) completed series.

Lightning Strikes

Thunder Rolling

The Deluge

Stand Alone Titles

Under The Lights

No Quitting Allowed

Mr. Wrong

Bite Marks

Bitten Surrender

The Vampire and The Virgin

Demon Within

Crimson Lust

Call Me Crazy

The Men of Elite Metal

www.ingramcontent.com/pod-product-compliance
Lightning Source LLC
Chambersburg PA
CBHW010818250626
47156CB00011B/3112